Jonath[...] he answere[d...] do. Like I s[aid...] men are th[at...] will." Jonat[han put his hand] on Sonora's. "All I can say is the rest of us need to pray. God is the only one that knows where your son is. We can pray for protection for your son and that God will lead Tivy to him."

Sonora snatched her hand back and got up from the table. "Seems like that's doing nothing. I've been praying, and so far, I'm no closer to getting Timmy back." Sonora looked Jonathan in the eyes. "Praying doesn't seem to have accomplished anything. God should have protected him and not let him get kidnapped in the first place."

Tobias came to stand beside his niece. He put his arm around her shoulder. "Girl, this is no time to go talkin' against God and prayer. You don't know what God has protected that boy from because someone has been prayin'. At least we know he's still alive because I believe the little boy they saw was Timmy. If we hadn't been prayin', who's to say those bandits wouldn't have killed him."

Sonora said nothing more. She knew her uncle was right but right now she was angry. She was angry with herself for not protecting Timmy. She was angry with Daniel Forrester for pursuing her and the child, causing them to have to leave the comfort of her father's home. She was angry with Jonathan and the whole stinking army for not finding her son and bringing him back to her. She was angry at the comancheros for taking Timmy away from her, and yes, she was angry with God for allowing all of this to happen in the first place.

Sonora

by

Elaine Bonner

God Bless You,
Elaine Bonner
Isaiah 59:1

This is a work of fiction. Names, characters, places, and incidents are either the product of the author's imagination or are used fictitiously, and any resemblance to actual persons living or dead, business establishments, events, or locales, is entirely coincidental.

Sonora

COPYRIGHT © 2007 by Elaine Bonner

All rights reserved. No part of this book may be used or reproduced in any manner whatsoever without written permission of the author or The Wild Rose Press except in the case of brief quotations embodied in critical articles or reviews.
Contact Information: info@thewildrosepress.com

Cover Art by *Kim Mendoza*

The Wild Rose Press
PO Box 708
Adams Basin, NY 14410-0706
Visit us at www.thewildrosepress.com

Publishing History
First White Rose Edition, 2008
Print ISBN 1-60154-194-5

Published in the United States of America

Dedication

To my long time friend, Kassy. You have been there through all the bad times, the good times and just the times I needed to talk. I am so blessed to have you for a friend and sister in Christ.

Chapter One

The Dakota Territory

Sonora lay in the darkness. She felt the cold, gritty earth beneath her. As agony shot through every inch of her body, she tried to clear her scrambled thoughts and understand what had taken place. Wincing with pain, Sonora finally managed to force herself into a sitting position. Her right eye was swollen shut, but through the blurred vision of her left eye, she could see the smoke rising from the embers of what was once her home. Now she remembered. Everyone and everything had been taken from her in one evening.

"God, this can't be happening." Sonora cried out in torment. "It's no use. There's no reason to go on." She fell back to the cold ground and passed once again into unconsciousness.

****

The soldiers noticed the smoke rising into the dawn of the early morning sky. They surveyed the area carefully before riding into the now deserted remains of someone's home. Slowly, staying alert to their surroundings, the two uniformed men carefully searched the immediate area.

"Hey, there's a woman over here."

"Is she alive?" The captain asked as he watched his young corporal kneel by the lifeless form.

"Just barely," the young man replied.

"Let's get her back to the fort." The captain mounted his horse and the corporal gently handed the battered young woman up to his superior officer. Settling the fragile maiden in front of him as best he could, the captain called, "Let's ride, Corporal. I'm afraid time is of the essence here."

Captain Jonathan Parker couldn't keep the young

woman from jostling but he tried to brace her as best he could. Her head rested on his shoulder and he could feel her faint breaths against his neck.

"Father God, please let us get her to the fort in time," he softly prayed.

****

Fort Benton

"Riders approaching," the sentry called. "Open the gates, it's Capt'n Parker and Corporal Tivy."

Jonathan slowed his horse to a trot as he passed through the massive wooden gates that helped secure Fort Benton from unwanted guests. He pulled his mount to a stop in front of the log building serving as the infirmary. The corporal dismounted first and the captain gently lowered the young woman into the corporal's waiting arms.

"Doc, get in here," Jonathan yelled as Corporal Tivy lay the woman on the exam table in the doctor's office. "Corporal, you're dismissed. Take care of the horses, and then go get something to eat. I'll let you know how she is after Doc gets through with her."

The doctor came through the door that led from his private quarters into his office. "My word, who's this?" he asked as he approached the table.

"Don't know. Found her in the woods by a burned out cabin." Jonathan watched quietly as Doc Thomas began to examine the patient.

"Indians?" The doctor questioned as he walked to the washstand and filled a pan with sparkling clear water.

"Don't think so." Jonathan looked from the patient to the doctor. "If it had been Indians, they'd have taken a strong, young woman like this captive and made a squaw out of her, not beat her and leave her for dead."

"Comancheros?" The doctor continued his one word interrogation as he began to clean Sonora's wounds.

"Maybe, but they haven't been around here in months. They usually take the women, too. Course I guess one of them could've gotten a little too rough with her, thought he killed her and just left her there."

The doctor cleaned the dried blood from the young woman's face. "I don't think whoever did this was just a little carried away." Doc Thomas walked toward the cabinet that held his medicines.

"Will she be all right?" Jonathan gently reached over and touched the woman's bruised hand.

The doctor lightly scratched his neatly trimmed beard. "Can't say. She's hurt real bad. From the look of those bruises on her stomach, she's bleeding inside. She needs surgery."

Jonathan stared into the ashen face of the young woman lying on the examining table. "Well, what are you waiting for?"

Doc Thomas stopped in his tracks and looked the captain in the face. "Captain, I'm pretty good at bullet and arrow holes, but I haven't done surgery like this since I joined the army. I'd probably kill her."

Nathan Thomas was almost six-foot tall. Jonathan had not only seen him patch up badly wounded soldiers but the doctor had been in a few fights himself. Fear was not a part of the doctor's personality, but today, Jonathan saw the fear in his friend's hazel eyes and heard it in his voice. He still had to ask. "What chance does she have if you don't cut on her?"

The doctor sighed heavily. "None."

Again Jonathan looked down at the helpless, young woman. He stood to his full height of five-foot ten inches and looked directly at the doctor. "Then she's got nothing to lose. Now get on with it."

"Why is this girl's life so important to you?" Doc wanted to know. "If she recovers, she'll probably wish she'd died when she remembers what those heathens did to her."

"She's a creation of God, Nathan. You've got to do what you can to save her life. Now let's get busy." Jonathan took off his coat and began to roll up his sleeves. "I'll help. What do you need me to do?"

"Pray," the doctor replied. He walked over to the potbellied stove in the corner of the room and put more logs on the fire. He removed the kettle and poured steaming water into the wash pan and washed his hands and arms up to his elbows. "She's in a coma now and if we're lucky she'll stay that way. If she does start to wake up while I'm operating on her, I don't have any medicine that'll put her to sleep. You'll have to hold her down." The doctor set a bottle of whiskey beside Jonathan. "You might try to force some of this down her throat. It'll help numb the pain a little bit."

Jonathan watched as the doctor began. The captain had never seen his old friend this nervous. He watched as the beads of sweat began to roll down the doctor's face. Jonathan picked up a cloth and wiped the sweat from his friend's brow.

Jonathan prayed, not only for the young woman, but also for God to guide Nathan's hands. The doctor was very meticulous with the procedure. Jonathan didn't know anything about doctoring, but from what he observed, he felt he was in the presence of greatness no matter what the doctor had declared about his inadequacy.

The young woman began to stir and Jonathan braced himself against her shoulders and began to whisper softly into her ear. The words he spoke were for the patient's ears only. He wasn't actually talking to Sonora. He was asking God to calm the young woman lying on the operating table. God answered quickly because Sonora began to relax and breathe with ease.

As the doctor placed the last suture, Jonathan looked up into his worried face. "Well?"

"Well...now we wait. I think I stopped all the bleeding. The rest is up to God. We wait and pray."

****

The sun was barely coming over the horizon when Captain Parker came into the infirmary to check on the patient. "How's she doing?"

"Been restless from time to time but that's to be expected. I sure wish my supplies would get here. I'm down to nothing. I don't have anything to help ease her pain except this bottle of whiskey." Doc stood and stretched the kinks out of his back. "It's all right for the burly men I treat but doesn't do much for a fragile thing like her." He leaned over and pulled the covers up around his patient's shoulders as she began to thrash about once again. "Sure wish I could ease her pain some."

Jonathan looked into the face of his friend. Fatigue was very evident. "How about I sit with her for a while and you go get a little shut eye?"

The doctor walked over to the stove and poured two cups of coffee. "Aren't you gonna go out and try to find who did this?"

Jonathan accepted the cup of coffee the doctor held out to him. "A patrol's leaving in fifteen minutes. Corporal Tivy's taking some men and going back to the place we found her to see what trail he can pick up. There were so many tracks it'll be hard to figure out which ones to follow." Jonathan took a slow drink of the hot coffee.

"If anyone can figure it out, Tivy will. He can find a trail in a blizzard." The doctor slumped into the chair that sat behind his cluttered wooden desk.

Jonathan seated himself in the straight-backed chair in front of the desk. "Yeah, Tivy's the best tracker I've ever known. That's why I sent him out." Then looking at the young woman lying on the cot by the stove, he added. "I'm hoping when she comes around she'll be able to tell us who did this to her."

The doctor went into his quarters for a much-needed rest while Jonathan watched the dark-haired young woman as she slept. In his mind, Jonathan was trying to put a story to the face he saw before him. Under all the bruises he could tell there was a beautiful woman. *What happened? Who did this to her?* He could only speculate, but if he had it in his power, he'd find the ones responsible and bring them to justice.

The young woman began to stir and Jonathan pulled a chair to her bedside. He began to pray softly. "God, restore your child to health. Heal her from the top of her head to the soles of her feet, inside and out." As his prayer poured forth, the girl's breathing slowed and her body relaxed in peaceful slumber.

"You certainly have a way about you," Doc Thomas commented as he came back into the room. "Whatever it is you say to her, she responds in a very positive way."

"I don't really say anything to her. I talk to the Father and He calms her." Jonathan stood and walked toward the door. Taking his hat from the peg on the wall, he told the doctor, "Well, I'd better get about my duties. Call me if you need me or if she wakes up. I'll check back later." Jonathan ran his hand through his light brown hair before placing his hat on his head and leaving the infirmary.

****

The cool, late summer breeze filled the room before Jonathan could get the door closed. The doctor watched the young captain leave and then looked down into the pale face of his patient.

Softly to himself, he murmured, "I just hope your prayers work, Jonathan. I just hope she wakes up."

Nathan Thomas leaned down and pulled the blanket up over Sonora's shoulders and then sat down in the chair beside her cot. He sat for what seemed like hours staring at his patient. She was very beautiful. Her dark black hair and dark skin tone made him wonder if she had some Indian blood in her. That was not the only thing he wondered about this young woman. Surely she hadn't been living out there in the wilderness alone. Maybe someone had begun searching for her. The doctor just hoped that if that someone did come to the fort looking for her, she would still be alive.

He sighed as he stood to his feet. If he were completely honest with himself and Jonathan, he didn't give her much of a chance right now.

Chapter Two

The days wore on and Doctor Thomas' patient showed little sign of improvement. She woke up enough a couple of times to take a few spoonfuls of broth offered by Amanda Stone. Amanda ran the fort's general store and was one of only three women who lived at the fort full time. When she heard about the young woman Doc was caring for, Amanda offered her services. "There's just some things a woman can do for another woman that a man can't do or at least shouldn't do," Amanda had said when she offered her help.

"Shouldn't she be waking up more?" Amanda asked as she made her usual morning visit.

"I had hoped she would be more awake by now but she lost an awful lot of blood and took a very bad beating. Her body just has to heal and that will take a while. As her body mends she'll start waking up more." Doc assured as he placed his hand on his patient's forehead to check her temperature.

****

Sonora heard voices. They were not familiar voices but she could tell they meant her no harm. In the cobwebs of her mind, she remembered seeing a red-haired woman spooning liquid into her mouth a few times. She also vaguely remembered a soft male voice talking to her in moments of semi-consciousness.

What's happened to me? Sonora tried her best to remember but no memories came. Heaviness overtook her once again and she fell into a deep slumber.

****

"Stagecoach approaching," the sentry called. The big wagon lumbered through the gates. Jonathan laid aside the papers he was sorting and went outside to greet the stage.

"Hey, Amos, have a good trip?" Jonathan called to the

stage driver.

"Good trip, Capt'n. Nary a sign of no Injuns." Amos called as he stepped down from the coach.

"Boy, am I glad to see you," Doc said as he approached the stagecoach. "Have you got my supplies?"

"There's a package fer ya under my seat. Can't say what's in it. Maybe it's what yer lookin' fer though." Amos stepped up on the wheel and retrieved the parcel wrapped in brown paper for the doctor.

There was only one passenger on the stage. He was a salesman who had disappeared into the fort's general store to visit with Amanda. Doc sat down on the wooden bench in front of the store to open his package and examine the supplies.

Jonathan surveyed the scene before he asked his next question. He didn't want to cause any more alarm than absolutely necessary. "Amos, you didn't see any sign of comancheros did you?"

The old stage driver gave the captain a startled look. "Comancheros? What'cha talkin' about? Ain't been no comancheros in this part for nigh on two years."

Jonathan looked around once again before speaking. "I know we haven't had any trouble for a while but we came across a young woman the other day that may have been attacked by them."

Amos scratched his gray beard. "What makes ya thank it was comancheros and not Injuns?"

"Just a gut feeling I guess," Jonathan admitted.

The old driver walked to the back of the coach and began to unload the rest of the fort's supplies. "The woman dead?"

"No, but she hasn't come around enough yet for us to find anything out."

"I ain't seen no signs of them dirty, low-down rascals but I'll keep my eyes peeled. Specially if ya think they're back in this here territory." Amos set a wooden crate down on the porch. "Now how about gittin' some of yore boys to help me unload the rest of Mandy's goods."

The crusty old driver turned to look at Doc Thomas. "Was that what ya wanted?"

Doc looked up at the old man. "Well, part of it at least."

Amos pulled a handkerchief from his hip pocket and wiped his brow. "Well then, how 'bout buyin' me somethin' to wet my whistle?"

Doc Thomas grinned. "You'll have to settle for sarsaparilla; we haven't had a whiskey delivery in several months."

Amos shook his head, and then turned to look at Jonathan. "Capt'n, I don't know how you can keep yer fellers from desertin'. You got the driest fort in the territory."

Jonathan laughed. "I may have the driest fort, but I've got the most alert men. After a while, even you could get used to being on the wagon."

"I don't plan on bein' on any wagon 'cept that one there. 'Sides, a little somethin' to numb the senses makes it a lot easier to sit up on that there hard bench and stare at those horses behinds," Amos growled as he stuffed his kerchief back into his pocket.

Doc led the stage driver into the general store for a sarsaparilla and Jonathan started across the compound for his office when he heard the sentry call. "Riders approaching. Patrol coming in." The gates swung open and the patrol led by Corporal Tivy rode into the fort. Jonathan waited until Tivy reigned his horse to a stop beside him.

Stepping down from his horse, the corporal saluted Captain Parker. After returning the salute, the captain commanded, "Let's go into my office, Corporal. I want a full report."

The two men stepped upon the wooden porch and walked into the log building that housed Jonathan's office. The room was sparsely furnished. There was a hat rack to the right of the doorway and a washstand stood alone on the wall to the left. Jonathan's large wooden desk sat in the center of the room toward the back wall and he seated himself behind his desk.

After getting permission from the captain to be seated, Corporal Tivy began to tell what the patrol had found. "We followed the tracks south to the edge of the Badlands, sir. It had to be a band of comancheros. Some of the horses were shod and some not." Tivy paused a moment before he continued. "You know how it is in those hills, sir. They could probably see us comin' from miles away. I didn't want to lead the men into an ambush so we returned to the fort for further orders."

The captain smiled. "You didn't want to lead the men into an ambush but I've got a feeling you found out a little more than you just told me."

Tivy grinned as he ran his hand through his dark brown hair. "Well sir, I did a little reconnaissance work on my own durin' the night. I got close enough to tell we are dealin' with a mighty tough bunch. There's Indians, Mexicans, and a few white men in the bunch. They probably just got into this territory a few days before they raided that young woman's place. Probably that bunch we heard about that was in Texas and Oklahoma territory for a while."

Jonathan slumped back in his chair. The stories about the band that had been raiding down south were not pretty and he certainly didn't look forward to dealing with them. "You think they're the ones who burned her cabin and left her for dead?"

The corporal stood and began to pace the room. "I can't be sure. Couldn't get close enough to hear them talkin'. But if I was guessin', I'd say they're the ones. She hasn't told you anything yet?"

Jonathan leaned back in his chair. "No, she hasn't been awake enough to talk to anyone. Doc says it may still be a few days before she's able to talk to us."

The corporal seated himself once again in the chair in front of Jonathan's desk and stretched his long legs out in front of him. "Well, if you want I'll take a company back out and we'll see if we can't bring those renegades in."

"No, Corporal. You're right about the Badlands. They could see you coming from miles away and I'm not going to sacrifice a whole company of men in vain. Rest up tonight and then at first light in the morning, I want you and a couple of men, of your choosing, to get as close to their camp as you can without being seen. Whenever they break camp, follow them from a safe distance. Send one of your men back to the fort. I'll have a company ready to ride in a moment's notice. We'll have to catch them on the outside to do any damage to their ranks."

"Yes, sir. I'll do my best. I'll take Baker and Calhoun

with me."

"Take plenty of provisions. You don't know how long you may be out. Although I'd bet they'll be on the move before many days pass. Those kind are too greedy to sit in the hills for long. They probably have a scout out now searching for a likely prey."

Tivy nodded his head. "If I were a bettin' man, I'd say the Miller spread would be a likely target. Big spread, lots of wealth."

The captain stood and walked to a map nailed on one wall of his office. "You're probably right. I'll send a man out there to warn Miller so he can get his men ready." He pointed to the map. "There's a couple of small spreads like the woman's between the Badlands and the Miller place. They're the ones that will need our protection."

Tivy walked over to stand by Jonathan. "Maybe you should send some men over to help out at those little places."

Jonathan nodded. "I'll do that. They could dress like ranch hands so they wouldn't be so conspicuous. I'll talk to Lt. Blake." Jonathan walked back over to his desk. "Now you get some rest, Corporal. You've got a big job ahead of you but I know you can handle it. Maybe the woman'll wake up soon and be able to give us some more information."

The corporal saluted his commanding officer. "We'll leave at first light."

Jonathan returned the salute. "Godspeed." He called as the corporal left his office.

****

Sonora propped herself on one elbow and looked out the window. She knew she must be at Fort Benton. She couldn't remember how she got here; actually right now everything about her memory was rather fuzzy.

"Well, it's good to see you awake for a change," A man said as he approached the cot. "Let me take a look at you."

The young woman began to withdraw a little so he introduced himself. "I'm Nathan Thomas. Most folks just call me Doc. You were brought here a few days ago. You'd been hurt real bad and I've been taking care of you along with some help from a few other folks." The doctor paused and looked into Sonora's eyes as he sat down beside the small bed. She couldn't help but feel a bit of fear at this large man beside her.

"Now don't be afraid, I just want to look at your wounds."

Sonora relaxed a little as the doctor spoke softly to her. She saw kindness in his soft hazel eyes. "You're doing a lot better. Now we need to get some food into you."

Still she was silent. "Will you at least tell me your name?"

Sonora just stared at him and said nothing. She didn't feel he meant her any harm but for some reason she just couldn't speak right now.

"It's all right," the doctor continued. "We have plenty of time to talk later. I'll go get Mandy and she'll bring you something to eat. I'd fix something for you myself but I want you to get better. My cooking's likely to keep you in that bed a lot longer." Nathan chuckled at his little joke but Sonora showed no expression. He gave her another big smile before walking out the door and closing it behind him.

Sonora tried to sit up on the side of the cot but thought better of the idea. The pain in her abdomen was severe and she lay her head back onto the pillow as gently as she could.

Chapter Three

Sonora was sitting on the cot with pillows propped behind her back. Amanda was spooning broth into her mouth when a man in uniform walked into the room.

A big smile covered his clean shaven face when he looked at her. "It's good to see you doing better."

As he crossed the room to stand beside the cot, Sonora watched his every move. That was the voice she had heard whispering words of comfort to her. Sonora continued to stare at him as Amanda spooned a few more bites of the bland liquid into her mouth.

"Well, that about does it for this time. I'll be back this afternoon and I'll help you get cleaned up," Amanda turned to the man and added, "I've been talking to her, Jonathan, but she acts like she don't even know what I'm saying."

"Maybe she doesn't speak English," the captain offered. "With her dark hair and eyes, I guess she could be Indian or even Mexican." The man Amanda called Jonathan sat down in the chair beside the bed. He asked her name in Spanish but Sonora just stared at him.

"Maybe she's Indian." Doc said as he walked to stand behind Jonathan.

The only dialect of Indian Jonathan could speak was Comanche so he tried again to find out her name. Still she did not respond.

Sonora stared deep into Jonathan's green eyes. He had prayed for her. She remembered hearing him talk to God on her behalf. She could trust this man.

"Where's Timmy?" she choked out. Tears began to run down her face as she cried once again, "Where's Timmy?"

Jonathan pulled his handkerchief from his back pocket and handed it to the young woman. "Who's Timmy?"

"My son," was all she could answer before the sobs overtook her. Jonathan tried to reach for her but she pulled away. He sat helpless as her tears flowed.

When finally her tears began to abate, Jonathan asked, "Can you tell us your name?"

"Sonora," she whispered as tears ran down her cheeks.

"Sonora, I'm Captain Jonathan Parker. I want to help you. Can you tell me what happened to you?"

Sonora wiped her eyes with Jonathan's handkerchief, and then in broken sentences she spoke. "The men; they came; they took Timmy. Couldn't stop them. Tried but couldn't. I tried." She sobbed and shook uncontrollably.

"It's all right. I know you tried. It's not your fault." Jonathan spoke but his words meant little to Sonora. She could not be comforted.

The doctor was still standing behind Jonathan. He placed his hand on the captain's shoulder as he spoke. "Let her rest now. You can try again later. I can't have her upset like this. It's not good for her."

****

As Jonathan was leaving he noticed Amanda standing silently in the background before she too turned to follow him outside.

"What do you think?" she asked.

The captain stood on the edge of the porch. "About what?"

Amanda flashed her blue eyes at him. "The woman."

"I think something bad happened and she can't talk about it yet." Jonathan looked out across the compound, and then back at Amanda. "What do you think?"

Amanda studied Jonathan's tanned face for a moment, and then looked across the compound at the soldiers cleaning the stables. "I don't know. Reckon those men made off with her son." Amanda looked back at Jonathan. "Where's her husband? Did they kill him or was he not at home, and why did he leave her and the boy alone?"

Jonathan had been asking the same questions in his mind but when he had looked into the eyes of the hurting young woman he didn't have the heart to badger her for answers. He hoped Sonora would be able to answer all those questions in time. Jonathan looked away from Amanda's intent gaze before he spoke.

"Well, Amanda, I don't have the answers to all your questions. All I can say is that we didn't find another body around that cabin. It's not uncommon for a man to leave his family alone. He has to find food from time to time you know."

Amanda shrugged, and then stepped off the wooden porch in front of the infirmary onto the dirt. "There's just a lot of unanswered questions," she remarked as she strolled away.

Jonathan agreed but kept his thoughts to himself. Something made him very protective of the mysterious young woman lying helpless in the infirmary.

****

Doc Thomas sat quietly as Sonora awoke from a long restless sleep. He had watched her thrash about and heard her cry out that it had not been her fault. He had tried to comfort her as she slept but was not nearly as successful as Jonathan always seemed to be.

"Can I get you anything?" he asked as Sonora attempted to sit up.

She grimaced in pain. "No. How long have I been here?"

Doc stood and walked over to the water pitcher to pour his patient a cup of water. "You were brought in about a week ago by the captain and Corporal Tivy." Doc leaned down to assist her into a sitting position.

Sonora's hands shook as she took the tin cup full of water from the doctor. The clear liquid helped ease the cottonmouth feeling she had. She took another slow sip of water before she spoke. "I hurt really bad. What's happened to me?"

Doc Thomas pulled the straight-backed wooden chair over next to the bed. He seated himself beside his patient. Looking into her questioning face, he explained, "You were badly beaten. You were bleeding inside and I had to operate on you." Nathan paused. The fear in her face increased.

"You're recovering nicely though," he assured her. "Why don't I get Mandy to come over and help you clean up a bit?"

Sonora took another sip of water. "Not right now. Could you get the captain first? I'd like to talk to him."

Immediately, Doc stood to his feet. "Sure thing. I'll be right back."

****

Sonora sat for just a moment after the doctor left, and then attempted to stand. She managed to get to her feet by using the chair beside the bed for a crutch. After taking a few moments to get her balance, she tried to straighten her back. Finding it difficult to stand completely erect, Sonora walked bent over to get to the washstand where she splashed water on her face and washed her arms and hands. She caught a glimpse of herself in the small mirror hanging on the wall above the stand. Her face appeared to be one giant bruise with a few cuts here and there. She could see out of both eyes but her right eye remained very puffy.

Beginning to feel somewhat nauseated, Sonora slowly made her way back to the cot. She had just seated herself on the edge of the lumpy little bed when Captain Parker came into the room.

"Doc said you wanted to see me." The man pulled off his hat and hung it on the rack by the door.

Finding her little stroll had taken most of her strength; Sonora took a moment to catch her breath. "Yes, I have some questions. Your name is Captain Parker, if I remember correctly."

Nodding, Jonathan seated himself in the chair beside the bed and looked into Sonora's badly bruised face which she knew had now turned to a sickening yellow. "What do you want to know?"

Sonora winced with pain but managed to speak. "The doctor said you brought me here. Was anyone else around the cabin when you found me?"

Jonathan leaned forward in his chair. "No, we found no one else. Was someone supposed to be there?"

Sonora knew no one else was there but she just had to ask. Finally she murmured, "No."

"Sonora, can you tell me what happened?"

As Sonora began to relate the story, tears filled her dark brown eyes. "The wild men came up to the house. I bolted the door and tried to get Timmy and me in the cellar but there were so many of them and they wanted in very badly. They broke down the door. One big man grabbed Timmy as I fought and fought. They hit me...hard...over and over." Sonora paused and fought back the tears that continually threatened.

Taking a deep breath, she continued. "Timmy screamed and screamed until the big man stuffed a rag into his mouth." Loosing her battle to fight off the tears, sobs racked her body once again and with the sobbing came great throbs of pain. Sonora found it difficult to breathe.

Jonathan reached out to her but she still pulled away. "It's all right, Sonora. It's all right to cry. You've been through a lot." Jonathan watched her face. She knew he wanted to help but the pain was beginning to overwhelm her. "Doc, get in here."

Doc came through the door and rushed to the cot. He eased Sonora down onto the thin mattress, and then walked to his medicine cabinet. He poured some powder into a small bowl, added a little water, and then spooned a small amount of the liquid into Sonora's mouth.

"The men, did you find them." Sonora spit out between gritted teeth as Doc tried to make her comfortable.

Jonathan took a deep breath and leaned back in his chair. "We think we've found their camp. Sonora, do you remember what any of the men looked like?"

Nathan looked at the captain. "Jonathan, this needs to wait; Sonora needs her rest now."

Sonora reached up and grabbed the sleeve of the doctor's shirt. "It's all right, Doctor. I want to help all I can. I have to get Timmy back." She took a deep breath. "The one who grabbed Timmy was big. He was white, had long dirty brown hair and a thick beard. He had a scar over his right eye. I saw him clear because I tried to pull Timmy from him. It was a Mexican man that pulled me off him. The rest I don't know; that's when the fight started and they started hitting me. I think some of them were Indians."

Jonathan's voice was tense. "We're pretty sure it's a band of comancheros. They're camped out in the Badlands. I have men watching them but right now that's all we can do."

Sonora's anger began to show as she lifted her head and yelled at the army officer. "Just watching them! Why don't you arrest them and get my son back?"

With a thud, Sonora fell back onto the cot and winced with pain. Again, Doc warned Jonathan this conversation needed to wait but Jonathan continued to try and explain his situation.

He stood and began to pace beside her bed. "Calm down, Sonora. We can't ride into the Badlands after them. My men would be slaughtered. It won't be long before they start to move again and then we can make our move."

His explanation seemed to calm Sonora a little. "Do you know if Timmy's with them?"

Jonathan sighed deeply as he stopped and looked down at Sonora. "No, I don't. One of my men got close enough to tell it was a band of comancheros but that's about all. We didn't know to look for a child then." Jonathan paused, "Tell me about Timmy if you feel up to it."

Doc raised his hands into the air. "I give up." He looked at his patient. "Sonora, you need to rest but I'll leave you two alone." Looking at Jonathan before he left the room, he added, "Keep it short, Captain."

A faint smile covered Sonora's face as she thought about her son but the smile was quickly replaced with fear. "He's five. Has blond hair and brown eyes." Again she lost control and wailed, "I should have protected him."

Jonathan sat down beside the cot once again. "Sonora, you did your best. Did you and Timmy live alone in the cabin?"

Sonora finally managed to answer between sobs. "No. We lived with Uncle Tobias but he was out hunting."

"Do you have any idea which way your uncle went when he left the cabin?"

"North, I think." The medicine the doctor had given her was beginning to take effect.

"Sonora, you need to rest. We'll talk more later. I'll get word to my men to be on the look out for your son and your uncle."

Sonora's eyes fluttered closed as she murmured,

"Please find Timmy."

Jonathan tucked the woolen blanket around her shoulders. "We'll do our best, I promise."

Chapter Four

"Thad, go out to the Saunders' place and tell Lt. Blake to be on the lookout for Timmy whenever he has any contact with that bunch of renegades." Captain Parker looked up at the private standing before him in his office.

"Yes, sir, and what about the woman's uncle?" The private wanted to know.

"Well, the Saunders' place is to the north of Sonora's cabin so keep an eye out for him. I can't launch an all out search for him while those rebels are still on the loose. Just tell everyone to keep their eyes open. Something must've happened to him or he would've surely come looking for his family by now."

The private saluted his superior officer and turned to go. "Godspeed," Jonathan called as he always did when he sent anyone from the protective walls of the fort.

****

"So, honey, you feelin' better?" Amanda asked Sonora as she assisted the young woman with her bath.

"A little I guess. Have the men left to find my son?"

"The men have been out since the day after Johnny brought you in." Amanda pulled a freshly laundered gown from a basket.

Sonora looked up at the woman with the red hair. "Who's Johnny?"

Amanda smiled. "Oh, that's what I call Capt'n Parker. Me and him are well...kinda close."

Sonora made no comment as she pulled the clean gown over her head and fastened the buttons all the way up to her throat.

"You better get some rest now," Amanda instructed as she fluffed the pillows behind Sonora.

Sonora moaned as she slumped against the pillows. "That's all I've been doing."

"Well, you gotta get your strength back. Now if you'd like I'll brush your hair." Sonora nodded and Amanda began to brush Sonora's long dark hair. "You surely have pretty hair. Real black. Was your momma Mexican?"

"No," was all the answer Sonora offered.

Evidently disappointed, Amanda tried again. "Then your daddy must've been."

Once again Sonora only gave Amanda a negative answer. When Amanda finished brushing the tangles out of Sonora's hair, Sonora eased herself back onto the cot and closed her eyes. Sonora hoped that would stop Amanda's prying into matters she certainly didn't care to discuss with the overly curious shopkeeper.

****

Amanda left the sleeping Sonora and walked out into the warm air. "She's not very talkative." Amanda commented to Doc Thomas when she noticed him sitting on the bench in front of his office.

He looked up at the slightly upset lady. "Mandy, no one is very talkative when they don't feel good."

Amanda leaned against one of the poles supporting the roof of the porch. "Well, she could tell us a little bit about herself."

Doc took a puff from the pipe he held in his hand. "Why is it so necessary for us to know anything about her, other than she was hurt and apparently her family is missing? She needs our help, Mandy."

Amanda sighed. "Well, I'd just feel better if I knew a little bit more about her." Chuckling, Doc couldn't help but tease the frustrated woman. "You're just like every other female I ever knew. Sometimes you're too nosy for your own good. You act like an old hen trying to protect her territory."

Amanda pretended to be hurt. "Well, maybe I am a little curious, but if you men were truthful, you'd admit you are, too."

Doc uncrossed his long legs and stretched them out in front of him. "I guess everyone is a little curious from time to time, Mandy, but right now, my patient is still very sick and she's real worried about her boy."

Amanda tuned away from the doctor's gaze and looked across at the corral. "I understand why she's anxious about her boy, but what about her uncle? I haven't heard her say two words about him. Don't she care what happened to him?"

Doc took another draw from his pipe. "I'm sure she does, but she's a momma and her boy is all she can think about right now. Actually nobody but Jonathan has heard her say more than a few words about anybody. I think she feels more comfortable confiding in him for some reason."

Amanda quickly turned and looked at the doctor. "Huh. She best not get too comfortable confidin' in him."

"Ah, could it be you're a little jealous?" Doc teased. "You think you have some claims on Jonathan Parker, Mandy?"

"Got no claims on him...yet." Amanda smiled as she turned her reddened face away from the doctor's knowing look.

"I see how it is." Doc laughed as he stood to his feet. "Well, I'd best be checking on my patient. See you later, Mandy."

"See ya, Doc." The doctor was closing the door to his office as he faintly heard, "Got no claims on Johnny yet, but give me time."

****

"Rider approaching," the sentry yelled. "It's Baker, open the gate."

Private Baker reined his horse to a stop in front of Captain Parker's office. He dismounted and hit the ground on a run that ended in front of Jonathan's desk. Disregarding formality, Baker began to speak. "Sir, they're movin', or at least will be by the time we git back. They were havin' a big party. Celebratin' their next big conquest I reckon. They'll be ridin' out at first light."

The captain looked into the eyes of the young man in front of him. "Any idea which way they'll be heading?"

Baker shuffled from one foot to the other. "Tivy got close enough to hear 'em talkin' 'bout a little spread to the east. Best we could figure they musta been talkin' 'bout Saunders' place."

Jonathan nodded in agreement. "Any sign of a little boy with them?"

The young man's brow wrinkled. "Not that we seen. Why?"

Jonathan stood and walked around his desk. "The woman we brought in said they took her five-year-old son."

Baker shook his head. "We ain't seen no kids, Capt'n."

"Okay. We can't waste any time." Jonathan grabbed his hat and sword from the rack behind his chair. "Get a bite to eat at the mess hall while I rally the troops. We'll leave in fifteen minutes." Walking out onto the porch, Jonathan yelled orders to the men standing nearest his office. As the bugler sounded the call to alert the troops, Jonathan ran across the yard to the doctor's office.

Doc met him at the door. "What's going on?"

"The comancheros are moving, probably heading toward the Saunders' place. We're leaving to give Blake a hand," Jonathan informed as he moved toward the bed where Sonora lay. "Is she asleep?"

"No," a soft voice answered. Sonora opened her dark brown eyes and looked up at the captain. "Is Timmy with them?"

"My man doesn't know. We'll do our best to find him, Sonora. You just rest so you can take care of him when we get him back."

She sat up on the cot and looked into Jonathan's eyes. "You think you'll get him back?"

Jonathan walked to the door and then looked back into the worried face of a young mother. "We sure will try. Now you rest up." Jonathan opened the door.

"Be careful, Captain," Sonora called. Jonathan turned back once again and gave her a warm smile before he left the room.

Once outside on the porch, Doc wanted to know. "What were you not saying in there?"

Jonathan pulled his hat on his head. "The men didn't see any sign of a boy."

Doc stood beside Jonathan. "Well, does that mean they don't have him?"

"Not necessarily. They could've stuck him back in a cave somewhere out of sight." The captain looked out over the yard where the troops were assembled. "Doc, take good care of our patient. I don't know how long we'll be out."

"You take care. I don't want a lot of doctoring to do when you boys get back here."

Jonathan slapped his friend on the back before he stepped off the porch and gave the command for the troops to mount their horses. The big wooden gates swung open and the Tenth Calvary rode out of Fort Benton under the command of Captain Jonathan Parker.

****

Amanda stood on the porch in front of her store and watched as the big wooden gates swung shut. Her stomach churned each time Jonathan rode out of the safety of the fort. She had never confessed her feelings to the captain, at least not in words, but she cared deeply for him. Amanda had to admit that as far as Jonathan was concerned he only treated her as a friend but Amanda hoped someday that would change. Now she just prayed God would bring him back to the fort safe and sound.

Although she knew her feelings were unwarranted, Amanda couldn't help but blame Sonora for Jonathan being in danger. If it hadn't been for Sonora's plight, the captain wouldn't have had to lead a troop out to capture the renegades. Deep inside, Amanda knew Jonathan would have gone after the scoundrels no matter what, but for now it was just easier to blame Sonora.

****

The sun felt good on Sonora's face. It seemed like an eternity since she had been outside. Her mind raced as she wondered what her future held. Would Captain Parker find Timmy? That little boy had been her life for five years now.

What would I do without him? Tears filled Sonora's eyes as she thought about her son. *What could those people be doing to him?* A wave of nausea overcame her when she thought of the fear Timmy was probably feeling and wondering why his mommy or Uncle Tobias didn't come to get him. Sonora could hold back her sobs no longer. Her body became racked with pain as her wailing increased.

Doc must have heard Sonora's cries from inside and stepped out onto the porch. Kneeling beside her chair, he tried to console her. "Now, now, Captain Parker'll bring your son back. He's a good man and he has a good bunch of men riding with him. They'll find him. Don't you cry anymore, you hear." Doc put his arm around her shoulders and held her until her tears subsided.

"Thank you. I'll try not to be a bother to you anymore and not to cry. I'm feeling much better now." Sonora pulled away from the doctor's embrace and tried to force a smile.

The doctor stood to his feet. "Sonora, you're no bother and you can cry all you want to. I just wish there was something I could do to make you feel better."

Sonora looked up into the doctor's face. He was not a young man. His brow had a few wrinkles and his beard had more gray in it than not but he had a kind face and the gray hair at his temples gave him a distinguished air. "You've done enough for me and physically I do feel better. The soreness has eased up a lot and the pain is not nearly as severe." She forced a smile to her face. "I would like to do something to start earning my keep around here. Maybe I could cook and clean for you."

Doc Thomas pulled a chair up beside where Sonora was sitting, "I don't think you're up to that just yet. I want you to take it easy for a few more days. You had some very serious injuries." Doc paused and pointed his hand at the large building to the east of his office. "Besides, I take most of my meals over there at the mess hall with the other men. When you're doing better, we'll find you something to do around here but for now I want you to just continue to rest. Okay?"

Sonora nodded in agreement. "Okay. I just thought if I could keep busy I wouldn't have as much time to think."

"I can understand that." Doc was thoughtful for a moment and then smiled. "Hey, do you play cards?"

Sonora turned to face the doctor. A look of shock covered her face. "No. I never learned since I don't believe in gambling."

Doc smiled. "You can play cards without gambling. We could play just for the fun of it and to keep you occupied."

"Okay, it might help." Sonora was willing to give the doctor's offer a try although she was sure nothing could erase the thoughts of Timmy from her head.

****

"What are you two up to now?" Amanda asked as she walked into the infirmary.

"I'm teaching Sonora the fine art of five card draw, without using money, of course." Doc smiled and looked up at Amanda for just a second. "I'm glad we're only playing for fun because this young lady would have already put me in the poor house."

A faint chuckle escaped from Sonora as she smiled at Doc. "I'm not doing that good."

"You've won the last six hands. Are you sure you've never played poker before?" Doc grinned as he teased Sonora.

"Positive. My momma would faint if she knew I was playing now."

Seeing an opening to learn something about Sonora's past Amanda joined the conversation. "Where does your momma live?" Amanda pulled a chair up beside the table where the two were playing cards.

Sonora stared at the cards in her hand. She answered Amanda's question with a single word. "Heaven."

Amanda was taken aback for just a moment but her curiosity got the best of her and she tried a different tact. "I'm so sorry to hear that." Pausing for just a moment she continued, "Where did you grow up?"

Sonora realized there was no escaping the questions of this woman. She hoped if she gave Amanda a little information, maybe it would ease the red-haired woman's need to know. "I grew up in the South, along the Mississippi River."

Doc glanced across the table at Sonora. "I thought I could detect the gentile influence of the Southern Belle in your manner of speaking," Doc drawled. "I'm a southerner myself. My grandparents had a big plantation in Louisiana before the big war. My grandmother lost her mind when the Yankees came in and took over her house. She died before the war ended." Doc leaned back in his chair. He seemed to gaze off in the distance for an instant. "I guess it was a good thing though. Two of her boys never came back. My daddy and his brother Tom were the only ones that survived. Listen to me rattle on." Again Doc paused, and then he smiled across the table at his patient.

"Sonora, did your folks own a plantation?"

Sonora sighed deeply as she stared at the cards she held in her hand. "No. My grandfather operated a riverboat along the Mississippi." She lay a card on the table, and then glanced at Nathan Thomas. "My folks had a little black-land farm in the Mississippi delta."

Amanda huffed. "So you're not really a gentile Southern Belle, just a farm girl." She stood, smoothed the bodice of her dress over her slim waistline, and then walked over to the stove and poured herself a cup of coffee.

"I guess you could say that. I was never invited to the fancy balls and never associated with the belles of society." Sonora paused and watched as Amanda once again sat in a chair beside the table. Sonora looked Amanda directly in the eyes. "But I never felt like I missed a thing."

Doc must have sensed the tension between his two female companions. "I know you didn't miss anything, Sonora. I grew up with all those fancy trimmings and for the most part, it was nothing to brag about."

"I don't agree with you." Amanda looked across at the doctor, stood and walked to the window. For a few seconds she looked out over the compound before turning back to face the two people seated at the table. "I enjoyed the social life in Austin, Texas, where I grew up. I really miss all the folderol."

Sonora glanced at Amanda and looked across at the doctor. "The only thing I miss about my past is my family."

Amanda sat back down at the table beside Sonora. She gently pushed a strand of her red hair from her face. "If you'll excuse my curiosity, you don't look typically southern."

Sonora gave Amanda a sidelong glance. "My grandmother, on my father's side, was from Italy. My father always said I looked just like her."

Amanda still wanted to know more about the mystery woman in their presence so she continued her inquisition. "You've mentioned your son and your uncle but I haven't heard you say anything about your husband. Was he away when the comancheros raided your place?"

Sonora paled at Amanda's question. Doc obviously noticed the look on the young woman's face as well and came to her aide. "I think Sonora has had enough excitement and questions for today. I think it's time for her to go lie down for a while." Doc directed his comments to Sonora.

Relief flooded Sonora's face as she rose from her chair and started toward the cot.

Chapter Five

The Dakota Territory

Jonathan leaned against the hitching rail in front of the Saunders' cabin. "Mr. Saunders', we'll do our best to protect you and your family."

"I know you will, Captain Parker." Mr. Saunders stepped down off his front porch. "My men and I will help. I've instructed my men to follow your orders, so what can we do?"

"You've already done plenty. Your men have cooperated with the lieutenant and have the perimeter well guarded." Jonathan sighed deeply. "Now we just wait."

"That's the hardest part." Saunders shook his head as he made a low groan.

Jonathan slapped the rancher on the shoulder. "Well, Mr. Saunders, you might start praying." The captain forced a smile, and then excused himself and walked out into the cool night.

He walked a short distance from the cabin before he stopped and looked up into the star filled night sky. "Oh, Father, please help us. Protect the men and help us arrest the rebels with as little blood shed as possible. And, Lord, please let us find Timmy. Keep him safe until he is back in his mother's care again." Jonathan knew they needed the Lord's help to be able to capture the comancheros. They were too big a force for his troops and Saunders' men to reckon with without Divine intervention.

Jonathan continued to quietly pray as he walked toward the corral but his mind began to wander to a young woman waiting back at Fort Benton. Sonora was a mystery Jonathan very much wanted to solve. He knew he had feelings for her that he didn't understand. She was just a lady he had rescued in her hour of need and all he knew about her was that she had a little boy being held hostage by the renegades who had raided her home. He also knew that if she had a little boy, she must have a husband somewhere. Knowing that hadn't stopped his feelings from surfacing.

Sonora had not spoken of a husband and Jonathan had found that rather strange. In her state of shock, he hadn't pressed her for answers. Of course, since she was apparently living with her uncle, it was a strong possibility she was a widow. First, he had to get her son back safely. Once that was accomplished, he could find out more about the young woman he had rescued.

Jonathan was brought out of his thoughts when a young private ran up to him. "Capt'n, the lieutenant wants you to come up on the bluff. There's dust on the horizon. They're comin', sir."

"I'm on my way." Before walking off, Jonathan looked at the private. "Baker, go in the house and tell Saunders. Have him get his wife and children into the cellar."

Jonathan joined Lieutenant Blake and Corporal Tivy. "Capt'n, I hope you're prayed up," Tivy commented.

"Always." Jonathan glanced over at the corporal. "It wouldn't hurt if some more prayers were to join mine though."

Tivy smiled. "Mine's going up now."

The lieutenant had remained quiet. Jonathan knew Lieutenant Blake's opinion of Christianity. Blake respected the captain, but Jonathan knew the lieutenant was of the opinion God helps those who help themselves. The young lieutenant was experienced in fighting the likes of these rebels and Jonathan knew Blake was relying on that knowledge at this time. Blake had always said knowledge was his best friend. Jonathan knew knowledge was good, but having God on your side was even better.

The men held their positions until the comancheros were in firing range, and then a warning shot was fired over the rebel's heads. The bandit's commander quickly pulled his horse to a halt. He seemed at a loss for a few seconds as to what his next move should be.

Before he could make a move, Captain Parker called out to him. "Throw down your weapons, you're surrounded."

The captain held little hope of the capture being that easy. He didn't really expect the ruffians to comply. He was not surprised when the rebels dismounted and headed for cover as they began to fire aimlessly into the air. The battle began.

Tivy fired a few shots toward the bandits before he glanced over at his commanding officer. "Capt'n, I think I can take a couple of men and get up in those hills behind them."

Parker nodded. "Go ahead, Corporal. We'll cover you."

Once Tivy was in position, it didn't take long to bring the bandits under control. Jonathan knew they still had a problem. From what Tivy had told him, Jonathan knew this was only a small part of the original gang.

As the soldiers guarded the prisoners, Tivy and the captain stood off to the side alone. "Sir, they must've split up."

The captain nodded in agreement. "They were all still together when you left them last night and headed here, right?"

Tivy pulled his hat from his head and wiped his brow on the sleeve of his shirt. "Yes, sir. I saw no evidence of 'em plannin' to split up."

Lt. Blake walked up beside Tivy. "Well, Corporal, what do you think happened to the rest of them?"

"Either the others went back to camp because they didn't think the whole band would be needed or the rest are raiding another ranch. The later would be my guess." The corporal moaned as he pulled his hat down further on his head.

Lieutenant Blake took a long look around at his surroundings. "So what now, Captain?"

Jonathan looked at the prisoners, shook his head and sighed deeply. "Let's question this group, although I doubt we'll get any information from them. Then you take your men and check the surrounding ranches. I figure the Miller ranch would be the most likely target." The captain gave the corporal a sidelong glance. "Tivy, take Baker and Calhoun and see if you can pick up their trail again. Remember, be on the look-out for the little boy."

"Yes, sir," Tivy saluted before turning to go find his partners.

****

Just as the captain suspected, interrogating the renegades was an effort in futility. The captain and Company B escorted the bandits back to Fort Benton while the remaining troops scouted to find what damage the other comancheros might have done.

As he rode, the captain's thoughts were on the young woman waiting at the fort. Sonora was hoping for answers about her son and Jonathan had nothing to tell her. Sonora wasn't the only one who wanted answers; Jonathan had some questions about the young woman he had rescued and they needed answers, too.

****

Fort Benton

It had been a long two days since the Tenth Calvary had ridden out of those enormous wooden gates and Jonathan was glad to hear the familiar call, "Company B approaching," as they neared the entrance to the fort and the gates swung open. His heart went to his stomach as he rode up to the doctor's quarters. Doc Thomas stood on the porch with Sonora at his side. The look of disappointment flooding Sonora's face was almost more than Jonathan could stand. If he had his choice, he'd ride over to his office, go inside, close the door and not come out for days, but he knew that was not a choice now.

Captain Parker dismounted and turned to his troops. "Sergeant, dismiss the men." After passing the reins of his horse to the young private standing at his side, Jonathan removed his hat ran his fingers through his brown hair and approached Sonora. Normally, Jonathan's posture was erect and he stood to his full five-foot-ten but right now his shoulders drooped a little. "I'm sorry. There was no sign of the boy." Before his words cleared his lips, the young woman's body went limp. Jonathan stretched out his arms and caught Sonora before she fell to the porch.

"Carry her inside," Doc instructed. Jonathan did as he was told and laid the young woman on the cot in the doctor's front room. The doctor firmly patted her cheeks and called her name. Jonathan wet a cloth with cool water and applied it to Sonora's forehead.

Jonathan looked down into her pale face. "I think she's beginning to come around."

Sonora began to moan. The doctor continued to sponge her face with the cool cloth. "Are you all right?"

Sonora nodded. She looked up into Jonathan's face. Tears began to fill her eyes as she questioned Jonathan about the events of the past two days. His answers held no comfort for her.

Jonathan pulled a chair up beside the cot. "Sonora, the group split up. Only part of the gang attacked where we were. My men are searching for the rest of them."

Doc glanced over at Jonathan. "What about the prisoners you brought in?"

"You brought prisoners?" Sonora quickly sat up on the side of the cot. "Make them tell you where my son is."

"We have questioned them, Sonora," Jonathan looked into her dark eyes, "but we got nowhere. They're not talking about anything, much less the whereabouts of a little boy."

Sonora jumped to her feet as she looked from Jonathan to the doctor. "Maybe if I talk to them. Maybe I can get through. I've got to try."

Jonathan stood to his feet, grabbed her shoulders and held her firmly, "We're not dealing with ordinary men, Sonora. These men have no compassion. They could care less about your loss or your hurt. There's no use in you talking to them."

Determination covered Sonora's face as she looked into Jonathan's eyes. "Captain, I've got to try. Please let me talk to them. Maybe I can make them listen to me."

Jonathan saw no way of stopping the stubborn young woman standing before him. "Well, Doc, what'd you say? Is she well enough to talk to these men?"

"There's nothing physically that should stop her." Doc ran his fingers through his hair. "But, Sonora, I agree with Jonathan, I don't think it will do any good and it will probably just make you feel worse in the long run."

Sonora turned to face Nathan. "Doctor Thomas, I've got to try. If I can get any information out of them about my son, it will be worth any grief they cause me. If I don't learn anything, at least I'll know I tried."

The men looked at each other and knew they had no choice; they had to let Sonora talk to the renegades. It wouldn't be pleasant but it had to be done.

****

"Please tell me about my little boy." Sonora pleaded with the man Jonathan had told her was the leader of the group.

The man looked down his nose at Sonora as he growled. "Lady, I done told you I don't know nothin' 'bout no little boy."

Sonora faced the man and with tears in her eyes she shouted at him. "I beg you. He's just a child. He should be with his mother. Where did you take him?"

The man laughed in her face as he propositioned her. "What's it worth to ya to find this kid of yours?"

Sonora lowered her eyes and spoke softly. "Anything, mister. I'll do anything."

The comanchero turned to his buddies. "You hear that, boys. This little woman is willin' to do anything to git her kid back." The men in the cell began to whoop and whistle. "Take her for yore woman, Carlos," one of the bandits called.

Carlos leaned over the table toward Sonora, but before he could speak, Jonathan was at the young woman's side. "That's enough! Sonora, let's go."

Jonathan took her arm, but before her could escort her from the room, she looked her adversary in the eyes and threatened, "I know you were one of the men at my cabin. I know you were there so I know you know where Timmy is. I'll see you hang if you don't tell me what I want to know."

Carlos snarled at Sonora's threat as the guard shoved him into the cell with the other bandits. "Hey, Carlos, the little woman is real tough. You should be scared," one of the renegades called. He was soon quieted by Carlos' firm hand across his face.

****

Once outside, Jonathan stopped and turned Sonora to face him. "Is that man really one of the men that raided your place?"

"I can't be sure," Sonora confessed. "I only got a glimpse of a couple of the men. I gave you the descriptions of the ones I remember clearly." Sonora's voice grew weak. "I didn't see the big one with the scar in the cell."

Jonathan leaned against one of the posts on the porch. "It was pretty stupid of you to tell the man that you remembered him. He'll be out to get you now for sure."

"I should be safe from him." Sonora glanced over at Jonathan. "You have him in jail and he won't go free, will he?"

Jonathan pushed his hat back on his head. "Not if I can help it, but there's still a big part of his gang on the loose. You never know what will happen." He couldn't bear to look at Sonora as he added, "We have to be prepared for anything."

Sonora stepped off the porch. "I'm not worried about myself; I've just got to find Timmy."

The two walked silently across the compound to the doctor's office. "Sonora, let's sit down." Jonathan removed his hat and indicated the bench on the porch. "I have a few questions for you, if you feel up to it."

Sonora knew what was coming and wished with all her heart she could avoid the obvious. She knew if she ever hoped to get her son back she would have to give the captain some answers to his questions. She sat down on the wooden bench. As Jonathan sat down beside her, she looked into his eyes and knew she had to be convincing.

The captain glanced at the young woman seated beside him. "Sonora, you told me about your uncle but you have not mentioned a husband." He left the statement hanging.

Sonora took a deep breath; her voice breaking as she started. "I don't have a husband." She paused, waiting for a comment but when Jonathan remained silent she continued. "Timmy and I came out here alone; we had to get away. We've been out here about six months staying at my uncle's cabin. He was up in the hills prospecting when the comancheros attacked us." Again she paused and swallowed hard. "I think I told you he had gone hunting, but my mind was so muddled I don't know half of what I may have said." She hesitated just a moment before adding, "He should be back in a few days and he'll be worried sick about us."

Jonathan interrupted and assured Sonora he'd send

someone to find her uncle and tell him what had happened to her and the boy.

Sonora tried to smile. "Thank you. Uncle Tobias is a good-hearted man. He took us in at a very difficult time."

Jonathan leaned forward and propped his arms on his knees. "You said you had to get away. Were you running away from something?"

"Not something—someone. We were running away from Timmy's father." Sonora stood and walked to the edge of the porch.

Silence fell between the two people. Jonathan began to twirl his hat between his hands. "I thought you said your husband was dead?"

"That's not what I said. I said I didn't have a husband." Again silence fell between them. Sonora could see the confusion written on the captain's face. "I'll try to explain. I was never married to Timmy's father."

When Jonathan made no comment, she told him about growing up along the Mississippi River. "You see life was hard for us. We were what you might call dirt poor, but my folks were wonderful Christian people. I just couldn't stand being a farmer's daughter and thought there had to be more to life than that. I ran away to New Orleans. Not long after I got to the big city, I met a wealthy young man. He didn't want to marry me but he did set me up in a fancy room in one of the big hotels. Bought me expensive clothes and jewelry. Everything a girl could want. I was young and stupid and thought he would eventually marry me."

Sonora wanted to avoid looking into Jonathan's eyes so she turned her back to him. She was afraid she would be met with severe disapproval and right now she didn't need to be judged by this young captain.

Taking a long breath, she continued her tale. She spoke just above a whisper. "I discovered I was going to have a baby and then I thought the man would marry me. When he found out, he just laughed in my face and told me he wasn't even sure it was his child. After that he threw me out. I found out he was going to marry the daughter of the governor of the state so I guess he had to get rid of me before he walked down the aisle."

Jonathan sat quietly and listened. He patiently

waited for the end of her story before he commented.

"I went back to the farm. I didn't know if I would be welcome or not and when I got there, I found out my mother had died the year before of pneumonia. Daddy took me in and seemed really happy to have me home. We didn't know what to tell folks about the baby so we decided we'd say my husband had been killed and that's why I came back home. It was just one more lie to the sordid life I had lived and it wasn't hard to play the part of a grieving widow because of the way I had been treated by Timmy's father."

Sonora fell silent giving Jonathan an opportunity to speak. "Sonora, you did the right thing by going home to your family, but I don't understand something. If the man denied Timmy was his, why are you running from him now?"

Sonora again sat down beside Jonathan. "The young man did get married not long after I left town. They now have two little girls but no son. It seems his father was very disappointed he didn't have a grandson as an heir and threatened to cut his son off without a dime. I guess Daniel, that's Timmy's father's name, got nervous and he told his father about Timmy. Somehow he must have found out I gave birth to a little boy. Anyway, the old man wanted his grandson no matter what kind of scandal it might cause so Daniel came to claim the son he had previously denied. That's when I took Timmy and ran away."

Jonathan looked over at Sonora. "Why didn't you go to the authorities for help?"

"There's no way someone like me could win in court with these people. They own the courts. They have money and power; I have nothing. They can give Timmy the world while all I can give him is love." Sonora hung her head and sighed deeply.

"Sonora, what you've given Timmy is something money can't buy." Jonathan started to reach out to touch Sonora's hand but quickly pulled back.

"Timmy's gone now so I didn't do a very good job of protecting him." Sonora began to cry. Jonathan pulled her into his arms and let her cry on his shoulder.

"It'll be okay. We'll find Timmy," Jonathan assured.

She heard his words but was afraid this was one promise he might not be able to keep.

The tears finally stopped and Sonora got up the courage to look into Jonathan's eyes. "I know what you must think of me. I'm a terrible person for doing what I did. I don't deserve your help but please don't hold that against Timmy."

Jonathan smiled, as he spoke, "You are not a terrible person. You were just very young." He paused and looked into her still moist eyes. "Sonora, do you remember the story in the Bible where the men were going to stone the woman they caught in adultery?" Sonora nodded. "Well, Jesus looked at the men and told them that anyone who was without sin should cast the first stone. I guess Jesus would probably say the same thing today if He were here. I can't throw stones at you, Sonora, I have sinned, too, but the wonderful thing is Jesus has forgiven me. He can and will forgive you if you just ask Him, too."

Once again, there was silence between them. Sonora heard the words the young captain spoke and knew they were true. She had been raised in the church and knew Jesus would forgive her. For some reason, she prayed this young man sitting next to her would be able to forgive her when he learned the real truth. That had suddenly become very important to her.

"Am I interruptin' somethin'?" Amanda asked as she walked up in front of the doctor's office.

"No. Sonora is just upset we didn't find any traces of her son yet." Jonathan quickly answered Amanda.

Amanda seated herself in the chair next to Jonathan. "I saw you caught the renegades."

"We caught part of them. We're still looking for the rest of the gang." Jonathan paused and gazed out at the compound as he continued the conversation with Amanda. "Company A is still out on their trail."

Turning back to look at Sonora he said, "Sonora, why don't you go in and try to rest a while. I'll come over and check on you later."

Sonora was not unhappy to get away from Amanda. This woman still made her feel very uncomfortable. She stood and bid goodbye to Jonathan and Amanda before walking into Doc Thomas' office.

Chapter Six

The Dakota Territory

"We were sure those renegades had raided your place, Mr. Miller." Lt. Blake explained as he carefully scanned the area. "When only part of the group of renegades showed up at the Saunders' place, we figured the rest of them headed your way."

The rancher pulled his hat from his head and wiped his brow with his handkerchief. "Praise God, we ain't seen nary a one of 'em, but me and my men have been on the lookout since we heard about them raidin' that old prospector's place." Mr. Miller pulled his hat back on his head. "I guess them comancheros musta thought old Tobias had dug a lot more gold outa them hills than he had. I bet they sure were disappointed when they left there."

The lieutenant continued to scan the horizon ever on the alert. "Well, I don't know if they got any gold or not but they sure roughed up the woman who was staying there and they took her little boy."

Eli Miller shook his head. "Probably took the kid since they didn't find much gold. They'll probably sell him for a purty penny." Eli started moving toward the corral and Blake fell into step beside him. "That may be where the rest of the gang is. They probably headed up into Canada where they'll sell the boy to a trader who'll take him to the coast and put him on a boat for only God knows where." Eli Miller shook his head as he propped his booted foot up on the lower rung of the corral fence.

Blake leaned on the top rail of the fence. "You may be right but I sure hope not." The army officer looked over at Miller. "I'll leave a couple of men here with you. If there's any trouble I want someone to hi-tail it to the fort for help. You understand?" Lt. Blake waited for a nod of understanding from Eli. "We'll get you help just as soon as we can. In the meantime, stay on the alert."

Miller again nodded that he understood. "We're always on the alert. I thank ya for the extra help but I think me and my men can handle it."

Blake stood up straight and adjusted the hat on his head. "Captain Parker would want you to have the help. We will still try to pick up their trail." The lieutenant pulled his gloves from his belt. "It just seemed to disappear a few miles before we got to your spread."

Eli Miller looked over at the young officer. "Well if ya don't find it again maybe that means they've moved on to better pickins."

"I doubt that." Blake shook his head as he sighed deeply. "We have seven of their men in custody and I doubt they leave the area without trying to get them back. If we don't find a fresh trail soon we'll head back to the fort. We may need all our resources to protect the fort and hold on to our prisoners." The two men shook hands before Lt. Blake walked to where his men waited.

"God be with ya," Miller called as the soldiers mounted their animals and rode away.

****

Fort Benton

Another two days had passed when Sonora heard the sentry yell, "Company A approaching." The big gates opened and a tired group of men rode in. Sonora anxiously watched as each man rode past her spot on the porch but there was no sign of her son. Tears began to fill her eyes once again. She watched as Lt. Blake reigned his horse to a stop in front of Jonathan's office. She wished she could be there when the lieutenant reported to his superior officer but she knew Jonathan would tell her if there was news of Timmy.

****

"Lieutenant Blake reporting, sir."

"At ease, Lieutenant. Tell me what you found." The captain leaned back in his chair and looked his officer in the face.

Blake took a deep breath. "Absolutely nothing, sir. The Miller spread was untouched. We lost the comancheros' trail a few miles from the Miller place and never could pick it up again. I figure they'll show up here sooner or later."

Jonathan nodded his head. "I figure you're right, Blake. The question is, when?"

"I don't know, sir, but I would think it will be pretty soon."

Jonathan leaned forward and propped his elbows on his wooden desk. He knew as the commanding officer he should be good at not showing his concern but he was afraid he wasn't as good at it as he might hope. "Did Tivy meet up with you or is he still out scouting?"

"He met us a few miles from the Miller Ranch but went back out scouting." Blake sat down in the chair in front of Jonathan's desk. "He took his men and they headed back toward the Badlands. He figured they might have gone back to their hideout to regroup and plan their next move."

Jonathan nodded. "He's probably right. I sure hope they see some sign of the little boy."

Lt. Blake told the captain Eli Miller's theory of what might have happened to Sonora's young son.

Jonathan stood and started to pace the floor. "I sure pray he's wrong. Sonora is at the end of her rope as it is. I don't know if she can hold herself together much longer." Jonathan tuned to face Blake. "Lieutenant, why don't you go get cleaned up and get yourself something to eat. Then double the guard starting tonight."

"Yes sir," Blake stood to his feet. He saluted his superior officer and then exited the room. Jonathan walked back to his desk and sat down. He slumped back in his chair and prayed for God to return little Timmy to his mother.

****

The Badlands, Dakota Territory

Three soldiers sat quietly in a small covering of trees. Private Pete Baker looked over to where the corporal sat keeping watch. "What do you think, Ben?"

"What I think is that that smoke over on the horizon is comin' from their camp," Corporal Tivy responded.

"I guess we might as well git comfortable until

nightfall." Private Aubrey Calhoun pulled his hat from his head as he leaned back against a small tree.

"Yeah, and pray there ain't no moon tonight." Pete whispered as he too tried to get comfortable for the long wait.

"We'd better try to git a little shut eye," Tivy encouraged. "It's a long way across that flatland. It'll take most of the night to cross it so we better rest now."

The Badlands of the Dakota Territory had been the perfect hideout for criminals for many years. Once a gang was in the midst of the hills there were plenty of hiding places. The other benefit was the area surrounding the Badlands was flat. All the renegades had to do was post a guard and they could spot a rider coming for miles around. The soldiers would try to get to the hills in the cover of night. Now they would just wait and pray that the night would be black.

Nightfall came and the soldiers began their quiet journey across the flat open terrain. God had been good; the moon was obscured behind a large bank of clouds. As Tivy had commented before they set out, it was pitch black. The men opted to walk. They had to tread cautiously due to the blackness. It wouldn't do to be riding and have one of the horses step in a hole and break a leg. If they were extra careful, men and horses alike should arrive at the destination safe and sound.

It was a slow cautious journey. The men dared not speak above a very soft whisper so for the most part they kept silent. A strange happening occurred when the men finally reached the edge of the hills and took cover among the rocks; the moon came from behind the clouds. They silently made their way closer to where they had found the comancheros' hideout before and where they had seen the smoke rising.

As they neared the area, the soldiers hid their horses a safe distance from the hideout. They couldn't afford to have even the whinny of a horse give away their position.

"You see that little knoll up there?" Tivy whispered. The other two nodded. "We'll meet on it. Now stay low and keep very quiet," Tivy warned as the trio split up.

Tivy was an expert at getting to places without being seen or heard. He was so quiet it was sometimes hard to tell if he was even breathing. The other two men were rapidly becoming experts under Tivy's guidance. Ben Tivy slowly inched his way toward the knoll. He silently prayed as he went along that they would find the little boy and he would be all right.

It was almost daybreak when the three rendezvoused on top of the little hill overlooking the renegade's hideout. They had easily slipped by the guard. The bandits had apparently either celebrated or drank themselves into a stupor for consolation. Either way, their drunken state made it much easier for the scouts to get close enough to have a good view of the hideout.

The bandits were slow in rising that morning. When they finally did come to life, the leader began to demand food. The women with the group hurriedly raced around and prepared a meal for the unsavory crew. The food smelled good to the three scouts hiding up in the rocks. A warm meal would certainly taste good but they pulled some beef jerky from their pockets and tried to alleviate some of their hunger.

It appeared nothing exciting was going to happen for awhile so the soldiers decided to try and get some rest. Tivy and Calhoun closed their eyes after Baker was chosen to take the first watch.

There was very little activity in the comancheros' camp. Shortly after the gang had finished eating, the leader, or at least the one with the loudest mouth, disappeared into the cave with one of the women. The others drank some more, and some of them appeared to have some kind of contest throwing knives. Another group had a card game going and one fellow played a guitar while a couple of the girls danced around the fire. From time to time, one of the men would grab a girl and twirl her around for a while then go back to his drinking and playing.

Baker had just awakened Tivy to take the next watch when five men were led into the camp by two of the comancheros. It was a strange site. The new arrivals were definitely not part of the gang. They were well-dressed white men. One of the bandits disappeared into the cave and shortly returned with the leader. Tivy gently tapped Calhoun to wake him so he too could observe the happenings.

The three scouts watched as the leader of the comancheros talked with the man who must have been the leader of the new arrivals. Several times, the bandit walked away from the man shaking his head. It appeared they must have been trying to strike a deal about something. The comanchero would walk away for a moment and then return to face his nemesis. They would talk a little more, followed by the bandit repeating his performance. The negotiations went on for several minutes but finally the bandit seemed to be satisfied.

The well-dressed man walked over to his horse, reached into his saddlebag and brought out a pouch which he tossed to the bandit. The bandit looked inside, and then began to shout and wave his hands. The other man shouted back and apparently satisfied the bandit once more. The comanchero shouted orders to two men standing by the cave entrance, and in just a few minutes, the two returned almost dragging a small boy between them.

Even from his far away vantage point, Tivy could tell the child was scared and crying. The leader of the bandits grabbed the boy and shoved him toward the well-dressed white man. The man grabbed the child just before the little lad fell to the ground. He lifted the boy up into his saddle and then mounted behind him. The white man shouted a few orders and the group rode out of the camp followed by the same two men who had escorted them in.

Tivy shook his head as he witnessed the scene playing out before him. It didn't look good. The boy they had just seen had to be the son of the woman back at the fort but it didn't look like the young woman would be seeing her son anytime soon. Tivy wished one of them could follow the men who had just left the camp but it was too far back to the horses.

Tivy would guess the fellow just bought that little boy but apparently didn't give the comancheros all the money. Of course, if he had brought all the money into camp with him, the chances of him and the boy riding out would have been slim. Whoever this man was he must be accustomed to negotiating with the likes of the comancheros.

After the men left with the little boy, it was apparent the bandits were going to do nothing else this day. Tivy's best guess would be they would ride out the next morning and he would also guess they would be headed for Fort Benton to rescue their comrades. Of course, if they had gotten a good price for the little boy, they might just leave the rest of the gang to be hung by the army. That would lessen the number with whom they had to split the money.

With nightfall, the scouts made their way down the hills and back across the flatlands. They once again took cover in the little grove of trees and waited for the bandits to move. They didn't have to wait long. Just after sun-up, the bandits rode out of the hills but this time they had the women with them. Instead of heading northeast, which would take them to Fort Benton, the comancheros headed due north.

"What do you make of that?" Calhoun wanted to know.

"Looks like they're gonna leave their comrades to face a hangman's noose. They musta got a good price for that boy and decided the fewer they had to split it with the better," Tivy offered.

"Well, I guess we head back to the fort and tell the Captain," Pete Baker moaned as he started to saddle his horse. "I'm sure glad it's the captain who will have to tell that lady about her little boy and not me."

Tivy threw his saddle on his horse and then turned to face the two men with him. "You two go back to the fort and fill the captain in. I'm gonna trail this group for awhile."

Aubrey Calhoun stopped what he was doing and looked at the corporal. "But Ben, you don't have orders to trail them."

"I had orders to find them and keep an eye on them. Now they're headed north but who's to say they won't turn east a little ways up the trail. If I trail them, they may lead me to the kid again." Tivy tightened the cinch on his saddle. "I know from what I saw yesterday they haven't gotten all the money yet. I'd bet they're headed to collect the rest now. Maybe I can find the little boy or at least get a lead on the men that bought him."

"You be careful." Pete instructed before Tivy mounted his horse and rode due north after the bandits.

Chapter Seven

Fort Benton

The days seemed to drag on as Sonora waited for news she knew might never come. Uncle Tobias had arrived at the fort just yesterday. It was good to have him with her. Captain Parker had to talk fast to keep the old man from riding out and trying to track down the bandits, but the captain had finally convinced Tobias he could do more good being here to support Sonora right now than he could being out on the trail.

"Interrupt your thoughts, girl?" Tobias asked as he sat down beside Sonora on the porch.

"My thoughts are always the same these days, Uncle Toby." Sonora looked up into the rugged face of her uncle.

"Thinkin' bout Timmy, I'd reckon." The old man gave her a knowing smile as he reached over and took her hand in his.

"Uncle Toby, what will I ever do if I don't get that child back? He's my whole life." Sonora showed signs of all hope being gone.

"I know he is child." Tobias gave her hand a squeeze. "I've been talkin' to that young captain and he's a good man. He'll do all he can to git Timmy back to us."

"I know he will, but so far, no one's even seen Timmy. What if those men don't have him anymore?" Sonora started to cry uncontrollably. Tobias took his niece in his arms and tried to comfort her. "Oh, Uncle, what if they killed him right after they beat me senseless."

"Now, now, child. Don't go saying things like that. The Good Book tells us to speak good things, to call those things that are not as though they are. We have to hold on to the belief Timmy's gonna be all right. We gotta keep believin' that ya hear. Speak life to his situation; don't go speakin' no death into my great-nephew's life." The old man did his best to comfort his sobbing niece.

****

Calhoun and Baker went straight to Captain Parker's office when they returned to the fort.

"So you saw the little boy?" Jonathan looked up into the faces of the two men standing before him.

"Yes, sir." Baker nodded. "It had to be the woman's son. Of course, we didn't see him up close but he had blonde hair and looked to be about the same age as the woman had said her son is."

Jonathan tapped his fingers on his desk. "Could any of you identify the men that took him if you saw them again?"

Calhoun and Baker looked at one another before Calhoun answered the captain's question. "Probably not, sir. Like Baker said, we weren't close enough to see details of their faces. We couldn't even tell you the color of their hair cause they all had on hats."

Jonathan rubbed his forehead with his hand. "Well, maybe Corporal Tivy will discover something. We have to pray he does, not only for that little boy's sake but for Sonora's also."

Baker rolled the brim of his hat in his hands. "Capt'n, you don't think we can get those fellows in the cells to talk?"

Jonathan shook his head. "We haven't had any luck so far."

A glimmer of hope crossed Baker's face. "But what if we tell 'em what we saw. I mean about the rest of their gang takin' the money for the boy and headin' to Canada instead of comin' here to bust 'em out?"

Jonathan stood and began to pace the room. After what seemed like a long time he stopped and turned to face his men. "We could try. I'd be willing to try most anything to get that little boy back to his mother."

Calhoun nodded. "We can go talk to them right now."

The captain shook his head. "Why don't you two get something to eat and get a little rest first? Then we can pull Carlos, the leader, out of the cell and talk to him here in my office where the others can't hear. If he doesn't tell us anything, we may have to talk to them one by one. Maybe one of them will crack."

Calhoun and Baker nodded in agreement and then saluted Captain Parker before they left his office. After returning his trooper's salutes, Jonathan leaned back in his chair and began to pray for God to give him strength and the right words to tell Sonora what he had just learned.

****

"Doc, I'm glad you stopped by." Jonathan looked at Nathan seated in the chair in front of his desk.

"I saw Baker and Calhoun ride in and I'm curious enough to want to know what they found out," Doc confessed.

Jonathan shared the recent events with the doctor. "Any suggestions on how I break this to Sonora?"

Nathan stood and walked to the window and looked across the compound toward his office. "No suggestions but I'll be present for the conversation if you want me to. I would also suggest you make sure Tobias is there."

"Thanks, friend. I'll take you up on your offer and your suggestion. Where is Sonora now?"

Doc nodded toward his office. "Last I saw, she and Tobias were over at my office. I came straight here from the mess hall." Doc pulled his hat on his head. "Shall we go find them?"

Jonathan sighed heavily. This was not a job he looked forward too. Rank might have its privileges but it also had its drawbacks. Slowly, he stood to his feet and took his hat from the rack behind his chair. "Let's go, old friend." Jonathan hesitated and then added, "I know you say you're not much of a praying man, but if you pray at all, now would be a good time to do it."

Doc patted his comrade on the back. "I know, old friend; how well I know."

****

Sonora and Uncle Tobias were just finishing supper when Jonathan and Doc found them at the mess hall. Sonora instantly knew by the look on Jonathan's face that something was wrong.

Fearing the worst, she asked, "They found him, didn't they?"

Jonathan took a deep breath as he looked down into Sonora's face. "We think so."

"So where is he?" Tobias jumped in before Jonathan could continue.

Taking a seat at the table, Jonathan told Sonora and Tobias the story Baker and Calhoun had relayed to him. "So you see Tivy is still tracking them to see if he can get a line on where they took Timmy, if indeed it was Timmy."

"You know it was Timmy." Sonora moaned as she rubbed her temples with her fingertips. "Who else could it have been?"

Tobias jumped to his feet. "When do we leave to find Tivy?"

"I can't just take off after Tivy." Jonathan looked from Sonora to Tobias. "Tivy will get word to us as soon as he has anything solid to go on."

Sonora slammed her hands on the table. "And just how will he do that?"

Jonathan's voice was even and he sounded very sure of himself. "Believe me, Tivy'll find a way. He's very resourceful."

Sonora shook her head and sighed very heavily. "So once again we just sit here and do nothing while God knows who has my little boy."

Jonathan looked directly into her cold, brown eyes as he answered. "Sonora, right now I don't know what else to do. Like I said, if anybody can find a lead on who those men are that rode out of the camp with the little boy, Tivy will." Jonathan reached across the table and laid his hand on Sonora's. "All I can say is the rest of us need to pray. God is the only one that knows where your son is. We can pray for protection for your son and that God will lead Tivy to him."

Sonora snatched her hand back and got up from the table. "Seems like that's doing nothing. I've been praying, and so far, I'm no closer to getting Timmy back." Sonora looked Jonathan in the eyes. "Praying doesn't seem to have accomplished anything. God should have protected him and not let him get kidnapped in the first place."

Tobias came to stand beside his niece. He put his arm around her shoulder. "Girl, this is no time to go talkin' against God and prayer. You don't know what God has protected that boy from because someone has been prayin'. At least we know he's still alive because I believe the little boy they saw was Timmy. If we hadn't been prayin', who's to say those bandits wouldn't have killed him."

Sonora said nothing more. She knew her uncle was right but right now she was angry. She was angry with herself for not protecting Timmy. She was angry with Daniel Forrester for pursuing her and the child, causing them to have to leave the comfort of her father's home. She was angry with Jonathan and the whole stinking army for not finding her son and bringing him back to her. She was angry at the comancheros for taking Timmy away from her, and yes, she was angry with God for allowing all of this to happen in the first place.

****

Jonathan had to get a breath of fresh air. He walked out of the mess hall and took a deep breath. He could understand Sonora's apparent anger and he wished with all his heart that he could do something about the pain and hurt she was feeling. He knew she had only lashed out at him and God because her heart was breaking. Something inside him made him want to protect this woman he barely knew. Something inside him made him feel her heartache and he wanted with all his heart to make things right in Sonora's world once again.

"What are your plans now?" Jonathan hadn't heard the doctor approach and his question startled the captain out of his thoughts.

Jonathan glanced over at his friend. "Find Baker and Calhoun and let them talk to Carlos. Then, I pray the bandit gets mad enough at his comrades to talk."

"Good luck." Doc slapped Jonathan on the back before he stepped down off the porch.

****

"You, stupid gringo," Carlos bellowed as he slammed his hands down on the table. "Why do you think I would believe anything you had to say?"

"You know your men had the boy and you know they were turnin' him over to someone for money. So if I know that much, why do you think I'd lie about the rest?" Private Aubrey Calhoun remained very calm as he talked with the bandit.

"So you say you saw a boy. So what? How you even know the men you saw was my men?" Carlos paced around the room.

"Let's just say that if they weren't your men, then some other fellows have taken over your hideout cause it's the same place we saw you before your raid on the Saunders' place." Baker added to the conversation as he kept his voice calm and even also.

"And how you know this? Can you be so sure you saw me at this hideout, as you call it? You gringos say all us Mexicans look alike." The comanchero grinned.

Pete Baker described the location of the hideout to the bandit seated before him. Jonathan could tell by the look Carlos tried so hard to conceal that the private had convinced the thief he indeed had seen the comancheros' carefully selected hideout.

"I tell you nothing, except beware. My men are not fools; they will be coming here soon to get me out of your prison. Then all of you will die." Carlos' words were threatening but there was also a hint of uncertainty in them. Yet, the bandit would not give in and had no intention of telling the soldiers anything they wanted to know.

Jonathan knew they were getting nowhere with Carlos but he had an idea. He left Pete and Aubrey to their interrogation. Walking across the compound to the guardhouse, he instructed four of his men to follow him. He had them to remove two of the big mouth prisoners from the cells. He had them take one prisoner to the stable and another to a secluded area at the far end of the compound. Once that was done, he returned to his office and ordered that Carlos be returned to his cell.

Once Carlos was out of the office, Jonathan faced Baker and Calhoun. "Men, I've got an idea. I don't know if it'll work or not but I thought it was worth a try. I've had two of Carlos' men taken to different parts of the fort. I wanted them removed before Carlos could give them any instructions. Now, Baker, you go question the one in the stable and Calhoun you take the other one. See if you can get anything out of them. If they believe a large portion of your information could have come from Carlos and that Carlos might have sold them out, maybe they will give us some information we can't seem to get any other way. I don't like deception but a little boy's life is in grave danger and we need some help finding him."

The men nodded understanding as Jonathan continued. "I think we'll keep them separated from the others for awhile. If this strategy doesn't work tonight, maybe after a few days of them wondering what Carlos said and Carlos wondering what they're saying, someone will crack and tell us something."

Pete and Aubrey smiled at the captain's well thought out plan and headed out to do their part. They questioned the other bandits but with little success other than to plant a few ideas in their heads. They would let things stew for a couple of days before questioning all three men again.

Chapter Eight

Canada

Tivy knew any protection the uniform afforded him ended right now. He had just entered Canada. Since he had no other clothes with him, he'd have to come up with a story if he needed one as to why an American soldier was in Canada.

The comancheros had been easy to follow. They had no clue anyone was watching them so they made no effort to take any precautions. The bandits made camp just outside a small town immediately across the border. Tivy watched carefully. It looked as though the gang planned on staying for a while. He figured their business must be in this small town but he didn't know why they didn't just ride on in since it was just a short distance away. He decided their reasons didn't matter. Their camp was set up and it didn't look like they were going anywhere soon.

Tivy decided it might benefit him if he rode into town before the comancheros. That way maybe no one would connect him to following them. Also, if the bandits had business in this little Canadian town, maybe the men who had the little boy were still there. It was worth riding into town to try and find out.

Before reaching his destination, Tivy had developed a plan. He reached up and pulled the corporal stripe from his uniform. If anyone asked, his cover would be that he was dishonorably discharged from the American army and he was fed up with his mother country and had fled to Canada. Life and death situations sometimes called for desperate measures.

It wasn't such a small place after all. The town consisted of a general mercantile, a bank, two saloons, a hotel and a livery stable. It seemed the most likely place to learn anything or find any strangers in town would be at the saloons. Tivy tied his horse to the hitching post and walked through the swinging doors into the Purple Garter Saloon.

He walked over to the bar and ordered a beer. Making himself comfortable at a table in the back corner of the room, he had a clear view of the room and the front door. He slowly took a sip of his drink as he scanned the room. Swallowing the distasteful brew, Tivy worked hard to control his face as he gagged. He hated the taste of beer and his fellow soldiers enjoyed teasing him about it. He would order a sarsaparilla when he was with them but for this situation he had to blend in as best he could and a soft drink wouldn't help him blend. Maybe no one would notice if he just let the beer sit on the table and he didn't drink anymore of it.

No one in the room resembled the men he had seen take the boy. He couldn't identify their faces but he thought he could recognize the stance and characteristics of the man who had done all the dealings with the comanchero leader. Tivy was lost in thought when a young woman approached his table.

"Would you like some company?" The young girl asked her question in French.

Tivy did not understand her words but he got their meaning from her actions. "No, thank you," he shook his head.

The young woman turned and stomped away. Tivy decided this might be a good time to leave and go check out the other saloon. Walking a short distance down the street, he entered the Road's End Saloon. Once again, Tivy seated himself at a back table with another beer he didn't really want before he scanned the room and came up empty. No one in here looked like the men he was hoping to find.

"Hello, soldier. Can I buy you a drink?"

Tivy looked up into eyes as green as the meadow near his family farm in east Texas. The woman standing before him also had the reddest hair he thought he'd ever seen. Her face was kind, nothing like the girl at the last place.

Tivy grinned. "I still have a drink but you can sit down if you like."

The woman pulled out a chair and sat down. "You're a long way from home?" Her smile was warm.

This was the perfect time to try out his cover story and see if it would be believable. "Don't really have a home no more."

A confused look covered the woman's face. "But your uniform, you're an American soldier, aren't you?"

"Well, I used to be but me and the army parted company on less than friendly terms." Tivy sighed and lifted his drink to his lips.

"So, you're on the run?"

Tivy managed a small sip of the drink before he set the mug back down on the table. "Nope. No reason to run, just no reason to stay down there anymore. Seems the union don't appreciate me so why should I stay in a country where I'm not wanted." Tivy paused and glanced at the woman to see if she was accepting his story. "Enough about me. I'd say from your manner of speech that you're not a native of Canada either."

The woman laughed. "You're right. I'm originally from Ohio."

Tivy kept watching the door out of the side of his eye as he tried to keep his focus on the woman sitting at the table with him. "So how did you wind up in Canada?"

"Married a gambler." The woman smiled broadly. "He got the bright idea of us moving on and opening up a place of our own. We'd stop somewhere, open a little place and when it'd start to grow he'd be ready to move on. When we crossed the Canadian border, I told him this was it. We would open a place here but this was the last place. If we could make a go of it, fine; if not, he'd just have to find a different line of work to support us. That's why the place is called Road's End."

Tivy glanced around the room. "Well, I'd say you made a pretty good go of it."

"We didn't do bad. Matt died two years ago, got bad sick and just died. Now I'm stuck up here. I make enough to get by but that's about all. I'd love to go back home but," she sighed deeply, "maybe someday." The woman blushed as she looked at Corporal Tivy. "Listen to me go on. I don't even know your name and here I am telling you my life story."

"Name's Ben." Tivy extended his hand to the lady seated at his table.

"Nice to meet you, Ben." She said as she shook his hand. "My name's Willow. It's not often I get an American in here to talk to, least not one who ain't on the run."

Tivy was just about to ask if she'd seen some men come through town with a little boy when the woman got called to settle a dispute at the bar. Willow didn't return to his table and Tivy knew it was getting late. The Road's End had a few rooms for rent upstairs; Ben secured one and walked up the stairs to bed. If nothing else it would be good to sleep in a bed for one night.

****

Fort Benton

Sonora lay awake most of the night. Her heart ached with such a longing to hold her son that she could hardly bear the pain of it. Not only did her heart ache but also her mind would not stop racing. She relived every moment she had spent with Timmy since the day he was born. Her mind was occupied not only with thoughts of her son but also a young captain.

Sonora had difficulty understanding Jonathan Parker. She had lashed out at him early in the evening when he had brought her the news of Timmy, but when he had come by later to check on her, he acted as though nothing had happened.

Jonathan had come by just to make sure Sonora was okay. She was sitting alone on the porch in front of the doctor's quarters when he arrived. Sonora remembered how soft-spoken he was but she could also hear pain in his voice. She believed the young army captain truly hurt for her and her son.

Why would this man feel so much compassion for someone he hardly knew? She recalled how often Jonathan had mentioned God and she knew that must be the answer to her question. Somehow through all the demands of army life, Jonathan Parker had managed to remain, or maybe even become, a Christian.

Sonora knew what it was like to be that close to God but right now it seemed God was so far away she couldn't reach Him. It had felt that way to her since the day

Daniel Forrester had shown up at her father's door and tried to take Timmy away. Sonora remembered how she had prayed that day that God would just fix everything and send Daniel back to New Orleans where he belonged. It hadn't happened. Instead, she had been forced to steal away in the dead of night with her little boy and come to this God-forsaken territory where the comancheros, people she had never heard of, almost killed her and took her son from her.

Sonora wept as she whispered aloud. "It would have been better for Timmy if I had let his father take him. At least with Daniel, he would have been safe and warm tonight."

****

Jonathan stood outside his quarters. The moon was partially hidden behind the clouds and the stars were few in the heavens tonight.

"God," he prayed. "Please take care of that little boy. You see him and know where he is. Just please let the little one know You haven't forsaken him. Keep Timmy safe in Your arms, and Father please help Sonora know You haven't forsaken her either, that you still love her and want to comfort her too. Please be with Ben Tivy as he searches. Just guide him on the path he should take. As always, I ask that You guide me in my duties. In Jesus name, I ask these things. Amen."

Jonathan didn't mention it directly in his prayer but he was confused about the feelings he had for Sonora. He was drawn to her and didn't know why. He knew he hurt for her and her loss and maybe that was all it was. Maybe he just felt sorry for her and wanted to help her find her son.

Jonathan looked across the compound and noticed the door to the general store open. It appeared Amanda was having difficulty sleeping tonight also.

Amanda...now there is a different story. Jonathan was well aware the woman had feelings for him. It was very obvious even to him. He had never acknowledged that he noticed her affection and he had never returned her affection, except as a friend. Maybe he was foolish. Amanda was a good woman and pretty in her own way. Most men would have been more than happy to have someone like Amanda interested in them.

Maybe I should rethink this, I could do a lot worse than Amanda Stone. She doesn't have the problems someone like Sonora would have. Jonathan shook his head. Why was he even thinking like this? He didn't want Amanda or Sonora. God would send the right woman into his life at the right time. He didn't have to settle for just anyone. God had things under control.

Lost in his thoughts, Jonathan hadn't noticed Amanda crossing the compound so he was startled when she spoke. "Havin' trouble sleepin'?"

"I don't know. I haven't tried to go to sleep yet." Jonathan glanced at Amanda and then looked up at the star-filled sky.

Amanda smiled. "I know you've got a lot on your mind. Would you like someone to talk to?"

"Oh Amanda, it's getting late and I'm about talked out for today." Jonathan looked at Amanda and gave her a faint smile.

"Well, you try and get some rest. Just remember I'm here if you need me."

Jonathan nodded his head and again gave her a little smile. "Thanks. I do appreciate it. It's good to know I have a friend. Now why don't I walk you back to the store and then I'll come back and turn in for the evening."

"You're tired. You don't have to walk me home. I think I'll be perfectly safe walkin' back across the yard. You just go get some rest. Goodnight," she whispered as she turned to go.

Jonathan watched until Amanda went inside the store and closed the door. Then he went into his own quarters to try and rest for a few hours.

Chapter Nine

Canada

Tivy woke early. He dressed and went downstairs to get a bite of breakfast. The saloon was empty at this time of day and he was just about to walk outside when he heard a soft voice behind him.

"Care for some breakfast?" Tivy turned to see Willow walking toward him. "I've got some bacon and eggs cooked. Was just going to sit down and eat when I thought I heard someone out here. Care to join me?"

"Sounds good to me." Tivy followed Willow through the door leading into the kitchen. "Not only sounds good but smells good, too," he added.

"Well, I just hope it also tastes good." Willow smiled as she motioned for Tivy to sit down at the small table in the kitchen.

Willow poured each of them a cup of coffee and then made herself comfortable at the table. She served her guest eggs, bacon and biscuits.

Tivy took a bite. "These biscuits just melt in your mouth." He took a bite of the bacon and eggs. "I can't remember when I last had a breakfast or any meal this good."

A broad smile covered Willow's face. "It's nice to have someone to share a meal with again." She picked up her mug of coffee and took a sip of the hot liquid.

Tivy took another bite of his delicious meal. "You don't normally serve breakfast to your overnight guests?"

"No." Willow smiled as set her coffee mug back on the table. "I figure they can get their meals down the street at the café. I don't usually cook breakfast for myself, either. For some reason this morning, I felt like cooking a big meal. I'm just glad I found someone to help me eat it."

Tivy wiped his plate clean with the last bite of

biscuit. After placing it in his mouth and swallowing, he smiled at his breakfast companion. "I'm real glad I was the lucky person that got to share this meal with you. Like I said I don't know when I've tasted better."

Willow blushed a little as she tried to steer the conversation in a different direction. "Are you staying here in town for a while?"

"Don't know. My plans aren't set in stone." Tivy took a sip of his coffee.

"Well, if you do stay, I guess you'll be needing a job. That is unless you're independently wealthy." Willow laughed.

Ben Tivy chuckled. "Not wealthy at all and I reckon I could probably use a job if I decide to stay."

Willow asked a very straightforward question. "What would it take to get you to decide to stay in our little town?"

Tivy looked to be deep in thought, as he seemed to stare into his coffee cup. "Oh, I don't know. Did you have somethin' in mind?"

"Well, I could probably use you around here." Her voice almost cracked as she spoke.

"I don't know. I don't much like to work indoors. I'm an outdoor kind of guy." Tivy picked up his coffee mug and took another drink of the dark liquid.

Willow stood and began to clear the table. "I could probably help you get on at one of the lumber camps."

"Well, if I decide to stay around here, I just might take you up on that. For now, I think I'll take a walk around town." Tivy stood up and thanked his hostess for the meal one more time.

****

Ben Tivy walked out onto the wooden sidewalk. The air was cool and crisp. He drew in a deep breath as he surveyed his surroundings. Just as he stepped off the plank walkway into the street, he noticed the leader of the comancheros along with a handful of his men riding toward him. Tivy walked on across the street and stopped in front of the general store. Without being obvious, he watched the bandits stop in front of the Road's End Saloon and tie their horses to the hitching post.

As the group entered the saloon, Tivy made his way

back across the street. Quietly, he entered the Road's End and silently walked to the staircase as if he were going to his room. The comancheros turned to look at him but Tivy heard Willow tell them they had nothing to worry about. She explained to the leader that Tivy was a guest and going to his room. He continued up the stairs at a snail's pace.

The bandits turned their eyes back to Willow and Tivy stopped when he reached the landing at the top of the stairs. He looked back just in time to see Willow hand over a large roll of bills to the leader of the renegades.

Could Willow be involved with these unscrupulous characters? Maybe dealing with the likes of them was her way of earning enough money to go back home.

Ben ambled on to his room. He had seen Willow pour the bandits drinks so he knew it would be a while before they left the saloon. Once inside his room, he moved a chair over by the window. He had a clear view of the street from where he sat. Several minutes passed before the men walked out and mounted their horses. They rode out of town in the same direction they had ridden in.

The next question on Tivy's mind was how to get information out of Willow. He had to find out how deeply she was involved with the comancheros and just why she was giving them money.

****

Fort Benton

"You know they ain't comin' to help us." The Indian shouted at Carlos as he paced around the small cell. "They sold us out. This way they don't have to split the money with us."

Carlos stood and looked the enraged Indian in the face. "So you told the gringos what they wanted to know."

"I didn't tell 'em nothin' they hadn't already got outta you." The Indian got right in the face of his leader.

Carlos didn't back down. "I told them nothing. I don't care if Ramon did sell us out we don't tell the gringos nothing. No matter what, we don't help these soldiers find nobody."

Another of the bandits stood and questioned the leader. "If nobody talked, then how did these soldiers find out so much information?"

Carlos walked over and placed both hands around the bars of the cell. "They're just guessin'. They don't know nothin'."

"They know about our hideout and about the boy," one of the bandits yelled.

Carlos turned to face his angry men. "Okay, so they had a couple of spies. But knowin' where the hideout is and that there was a boy is a long way from knowin' where that kid is now. If they knew that, they'd be out now tryin' to git him back."

The youngest of the bandits sat up on the side of the cot where he had been resting. "What difference does it make to us if they go after the boy? We ain't gonna git to enjoy any of the money for the kid. We ain't even gonna git outta this jail alive."

Carlos walked over and grabbed the young man by the collar and pulled him to his feet. Looking the frightened young man in the face, the leader snarled, "You are a weaklin'. You may not git outta this place alive but I have no intention of dying on the end of a rope. I don't need Ramon's help or anyone else for that matter. I can git out of this place without anyone's help." Carlos tightened his grip and then added, "We don't sell out to the gringo soldiers. Is that clear?"

The young man nodded his head as Carlos finally loosened his grip.

****

"Well, we're not making any progress with the bandits. What next?" Private Calhoun asked his captain.

Captain Parker looked up at the soldier standing before him. "Wait. I hope to hear from Tivy any day now. He seems to be our last hope at finding the boy."

"I sure hope he comes through," Private Baker moaned.

"Me too," Calhoun added.

"Enter," Captain Parker answered to the knock on his door.

Lt. Blake entered the office. "Everything's ready. The guards are bringing the bandits over now."

Captain Parker nodded. He sighed heavily as he thought about the following proceedings. The federal judge, along with witnesses from both Texas and Oklahoma had arrived yesterday and were ready to start the trial. Jonathan did not look forward to these proceedings even though he was certain of the outcome.

****

Canada

"Willow, I know it's none of my business but those men that were in here this mornin'...well do you know what kind of men they are?" Tivy questioned as he stepped up to the bar.

"You're right, it's none of your business, but it doesn't really matter what kind of men they are. I was just doing a favor for a fellow who came through here a few days ago." Willow finished drying the glass she held in her hand.

Tivy propped his foot up on the brass rail at the base of the bar. "What fellow?"

Willow's confusion showed in her face as she set the glass on a shelf behind the bar. "Why are you so interested in my business?"

Tivy hesitated. He didn't know how much he should tell this woman. He didn't know if she was really telling the truth or not but he had to try to get some information. This woman seemed to be his only lead. "The man you were doin' the favor for, did he have a little boy with him?"

Willow still appeared to be confused but she was also very curious. "As a matter of fact he did. Why?"

Tivy pushed his hat back on his head as he looked down into those dark green eyes. "The men you paid this morning took the little boy from his mother. They sold him to the man who gave you the money."

Shock covered Willow's face. Tivy could see that she wanted more information. "You didn't answer my question, why are you so interested in my business? How did you get all your information?"

Tivy swallowed hard. He might have to give himself away to get information from this lady but he would still try to evade telling the whole truth until he knew more about her. "Well, before I left the army, we found out about the boy bein' taken and we had tracked the comancheros this way." Tivy sighed deeply. "I didn't know what happened but when I saw those men this mornin', I recognized the leader. I just guessed about the rest."

Willow seemed to buy his story. "You mean those men stole that little boy and then sold him?" Tivy nodded; she continued. "But the man who gave me the money said he was the boy's father. He told me he couldn't hang around because he had to get the boy home. He said they had been gone longer than expected and his wife would be worrying about him and their son. He told me these men had done some work for him and asked me to give them the money when they came into town."

Tivy gave a sigh of relief. It appeared Willow was innocent of any wrong doing in this matter. "When did the man and the little boy leave town?"

Willow walked around the bar to stand beside Tivy. "The day before yesterday."

Tivy turned to face her. "Do you know which way they went?"

Willow nodded. "He and the boy left on the stage. The rest of his men rode east out of town."

"Where was the stage headed?" Tivy wanted to know.

"It goes east for about a hundred miles and then turns south. Eventually gets to Fargo."

Wheels were turning in Tivy's head. There was no way he could catch the stage but if it was headed back into the U.S., then maybe he could cut across country and head it off. He had to get word to Captain Parker but if he rode back to the fort it would be impossible for him to beat the stage to Fargo.

Tivy took hold of Willow's arm and led her to a table. He pulled out a chair for her and the two sat down. "Willow, do you really want to go back to the United States?"

She nodded and smiled at the young man seated across from her. "Yes. I have enough money now to go. I just need to sell this place and then I can be on my way."

Tivy looked across the table at Willow. He had to trust her; he had no choice. He laid out the whole plan for her. "So you see, this little boy could be in a lot of danger and we need to help his mother get him back."

Willow nodded in agreement. "Ben, you start for

Fargo. I'll get things in order and somehow get to Fort Benton and let your Captain Parker know what's going on."

Tivy shook his head. "Willow, you can't make a trip like that by yourself."

Willow smiled. "I won't be alone. Big Frank, my bartender, is going with me. No one will bother me if Frank's around. Now don't worry about me. You just get started to Fargo."

Tivy smiled broadly as he extended his hand. "Willow, you're a good woman. Thanks for your help."

Willow took his hand and returned his smile. "Thanks for trusting me with the truth and allowing me to do something good for the first time in a long time."

Willow watched as Tivy stood to leave. He stopped at the swinging doors and turned to look at the pretty red-haired woman once again. "Willow, what's your last name?"

A smile still covered Willow's face. "Ingram."

"Willow Ingram, I hope we meet again." Ben Tivy pulled his hat low over his eyes and turned to leave.

****

Willow walked to the swinging doors and watched as Tivy mounted his horse and rode away. "We will meet again if I have anything to say about it, Ben Tivy."

It had been a long time since Willow Ingram had found herself feeling this way about a man but, in the short time she had known him, Ben Tivy had opened her heart up to the possibility of love again. She walked back inside and surveyed the business that had been her life for many years. It wouldn't be hard to give this up. Her long awaited dream of returning to the United States Territory was finally coming true and she would be helping someone at the same time. Her life was taking a turn for the better; she could just feel it.

It took Willow the rest of the day to set everything in order. She made arrangements with the banker to sell her saloon. At first light the next morning, she and Big Frank would be leaving for Fort Benton in the Dakota Territory.

Chapter Ten

Fort Benton

The trial was over and just as Jonathan had anticipated the comancheros were sentenced to hang. The evidence the folks from Texas and Oklahoma offered against them was insurmountable. There were also witnesses who showed up proving they had raided and killed several people before they got to Sonora's place. The comancheros had been given one more chance to come clean about the whereabouts of little Timmy, but even with Sonora's pleas, the bandits just smirked in the faces of their captors.

Jonathan's stomach soured as he thought of the sentence that would be carried out at sun-up. He fell down on his knees beside the desk in his office and began to pour out his thoughts to his heavenly father. Justice had been rendered but in his mind he knew the death penalty had been given to some lost souls and that made his heart ache.

****

"It's a quiet night, isn't it?" Doc asked as he walked up to stand beside Sonora on the porch of the mess hall.

Sonora had spotted the doctor coming across the compound so she hadn't been startled when he walked up to where she was standing. "It is quiet and peaceful. I guess that seems strange considering what took place today and what's to happen in the morning."

Doc gave Sonora a sidelong glance. "Well, crime must be punished. Those men are killers and thieves and sentence has been passed. Now it just has to be carried out."

"I'm glad. Those men took my son from me and they have to pay for that even if I never see Timmy again." Doc could hear the bitterness in her voice.

When Sonora had first come to the fort, she was like a frightened wounded deer. The frightened side of her still showed through from time to time, but more and more, it seemed her heart was turning hard and cold. That was not a pretty thing to watch.

"Sonora, don't give up hope. Tivy is still out there looking. He won't give up until he finds your son," Doc encouraged.

Sonora made no comment. She had heard those words often from not only the doctor but also Uncle Tobias and the young captain. At first she wanted to believe them but now it had been too long. Timmy had been gone for well over a month now. Sonora held little hope of ever seeing her son again but at least tomorrow part of the men responsible for taking him away from her would have to pay for their actions.

****

Jonathan watched as Sonora and Doc crossed the fort to the doctor's office. Jonathan's heart ached for this young woman. More than anything he wanted to get little Timmy back but hope was dwindling for him. It had been too long. Tivy was still out so that left him one little ray of hope but the ray was getting dimmer every day. Jonathan noticed Nathan went into his office but Sonora had seated herself in the rocking chair on the porch.

Jonathan closed the distance between them. He wanted to offer whatever comfort he could to Sonora tonight. "Are you doing all right?" he asked.

Sonora didn't look at the captain and bitterness was evident in her voice. "No. I won't be alright until Timmy is returned to me."

Jonathan propped his foot up on the lowest step leading up to the porch. "I'm still praying we'll get some good news from Corporal Tivy real soon."

"You really believe God is listening?" Sonora began rocking the chair she was sitting in.

Jonathan had to swallow the lump that had come up into his throat. "Sonora, I know He's listening."

"Just how do you know that? If He's listening, why haven't we made any progress in finding Timmy? Let's just face it; God doesn't care about me or Timmy." She refused to look at Jonathan as her anger rose and she rocked the chair faster.

"Sonora, the Bible says God cares about all of us. It says he cares about the sparrows. Sonora, God even has the hairs on our head numbered. If He goes to all that trouble, then He has to care about us." Jonathan paused but it didn't appear his message was getting through to the angry, young woman. "The one thing that shows how deeply He cares is the fact He sent His only Son to die on the cross so we could be forgiven of our sins and live forever with Him. Sonora, that's the greatest love of all."

"I thought you were an army captain not a preacher." Sonora scoffed as she rocked her chair a little faster.

Jonathan smiled. "I'm not a preacher, just a witness whenever I get a chance."

"Well, I don't want a sermon or a witness. I just want my son back." Sonora shot back as she continued to rock the chair at a very steady pace.

Jonathan moved and sat down on the edge of the porch in front of Sonora. "Sonora, don't shut us all out. We all care about you and just want to help you get through this terrible time."

Sonora stopped the rocker abruptly and looked Jonathan in the eyes. He thought she might be going to say something but she kept quiet. He prayed she would come to realize he did care about her and would be here for her throughout this ordeal.

****

"Riders approaching," the sentry called. The big wooden gates swung open for two riders to enter the fort but a soldier stopped them as they entered the safe haven.

"State your business," the guard demanded.

"My business is with Captain Parker," the woman told the guard. "Now where is his office?"

The woman's determination showed on her face and the guard saw no reason to deny her access to the captain's office. The guard pointed the way to the captain's quarters and the woman and the man accompanying her moved their horses in the direction he indicated. The big man stayed outside with the horses while the woman entered the captain's office.

"Captain Parker, my name is Willow Ingram. I'm here with word from Ben Tivy."

"Miss Ingram, won't you be seated." Jonathan said as he stood and indicated for his guest to sit down in the chair in front of his desk. "Please, what is the message from the corporal?"

Willow told the story of the events that had taken place across the border in Canada. "So you see, Ben is on his way to try and head off the stage in Fargo and I came here to tell you what was going on."

"Miss Ingram, I do appreciate your help. I know you must be tired. Let me arrange a place for you to rest and get you something to eat." Jonathan stood and walked around his desk.

Willow stood as the captain came to her side. "That would be very nice, but please, call me Willow."

"Okay Willow, follow me." Walking out onto the porch, Willow introduced Jonathan to Big Frank. Jonathan took Willow to the guest quarters, usually saved for visiting brass, and assigned Private Hornsby to take Big Frank to the barracks. Captain Parker instructed Hornsby to have Lt. Blake to come to his quarters at once.

****

"So Tivy is on his way to Fargo?" the lieutenant restated.

"That's right. If we get started right away, we should be able to get there shortly after the corporal does." Jonathan stood at the wall looking at a map of the Dakota Territory.

Blake walked over to stand beside the captain. "Sir, do we have any justification for taking a company on what might be a wild goose chase?"

Jonathan turned to face Blake. "Lt. Blake, an American citizen was taken hostage and then apparently sold. It is our duty to protect all citizens no matter what age they are. We should especially try to protect children. Now alert Company B. I'll be leading them myself."

****

"I'm going with you," Sonora demanded, as she looked Jonathan directly in the face.

"Sonora, we'll be riding fast and hard. You stay here. This is the best lead we've had. You wait here, and with God's help, I'll bring your son back to you." Jonathan's look was determined and he looked deep into Sonora's eyes.

"He's right, Sonora. You stay here. It would be too hard on you but I'm goin' with you, Capt'n." Tobias walked up beside the two.

Jonathan turned to look at Tobias. "Fine, you can ride with us. Ask Private Calhoun to get a horse saddled for you. You'll find him down by the stable." Jonathan turned back and addressed Sonora again. "Now, your uncle will be with us. We'll be back just as soon as we can."

Sonora had to think fast. Jonathan had given her the description of the man the woman had said had the little boy. The description fit Daniel Forrester to a tee. *What would happen if the Calvary caught up with Daniel and he told Jonathan the truth? Whose side would the captain be on then?* Sonora had to do something and fast.

Sonora grabbed Jonathan's arm. "Please, can't you see, I have to go. I have waited and waited for some news. Now you want me to wait some more. I can't do it. I have to go with you. Don't ask me to wait longer than I have too. *Please.*"

Jonathan hesitated for a moment. "Okay, but you have to understand we will be pushing ourselves and everyone with us to the limit. That's the only way we'll have any kind of chance to make it to Fargo in time."

"You won't hear any complaints from me," Sonora promised. Jonathan sent her to the store for Amanda to outfit her with clothes more appropriate for the long ride.

****

Jonathan smiled when he saw Sonora standing by her mount dressed in jeans and a man's shirt and boots. Totally foreign clothing for a woman but even men's apparel couldn't hide Sonora's femininity. Jonathan stopped and took a good long look at Sonora. The jeans showed off her slim figure and Jonathan realized why it was better for women to wear dresses than pants. Her long hair was tied back with a yellow ribbon and a cowboy hat was pulled low on her head. A look of determination covered her face. Sonora was five-foot-six inches tall and the boots added another couple of inches. The captain uttered a short prayer for God to keep his mind on the task at hand and not on the beautiful woman riding with him.

Jonathan gave the orders to move out and the big gates swung open. Company B rode out of the confines of the fort and headed northeast. Jonathan prayed as he always did that their mission would be successful and that God would keep his men safe. This time he added a special prayer for Sonora and an extra special one for little Timmy.

"Please, God, let us reach Fargo in time to get Timmy back to his mother."

****

The Dakota Territory

It was a long day in the saddle. They had made good time, but Jonathan worried that no matter how good their time was, it wouldn't be good enough. He had never had hopes of actually catching the stage when it arrived in Fargo. Jonathan knew, barring some unforeseen trouble, the stage would reach Fargo at least two to three days before he and the Calvary would arrive. His hope was that either Tivy was able to detain the man and Timmy or that the corporal had left a detailed trail for him to follow. Jonathan wouldn't mention any of this to Sonora. She needed the hope right now.

****

"The night air is getting cooler. You'd better go bed down close to the campfire. We'll keep it burning all night," Jonathan told Sonora as they finished their evening meal.

"I am exhausted." Sonora stood and stretched her legs and back. "When do you think we'll reach Fargo?"

"Couple of days, if nothing happens." Sonora wished he could offer more hope and comfort. She knew the time was rapidly approaching when she would have to tell Jonathan the whole truth about Timmy and her. Her stomach churned as the thought crossed her mind. *I've just got to get Timmy back. I can't live without him, I just can't. He is my son.*

"Are you okay?" Jonathan questioned.

Sonora choked back the tears; "I'm fine. Just tired, like I said."

Jonathan spread a bedroll out near the fire. "You go

ahead and lay down. You need all the rest you can get."

Sonora didn't argue. She was afraid she wouldn't sleep, but at least if she lay down and pretended, she wouldn't have to talk and try to hide her feelings.

Dawn had barely broken when Sonora was awakened to the smell of coffee brewing over the open fire. She didn't know what time she had finally fallen asleep but it couldn't have been long ago for she didn't feel rested at all. Her back ached as she tried to sit up. Oh how she would love a warm bath, but such luxuries were not to be found out here on the trail.

"Feeling rested?" Uncle Tobias questioned Sonora as he poured himself a cup of coffee.

"Oh, sure. I always feel refreshed after a night on a soft feather bed." Sonora groaned as she tried to stretch the kinks out of her back.

"You've just had too soft a life, girl. We'll have to toughen you up some. When we git Timmy back, I'll have to make it a point to take you and him campin' out under the stars from time to time." Tobias poured another cup of coffee and handed it to his niece.

Sonora took a sip of the strong brew. Her face grew somber. "Uncle Tobias, do you really think we'll get to Fargo in time to get Timmy back?"

"All I know is this young captain is doing his dead level best to get it done. The other boys say if we don't make it in time, then we have nothin' to worry about 'cause that Corporal Tivy will still be hot on their trail. We're close to gittin' our boy back, girl. Real close." A broad smile covered Tobias' face.

"I sure hope you're right." Sonora sighed as she stood and rolled up her bedroll.

****

The call sounded and the soldiers readied to break camp and start another day in the saddle. The weather threatened rain but nothing would stop the cavalry and the mission at hand.

Jonathan rode beside Sonora. He wished she didn't have to endure this horrible weather. When the rain began it was cold against his face. He watched Sonora as she pulled the poncho tighter around her neck and her hat further down on her head. He wished there were something he could do to make things easier for her, but they had to keep moving. The weather was slowing them down considerably.

The further they traveled the worse the rain became. The dusty trail gradually turned to mud and the horses moved slower and slower. He would like to stop but whatever ground they could cover today would put them a little closer to their destination.

A loud clap of thunder burst from the sky and Sonora's horse began to act up. Jonathan quickly reached over and grabbed the reins. He finally had to jump down from his horse to get hers to settle down. He stood for several moments rubbing her horse's neck and talking soothingly to the big animal. He then turned his attention to the rider.

"Sonora, are you all right?" he asked.

She nodded her head. He could tell by the look on her face how frightened she was. He wished he could pull her from the horse into his arms and calm her but that was not a good idea.

"Do you think you can go on?"

Again Sonora did not speak, she only nodded.

Jonathan mounted his horse again but continued to ride close for the rest of the day.

****

The rain continued into the night. There was no way to keep a campfire burning tonight so it was cold rations all around. Sonora was afraid she would lose a tooth as she tried to bite off a small taste of the jerky Jonathan had given her. She shivered as she looked around her; there was just no shelter to be found. She was soaked from the rain and chilled to the bone.

Sonora jumped when Jonathan walked up behind her and called her name. "Follow me," he instructed.

Sonora followed Jonathan a short distance to a small grove of trees beside some large boulders. "It's not great but at least it will give you a little shelter from the elements," Jonathan smiled. He had made a lean-to up against the huge rocks. "The blankets are dry so maybe it'll help take a little of the chill out."

"Thank you so much." Sonora crawled into her little shelter. Once inside Jonathan propped more branches in front to give her privacy and block more of the rain. Sonora slipped out of her wet clothes and wrapped herself in the dry blankets. She lay down and tonight had no trouble falling to sleep once the chill started to subside.

****

The rain stopped as the next day dawned and Jonathan pushed hard to make up some of the time they had lost the day before. Every bone in Sonora's body ached. She hurt in places she didn't even know she had, but she never complained. She would do whatever it took to get her son back.

"You holdin' up all right?" Tobias asked as he rode up to the right side of his niece.

Sonora glanced over at her uncle. "I'm fine. How much farther do you think it is to Fargo?"

"I'd say we should be there sometime tomorrow."

Sonora nodded. It couldn't be too soon for her. She smiled as she thought about seeing Timmy once again. She could just imagine how glad he would be to see her. They hadn't been separated since the day he was born. Her heart ached at what the little boy must be going through but soon that would all be over. Soon they would be together and then no one would ever separate them again. If she had to, she would go to the ends of the earth next time just to keep Timmy with her. Daniel Forrester would never get his hands on Timmy again. Not when Sonora finally got him back.

Chapter Eleven

The cavalry camped on the outskirts of Fargo. Jonathan decided to ride into town alone and check things out. Not knowing what he would be riding into, Jonathan prayed for God's guidance.

Everyone in town watched as the army officer rode down the dusty street running through the center of town. Jonathan observed everything and everyone very carefully. He pulled his horse to a stop in front of the building where the stageline's sign hung. A tall, slim man walked out the door as Jonathan was securing his horse to the hitching post.

"Can I help you, Officer?" the man asked.

"Has there been a stage through here in the last few days from Canada?" Jonathan returned.

The man scratched his dark beard. "Yep. It was a day late but got in here about noon day before yesterday."

Jonathan took his hat off and wiped his brow with his handkerchief. "Could you tell me if there was a little boy on board the stage?"

"Sure was. Cute little feller, travelin' with his pa."

"Was the little boy about five years old with blonde hair?"

"These people relatives of yours?" the man wanted to know.

Since the man answered his question with another one, Jonathan tried to get more information. "Are the little boy and his father still in town?"

"I reckon they are. Ain't another stage outta here for a couple of days." The man indicated a large building across the street. "Reckon you'll find them over at the hotel."

Jonathan gave a long sigh of relief. It looked as though their search for little Timmy had finally come to an end. Jonathan was about to walk away when the man said, "They're probably over at the hotel but the little boy that got off the stage had brown hair not blonde."

Jonathan stopped in his tracks without turning around.

"Your name wouldn't happen to be Captain Parker, would it?"

Jonathan turned and looked at the man. "Yes, sir, I'm Parker."

"Well, the stagedriver give me this here letter to give to ya if ya showed up here."

Jonathan's hopes were dashed as he took the letter from the man. The handwriting was very familiar. It was from Tivy. Jonathan opened the note and sighed deeply as he read it. He thanked the stationmaster and then mounted his horse.

****

"Sonora, I'm so sorry." Jonathan sighed deeply. "I had prayed for a different ending when we reached Fargo but it's not to be."

"May I read Corporal Tivy's letter?" Sonora asked.

Jonathan gave her a nod and handed her the small envelope. Opening it, Sonora felt her heart tighten as she began to read.

Captain Parker,

The man and the little boy got off the stage just after the coach crossed the U.S. border. There was a private coach waiting for them with four men to escort them, not counting the driver. They are staying on the stage trail for now and I am following at a safe distance. I'll do my best to leave a well-marked trail for you if they leave the main stage route. Looks like they are keeping a steady southern course.

Tivy

Tears began to stream down Sonora's cheeks as she read the words Corporal Tivy had written. Once again her hopes were dashed. Daniel Forrester had her son, and if he got back to New Orleans with Timmy, there was no way she would ever get the boy back. The future looked dismal to her now.

"What do we do now, Capt'n?" Tobias wanted to know.

Jonathan hesitated and took a deep breath. It

seemed like several minutes before he could answer. "We'll start out right away and trail them on south. Maybe we can catch up to them in a day or two. I asked around in town and found out the private coach only left Fargo early yesterday morning. We're closing the distance between us," Jonathan encouraged.

"They still have a day and a half lead on us." Sonora pointed out as she folded the letter and placed it back in its envelope.

Jonathan nodded. "Yeah, but we can travel faster on horseback than they can in a coach."

Sonora turned to face Jonathan. "Are you real sure the little boy in town is not my son? Maybe they decided to wait for the next stage just to throw us off."

Jonathan could hear the hope in Sonora's voice and he hated to keep being the bearer of bad news. "I don't think it is. The boy in town has brown hair not blonde." Jonathan paused a moment and looked from Tobias to Sonora. "But I'll tell you what. I'll take you through town so you can look at the boy for yourself. The troop can ride around the outskirts and we'll catch up with them south of town. How about that?"

A faint smile crossed Sonora's face as she nodded her agreement with the plan.

****

Satisfied that the little boy staying at the hotel was not her Timmy, Sonora and Jonathan rode hard to catch up with the rest of the troop. It was a short day on the trail since they got such a late start but so far the trail Tivy marked couldn't be missed. Calhoun and Baker had found the signs Tivy had left all along the way. At least there was hope; Tivy still had Timmy in his sights.

Later that day, Jonathan watched as Sonora pushed her food around on the plate. His heart ached to do something to make her pain more bearable. He couldn't explain the feelings he had for this young woman. For years, he had been praying God would send him a wife but he didn't think Sonora could be the woman God had in mind. She came with way too many problems and as far as he could tell she certainly didn't have a strong faith in God.

Jonathan could forgive her for the life she had led

that had caused her to become a mother with no husband. After all Jesus said, *'ye who be without sin cast the first stone,'* and Jonathan knew he was definitely not without sin. But did he want someone like Sonora for his wife?

Jonathan shook his head. "Where's that thought coming from?" Jonathan murmured aloud as he poured himself a cup of coffee.

Lt. Blake walked up to stand behind Jonathan. "Did you say something, Captain?"

Jonathan didn't realize anyone was that close to him. He was startled to hear Blake's voice. "No, just thinking out loud I guess." Jonathan didn't realize he had given voice to his thoughts. He would have to be more careful but he was still confused as to where the thoughts of Sonora as his wife had come from. Sure she was attractive. He also had to admit he felt sorry for her and wanted to do all he could to reunite her and her little boy. But he had no feelings for her other than that, or did he?

Once again, Lt. Blake drew Jonathan out of his thoughts. "Sir, could I speak to you in private?"

Jonathan gave the lieutenant a nod and followed the young man several yards away from the campfire. "What is it, Lieutenant?"

Lt. Blake looked his captain in the face. "Sir, just how far do you plan to go in search of this little boy?"

"As far as it takes to find him," Jonathan answered.

"Sir, I don't mean to be insubordinate, but do you mean to keep a whole company of men tied up for who knows how long looking for one little boy? What about the fort and our duties to protect it and the territory surrounding it?" Blake questioned.

Jonathan dropped his head. He knew the young lieutenant was right but he just couldn't forsake Sonora and Timmy. "Lt. Blake, you have a point, but for right now, we're going to stay on the course we're on."

"But, sir, by late tomorrow, we'll probably be out of the Dakota Territory. Then what?" Blake continued to press the issue.

Jonathan was becoming somewhat agitated with his second in command. "Blake, this discussion is over for now. When I have further information for you, I'll let you know."

The young lieutenant saluted his superior officer and took his leave.

Captain Parker stood alone in the night. His heart was downcast. He knew Lt. Blake was right. He couldn't keep a whole company tied up looking for a little boy and especially in a territory that was not under his jurisdiction. He couldn't just give up the search; some force kept driving him on.

****

The ground was cold and Sonora found it difficult to get comfortable. She tossed and turned and even stood up to reposition her bedroll but nothing helped. Inside her heart, she knew it wasn't just the cold, uncomfortable ground that kept her from sleep. Daniel Forrester was ruining her life and Timmy's. She knew the coldness in that man's heart and that made her shiver even more than the dropping temperature.

She wanted her son back but was beginning to lose hope that would ever happen. There were no lengths Daniel wouldn't go to get what he wanted. Sonora thought back to a conversation she had with her sister before Timmy was born. Her sister had told her about how Daniel had wanted to buy a saloon in New Orleans and the owner refused to sell it. Daniel had made the man's life miserable. First, he had made sure the man lost a major portion of his business by paying his customers to frequent another saloon, and then Daniel had made it impossible for the owner to buy liquor. The man eventually had to close up and Daniel got the saloon for nothing. Daniel Forrester was ruthless.

Sonora wondered how long these soldiers would keep following the trail of her son. She knew Captain Parker really cared about her and her son but she also knew they had to almost be out of the territory the Captain presided over. What would become of her and her son if the army turned back? She knew Jonathan wouldn't want to turn back without finding Timmy but he might not have any choice. If the army did go back to Fort Benton, she and Uncle Tobias would have to go on alone. The two of them would be no match for Daniel Forrester and his henchmen. It was a long restless night for Sonora.

****

The wake up call sounded too early for Jonathan. His thoughts had caused him a very restless sleep. He knew before this day came to a close he would have to make a decision as to how much farther he and his troops could go. Jonathan had been seeking God's guidance in the matter, but as of now, he had no clear revelation. A new day was waiting and Jonathan prayed they would catch up to the man carrying Timmy away from his mother. If they could get Timmy back today, all his troubles would be over; at least part of his troubles would be over. Jonathan was afraid this unfamiliar feeling he was experiencing for Sonora would linger long after Timmy's return.

****

Private Pete Baker rode up beside Jonathan. "Capt'n, I found Tivy. He's about two miles ahead."

"Well, let's go," Jonathan replied as he turned to summon the troops.

"Wait a minute, Capt'n. I think maybe you'd better come and talk to Tivy yourself and check out the situation before you alert the woman."

Seeing the concern in the young private's face, Jonathan decided to follow without alerting the rest of the troops. Leaving Lt. Blake in charge Captain Parker and Private Baker rode off.

"Good to see you, Capt'n." Tivy smiled when his captain rode into his little camp. "It's been a long trail."

"Sure has, Corporal, now tell me what's going on here?" Parker asked as he dismounted his horse.

"Well, the private coach camped on Nebraska soil last night. I crept in close enough to hear them talkin'. They're headin' for Omaha and from the sound of things they plan on catchin' the train there and headin' on south." Tivy offered his captain a cup of coffee. "Capt'n, I think we have a real problem here."

Jonathan took the cup of coffee Tivy handed him and took a sip before he spoke. "We've always known we have a problem. That's nothing new."

"But, sir, there was a visitor last night, some kind of government official. This man has some real pull somewhere. I gotta feeling we may have come upon a hornets' nest." Tivy handed Baker a cup of coffee before pouring one for himself.

"Well, he kidnapped that little boy, so it don't matter who he knows." Baker interjected as he leaned against the tree behind him.

Tivy took a sip of his coffee and then looked up a Baker. "Technically, he didn't kidnap the kid; the comancheros did."

"Well, he paid the comancheros for the kid." Baker was quick to point out. "We saw him give those renegades money."

"He could just say he was paying a ransom." Tivy sat down on a fallen tree. "It seems this boy is pretty important to this fellow. I don't understand it. If he had bought the boy to sell him, I guess that would make sense, but I sure can't figure this out. If you ask me, I'd say this man plans on keeping the kid."

"Why would this man want a strange kid?" Baker took another sip of his coffee before speaking again. "Capt'n, what'd you think?"

Jonathan paced in front of where Tivy was seated. Jonathan shook his head. "I don't know. We know the boy was taken from his mother but this fellow could claim almost anything, especially if he has the government on his side."

Baker finished his coffee and put the cup on the ground. He took off his hat and scratched his head. "Who is this fellow anyway?"

Tivy looked up at Baker. "I heard them calling him Daniel last night. That's the name he used on the stage, Daniel Forrester."

"So, it is him," Jonathan murmured. "We really do have a problem." Jonathan squatted beside Tivy.

Tivy looked puzzled. "Who is he?"

Jonathan was silent for a long time. Thoughts were running wildly through his mind. The man who had the little boy was the boy's father. *What do I do now?* It really shouldn't matter. Daniel Forrester apparently paid the comancheros to take Timmy from Sonora and that was wrong. The man had wanted nothing to do with the boy until recently so any judge should understand the boy should be with his mother.

Tivy noticed the strange look on the captain's face.

"Capt'n, you all right?"

Jonathan was still somewhat distracted but finally managed to speak. "Did you say something?"

"Yes, sir, what do you think about this situation and who is this fellow?" Tivy asked.

"I don't know exactly. I need to go back and get Sonora. We need to ride in there and get the boy before morning and before they can take off again." Jonathan walked to his horse.

"But, sir, they're out of our territory," Tivy reminded him.

Jonathan turned to look at Tivy. "Well, they were certainly out of our territory when you followed them into Canada."

Tivy nodded. "Yes, sir, I know that, but if I had gotten busted I'd only been kicked back to private. You could be in a lot of trouble."

"Corporal, I'm in the United States Army. I am sworn to uphold the laws of the United States and Nebraska is a part of the United States. So I'm just in pursuit of a criminal and I'm pursuing him into Nebraska territory. Now, you two stay here."

Jonathan looked at Baker. "If anything happens before I get back, Baker, you come get me."

Baker saluted. "Will do, Capt'n, but you be mighty careful."

****

"What did you say?" Sonora choked out.

Jonathan stood facing the bewildered young woman. "Daniel Forrester is the man that has Timmy."

Sonora's head began to spin. It was true. Daniel had Timmy just as she had suspected. Jonathan would soon learn the truth. She would never get Timmy back. The tears began to stream down Sonora's cheeks.

Jonathan pulled the young woman into his arms. "Sonora, don't cry." He comforted her for a brief moment and then said softly. "Now get ready, we're going after Timmy."

Her crying increased. "Daniel will never let him go."

Jonathan held Sonora firmly by the shoulders and looked her in the eyes. "He doesn't have any choice. He stole Timmy from you and any court in the land will see to it you get Timmy back."

"No, they won't. Not with all of Daniel's money. I'll never get Timmy back." Sonora pulled away from Jonathan and walked a few feet away.

Jonathan walked and stood behind her. "Sonora, don't talk that way. Timmy's your son and you're the one that raised him. Daniel hasn't shown an interest in him before now. So why would a judge let Daniel have him?"

Sonora turned to face Jonathan. "Because Daniel will pay the judge off. Don't you see, I don't stand a chance against the Forrester money."

Jonathan gently placed his hands on her shoulders once again. "Sonora, we have to believe justice will prevail. Now dry your eyes and let's get going. We have to get Timmy back before they ride on."

In a matter of minutes, the troop was on the move. Sonora felt sick to her stomach. She knew she should have told the captain the truth before they left camp but at least this way she would get to see Timmy one last time. She couldn't worry about what might happen to her when the truth came out. As the cavalry came to a halt, Sonora knew it wouldn't be long before Jonathan and everyone else knew the whole story.

Chapter Twelve

The troops entered the sleeping camp after quietly knocking the sentries unconscious. Jonathan poked Daniel Forrester with his rifle to wake the sleeping man. "Don't yell; we've got the drop on you and your men," Parker cautioned as the man opened his eyes and looked around.

Although he was staring down the barrel of a rifle, Forrester had more gall than most men did. "What do you think you're doing coming into my camp in the middle of the night?"

The man tried to sit up but Jonathan nudged him back down with the rifle. "I think I'm coming in to get the little boy you took from his mother." Jonathan looked Forrester in the eyes. "Now, where is he?"

Forrester glanced over to the right. "He's asleep in the coach, but I did not take him from his mother."

Jonathan looked off into the darkness. "Sonora," he called. Sonora walked into the light of the campfire. "Timmy's in the coach. Wake him up so we can get out of here."

"Wait a minute," Forrester protested as he looked up into the eyes of the angry army captain.

Jonathan's anger surfaced. "Don't say another word, mister. You'll get your say in a courtroom."

Again the man attempted to sit up and this time Jonathan allowed it. "How dare you speak to me that way." Forrester stood to his feet with no resistance from the captain. "Apparently, you don't know who I am." Forrester dusted off his trousers with his hand, "and you must not know who she is either."

Jonathan shook his head at the audacity of this man. A man who had kidnapped a small boy shouldn't be shooting his mouth off like this fellow. "I know she's the boy's mother and I understand you claim to be his father."

Forrester picked his hat up off the ground and shoved it on his head. "Well, you're half right. I am the boy's father but that is not his mother."

An enthusiastic, "Mommy" interrupted the conversation. A small, blonde-headed boy sprang from the coach into the waiting arms of Sonora. "I knew you'd come, Mommy; I just knew you'd come."

Sonora was overcome with joy. Tears streamed down her cheeks as she hugged and kissed her small boy. "Oh, Timmy, how I've missed you. I love you." She pushed him away from her just a little so she could get a good look at him.

"I love you, too, Mommy." Timmy again put his little arms around his mother's neck and hugged her tightly.

The scene brought a large lump to Jonathan's throat but he managed to choke out his command. "Lt. Blake, place this man and his associates under arrest. We'll take them back to our camp and then head back to the fort at first light."

Forrester held up his hand in protest. "Just wait a minute." He glanced from Captain Parker to Sonora. "I told you she's not the boy's mother. She has no right to my son."

Jonathan looked at Sonora and her son. "Seems the boy thinks she's his mother." The captain looked back at Forrester and nodded his head toward a large boulder. "Now you just sit down; we'll be pulling out of here in a few minutes and I don't want to hear anything more out of you. You can tell your story to a judge."

The captain walked over to stand beside Sonora and her son. "Sonora, you and Timmy get in the coach. You'll be more comfortable in there. I'll have Private Calhoun drive you." Turning, Jonathan called, "Tobias, why don't you join Sonora and Timmy in the coach."

The older man had been standing back and observing his niece's reunion with her son. With tears in his eyes, he walked into the light of the fire.

"Uncle Toby," Timmy called as he ran and jumped into the old man's waiting arms.

Tobias walked to the coach, set Timmy down inside and then turned to offer Sonora a hand up. For the first time, Sonora had turned to face Daniel Forrester. His eyes were cold and his face showed signs of hatred and determination. Sonora swallowed the lump in her throat and then turned to face her uncle. Tobias felt her hand tremble as he closed his strong fingers around her slender hand. They both breathed a sigh of relief as they settled themselves in the coach with Timmy.

****

Daylight came all too quickly for Jonathan. He had slept very little after they had made camp for the evening. In his mind, he kept seeing Sonora's face as she cradled her son and hearing the happy cries of a young boy returned to the bosom of his mother. How could Daniel Forrester be so full of bitterness to say Sonora was not the boy's mother? Anyone with eyes could tell Sonora was the woman who had nurtured and loved that young boy.

The feeling Jonathan had been fighting was growing stronger with each passing day. He still wasn't exactly sure just what the feeling was but he prayed either God would take the feeling away or he would have time to get to know Sonora and her son better to see just where such feelings might lead. He also prayed that now that Timmy was back safely, Sonora would not be so bitter and would allow God to heal her wounded heart.

****

The day was cold and the ride was long as they traveled back to Fort Benton but Sonora was comfortable inside the coach with Timmy. The boy had a thousand questions and had filled Sonora in on most of the details of his capture.

"I was really scared when I was in that cave," Timmy told his mother as he snuggled closer to her. "I was afraid a bear would get me."

Sonora thought her heart would break as she listened to her son. The thought of him being alone and scared was almost more than she could bear. "Oh, Timmy, I'm so sorry Mommy couldn't be there with you." She hugged him tightly. "But you don't have to be afraid any more. Mommy and Uncle Tobias are here now."

Timmy looked up into his mother's face. "Mommy, why did that man say he was my daddy? My daddy lives in heaven. That's what you and grandpa said. That's what I told the man, too."

Sonora pushed his blonde hair back from his face. She tried desperately to smile. "Timmy, let's not talk about that now. You've had a rough time and it's a long way back to the fort. Why don't you lay down and try to take a nap?" She leaned down and placed a soft kiss on his forehead.

Timmy argued for just a few minutes but tiredness overtook him and he fell into a restful slumber with his head in his mother's lap.

Oh, what do I do? The truth will come out now. What will happen to Timmy when he learns I'm not really his mother? What will happen to him and to me if a judge allows Daniel to take him back to New Orleans? Tears began to stream down her face one more time as she pondered her and Timmy's fate.

"God help us," she whispered. Sonora realized that for the first time, in a very long time, she had called on God for help but would He really help someone like her? She was sure all the lies she had told didn't put her in very good graces with the Heavenly Father.

Looking down at Timmy's sleeping form, she smiled lovingly, *Maybe He will do it for you though. You're so young and innocent maybe God will help us because of you.*

****

Fort Benton

It was late afternoon when Company B and their wards and prisoners arrived back at Fort Benton. Amanda was watching from the porch of her store as Jonathan rode up to his office and dismounted. He gave the orders to dismiss the troop and the men moved toward the stable. Something between a faint smile and a frown covered Amanda's face as she watched Sonora and a little boy step down from the coach that had stopped in front of Doc Thomas' quarters.

"Sonora," Doc called as he rushed out to assist her up the office steps. "It's so good to have you back." He watched as Sonora turned and assisted the small, blonde-haired boy. "And this must be Timmy." A broad smile covered the doctor's face.

"Yes. Timmy, this is Doctor Thomas." Sonora smiled

at her son.

"Pleased to meet you, sir," Timmy said as he held up his little hand toward the doctor.

Doc shook the little lad's hand. "My, what a well-mannered little boy." Doc smiled. "I'm pleased to meet you, son." Nathan Thomas turned to look at Jonathan who had crossed the compound to join them. "I see your mission was a success."

Jonathan nodded. "Yes, it was." He looked toward the stockade as he added; "Now I just have to get in touch with the U.S. Marshal to come pick them up." Jonathan moved to stand beside Sonora and Timmy. He reached down and ruffled Timmy's hair. "Sonora, why don't you and Timmy take the guest quarters for now? You'll have more room and be more comfortable."

Sonora readily agreed and guided Timmy toward their temporary home. She had plans to make, but for right now, she needed a hot bath and some rest. She would be able to think much more clearly when she felt clean and rested.

Sonora turned back to look at her uncle. "Uncle Tobias, are you going to join us?"

Tobias smiled. "I'll see you two later. For now, you both just need some rest."

"Jonathan, it's so good to have you home," Amanda called as she stepped up on the porch in front of the doctor's office. "It was really quiet around here."

Jonathan gave her a little smile. "It's good to be back and especially since we were able to bring Timmy back with us."

Amanda gently lay her hand on Jonathan's arm. "How about I cook you a good, hot supper?"

He looked down into her soft blue eyes. "Amanda, that sounds good, but tonight I'm so tired, all I want is a hot bath and some sleep."

Very disappointed, Amanda smiled, before turning and walking back toward her store. She'd wait until tomorrow and then try again to have a little time alone with Jonathan. While he was gone, she had made up her mind to tell him how she felt about him but it would have to wait one more day. Then, she would be bold and declare her feelings for this man she had loved for so long from afar.

****

"Enter," Jonathan called, when he heard the knock on the door to his quarters.

"Capt'n, I brought you some grub. When you didn't show up to eat, I decided I'd better bring you somethin'," grunted Zeke, the company cook. "You gotta eat."

Jonathan was stretched out on his bunk and hadn't bothered to get up when Zeke came into his room. "Thank you, Zeke, but you shouldn't have gone to so much trouble."

The cook set the tray down on the small table beside Jonathan's cot. "Weren't no trouble, Capt'n. Like I said, you gotta eat. Guess I'd better git back to the mess hall and make sure it gits cleaned up. See ya in the mornin', Capt'n." With that the cook was gone as quickly as he had come.

Jonathan was hungry and he was grateful for Zeke's thoughtfulness. Zeke would have folks think he was a crusty old man but Jonathan had always seen through him. Beneath that rough exterior, Zeke was as softhearted as they came. He sat up on the side of his small bed. The stew smelled good and tasted great. After finishing, he lay back down. It would feel good to get a good night's sleep, and for the first time in several weeks, he thought he would sleep peacefully. Sonora and her son were safe and for now Jonathan had peace of mind.

****

Sonora settled her son down into bed and pulled the covers over him. "Mommy, when can we go back to Uncle Toby's? I need to check on Rascal."

Her son's question made Sonora's chest tighten. Through all the stress of the past weeks, she had never once thought about her son's dog. She remembered seeing the little pup lying lifeless beside the well just before she passed out. How could she tell him they had no home to return too and that his pet was gone?

Sonora sat down on the bed beside her son. "Honey, I don't know when we'll get to go back to Uncle Toby's. You see those men that took you burned down the cabin so Uncle Toby will have to build a new one."

Timmy frowned as he looked up at his mother. "How

long will that take?"

Sonora was glad Timmy didn't mention anything else about his puppy right now. She knew it would come up again but for now she could spare him that bad news.

"I don't know, son. Uncle Toby will have to cut down the trees and everything. It may take a long time."

Timmy had a very puzzled look on his face. "Then where will we live?" A smile covered his face as a thought came to his mind. "Can we camp out under the stars, Mommy?"

Sonora smiled as ran her fingers through his hair. "For now we'll stay here. Tomorrow we'll talk to Uncle Toby about his plans for a new cabin. Right now we need to get some sleep." Sonora leaned down, kissed her son, and then tucked the cover around him. She gave him a big smile just before she blew out the lamp.

As Sonora lay in the darkness, the worries for the future tried to overtake her but her exhaustion won out as she fell into a deep slumber. Any plans or thoughts of the future would just have to wait until morning.

Chapter Thirteen

"Good mornin', girl. What a glorious day," Tobias called as Sonora opened the door for him. "You two hurry up; breakfast is waitin'. Come on, Timmy, my boy. I'll bet the cook has some flapjacks ready for a growin' boy like you."

"Oh, boy. Come on, Mommy, let's go," Timmy encouraged as he raced out the cabin door.

Sonora laughed as she grabbed her shawl and put it around her shoulders. "I'm coming."

As they stepped out into the fresh, cool morning air, Tobias spoke. "You'll never believe what that young captain has done now."

Sonora glanced over at her uncle. She was really curious. "What has Captain Parker done?"

The trio stepped off the wooden porch and headed across the compound toward the mess hall as Tobias answered. "He's sending some of his men out to help me rebuild my cabin. You know, he's an awful nice man." Tobias smiled. Looking at Sonora, he grinned as he added, "The girl that gits him for a husband will be a lucky woman."

Blushing, Sonora tried to ignore her uncle's statement and hide her reddened face but she couldn't stop the missed beats of her heart. She had been able to hold her emotions in check up to this point and had to continue to do so, especially now. The young captain would never want a woman like her and she knew it.

"I think Miss Amanda has designs on the captain," Sonora informed her uncle as they walked toward the mess hall.

"That might very well be but don't mean he returns her feelings," Tobias observed.

Sonora was thankful they had arrived at the mess hall so she didn't have to reply to that statement.

Sonora

The little family group was seated and enjoying their meal when Captain Parker entered the room. He filled his plate and then walked to their table. "Mind if I join you? I'm a little late eating this morning."

"Pull up a chair, Capt'n. Glad to have you join us. Timmy's been tryin' to eat up all the flapjacks." Tobias smiled as he looked down at his great-nephew.

Timmy puffed out his little chest. "I'm gonna do it, too. I'm a big boy now; Mommy says so."

"Well, a big boy needs lots of flapjacks so you eat all you want," Jonathan encouraged. Then addressing Tobias, he added, "When do you think you'll be ready to leave for your place?"

"Anytime, Capt'n. You just say when. I'm grateful for you lettin' Sonora and Timmy stay here 'til I have the place ready for 'em."

Jonathan took a sip of his coffee before he spoke. "It's no problem. We'll be glad to have them. Besides Sonora and Timmy will have to give their statements to the marshal when he arrives."

Sonora couldn't swallow the lump in her throat. It took what seemed like several minutes before she could respond. "Hasn't Timmy already been through enough? I really don't want to subject him to reliving what he's been through."

The captain gazed across the table at the young mother. "I understand how you feel and I will do everything I can to protect both of you." He tried to look reassuring. "Tivy, Baker, and Calhoun will testify to what they saw and we have your statement from the trial of those comancheros but the judge may still insist on questioning both of you himself."

Sonora glanced over at her son to see if the talk had upset him but Timmy seemed oblivious to the whole conversation. He was still consuming flapjacks as fast as he could.

She couldn't help but giggle as she watched him eat. "Son, you'll get a stomachache if you don't slow down."

Timmy looked up at his mother and with his mouth full he spoke, "I gotta eat a big breakfast so I can help Uncle Toby build his cabin."

Sonora picked up her napkin and wiped her son's

face. "Timmy, you can't go out with the men to build the cabin; you're too little."

A frown covered the little lad's face. "But, Mommy, you said I was a big boy. Why can't I go and help?"

Before Sonora could reply, Jonathan attempted to console the boy. "Timmy, you are a big boy, but if you and Tobias both go out to build the cabin, who will look after your mother?"

Timmy looked at Jonathan, then at Uncle Tobias and finally his mother. "Well, I guess I could stay here and take care of Mommy."

"Good fellow." Jonathan smiled.

Timmy turned to look at his uncle. "Uncle Toby, will you take care of Rascal for me. He must be wondering where we all are. He's probably scared like I was when I was with those bad men."

Sonora choked back the tears. Once again, she was saved by one of the gallant men at her table. Uncle Tobias looked at Timmy and softly began to speak. "Timmy, Rascal's not at the cabin anymore."

"Where is he?" Timmy demanded.

"Well, son, Rascal got bad hurt when those men took you. From what I could tell by the markings, that dog tried his best to protect you and your mother. I'd say your pup was a real hero." Tobias paused. There was no mistaking the lump in his throat or the moisture in his eyes as he softly added, "He fought hard but he just didn't make it."

Sadly, Timmy hung his head as he murmured, "So Rascal's in heaven with my daddy?"

"I s'pect so," Tobias choked out.

Tears filled the boy's eyes as he added, "Rascal was a hero, Mommy."

Sonora put her arms around her son as she assured him, "Yes, Timmy. Rascal was a hero."

Even the big army captain had to choke back the tears as he watched the bravery of the small boy seated at the table with him.

****

Tobias and a small band of soldiers rode out of the fort shortly after breakfast.

Sonora and Timmy waved good-bye to them from the porch of the doctor's office.

"Timmy, how about helpin' me out for a little while this mornin'? I have to tend the horses," Private Baker said as he walked up to the porch.

"Can I help him, Mommy?" Timmy wanted to know as he looked up at his mother.

Sonora smiled. "I guess it will be all right, but Private, if he starts being a problem send him back over here."

"He'll be fine, ma'am." The private drawled as he took the lad by the hand and the two strolled toward the horse barn.

"Sonora, why don't you sit down and talk a spell," Doc Thomas offered as Timmy and Pete walked away.

Sonora seated herself in the rocking chair and looked out across the yard. Amanda was sweeping the front porch of her little general store. The woman glanced Sonora's way but made no acknowledgement that Sonora or the doctor were anywhere in sight.

"I think Amanda's waiting for Jonathan to come out of his office." Doc grinned as he pulled his pipe from his pocket.

Sonora looked puzzled. "What makes you say that?"

Doc chuckled as he poured tobacco into his pipe. "She's been sweeping that porch for at least a half an hour now. Never has taken her that long to get the dirt swept off before."

"Maybe she's just being more particular this morning." Sonora grinned. She was ashamed of herself for making light of another woman's feelings.

"That woman's got it bad for the captain but I'm afraid she'll be real disappointed. Jonathan thinks of her only as a friend." Doc began to puff on his pipe as he struck a match to light the tobacco.

Sonora rocked back and forth in the chair. "You seem real sure of that."

Nathan laughed. "Well, some men aren't as ignorant of their surroundings as you women seem to think we are. I've watched Jonathan when Amanda's around and there are no romantic notions on his mind, but she definitely has romance on hers."

Sonora grinned. "Women have been able to change a man's mind before. If Amanda sets her cap to winning Jonathan's heart she can probably do it. She's a lovely woman."

With a longing in his eyes and voice, Doc Thomas murmured, "Yes, she is." Snapping his mind back to the conversation at hand he added, "Well, Amanda might be able to win Jonathan but I doubt it. Jonathan has high expectations for a wife."

"What do you mean...high expectations?" Sonora wanted to know as she began to rock her chair a little faster.

Doc's gaze was still focused across the compound on Amanda when he answered Sonora's question. "Oh, it's his Christian values. He wants a woman who shares his beliefs and that'll be tough to find out here."

Sonora looked somewhat puzzled as she asked the doctor, "Aren't there any Christian women out here?"

Doc took a puff off his pipe. "As you should well know, there's hardly any women at all out here. The few who are good women are already taken; most of them came out here with their husbands to start new lives. The other women are the type you find in the saloons." He took another drag from his pipe as he looked across at the general store.

Sonora wondered just what class she would fall into if the doctor knew her deceitful story but she kept her observations to the subject at hand. "Amanda seems like a good woman."

"She is, but I think she's lacking in a real faith in God." Then the doctor looked Sonora's direction as he asked, "What about your beliefs, Sonora? Are you a Christian?"

Sonora sighed heavily. "The fact you have to ask me should answer your question." She stopped rocking for the moment and sadly shook her head. "I believe in God but He and I have kinda parted ways lately. I guess I blame Him for most of my problems of late." She gave Doc a sidelong glance. "What about you, Doc?"

"Well, like you said, if you have to ask then that should answer your question, too. I guess you and I have something in common. I believe in God and although I don't blame Him for anything, I've just never felt the need to have a close relationship with Him."

Sonora could sense sadness in the doctor's voice as he continued. "I decided long ago that I could handle most things by myself. Figured that's why He gave me the brains that He did. Although I have been known to pray on occasion if something comes up I can't handle." He glanced around the compound. "Don't know if it really does any good or not because I don't know if God would really listen to anything I have to say, but it makes me feel better."

Sonora sat quietly for a time. She didn't know why talk of God disturbed her but maybe it wasn't the talk of God that bothered her. Maybe it was the talk of Amanda and Jonathan that had her feeling strange. Whether or not Jonathan liked Amanda was no concern of Sonora's; she certainly had no claims on him. Also, the doctor had confirmed her own beliefs; Captain Parker could never be interested in someone like her. Besides she had to decide what to do about her own problems and she didn't know how much time she had. She certainly couldn't waste time wondering what might or might not be between herself and Captain Parker.

She finally came back to the present as she gently began to rock her chair back and forth. "Doc, how long do you think it will be before the marshal gets here?"

"I don't know." Doc looked across the compound towards Jonathan's office. "Why don't we ask the captain? Here he comes now."

"Morning, Jonathan," Doc Thomas greeted.

"Good morning, Doc." Jonathan walked up and propped his booted foot on the edge of the porch. "The two of you look comfortable, like you don't have a care in the world."

"We're just folks of leisure." Doc leaned back and puffed on his pipe. "Besides, since you brought Timmy back, we don't have any cares; do we Sonora?"

Sonora was a little preoccupied with her own thoughts but finally responded to the doctor. "Uh, I guess not." She looked at Jonathan. "Captain Parker, when do you expect the marshal?"

Jonathan sat down on the edge of the porch. "Haven't

gotten a reply from him yet, but I suspect it will be anywhere from a week to ten days."

"That long?" Sonora wondered.

Jonathan noticed a strange look on Sonora's face. "At least. We're not usually top priority with him. I guess he figures if we have someone in custody we're more than capable of taking care of him."

Sonora nodded understanding. "How long do you think it will be before the men have Uncle Tobias' cabin ready?"

"Are you anxious to leave us?" Doc asked with a smile.

Sonora tried to hide the anxiety in her voice when she had been questioning Jonathan. Now she still tried to keep her voice calm. "Well, I would think you'd be pretty tired of me and all my problems by now."

"Why would you think that?" a female voice inquired. Amanda walked up to stand at the edge of the porch where Jonathan was seated.

"Sonora, you and Timmy are welcome to stay here as long as you like." Jonathan looked from Sonora to Amanda. "I don't know how long it will take the men to build a cabin. I know you're uncle is anxious to have a place of his own again."

"I can certainly understand why Sonora would be anxious to have a home again and get away from the confines of this fort." Amanda smiled.

Sonora saw no need to reply to Amanda's comment. She just sat quietly and smiled as the doctor began to tease Amanda. "Mandy, would you like a home out of the confines of this fort?"

Amanda smiled as she looked at the doctor. "I have a home and I'm used to all you men and your heathen ways." She looked down at Jonathan as she added, "I like it here but most women would prefer the company of other women."

"Sonora doesn't have the company of other women at the cabin. She just has Tobias and Timmy so maybe she likes our company for a change." Doc grinned as he continued to somewhat torment Amanda. "Besides seems to me, you'd be wanting her to stay so you would have another female to talk to for a change."

Amanda was becoming a little flustered. "Look, you're blowin' everything out of proportion here. I didn't say I didn't want Sonora to stay. I just said I could understand why she might be ready to leave."

"Doc, one of these days someone's gonna knock you upside the head when you start your teasing, even though it is good-natured in spirit." Jonathan chuckled.

"Well, that's about all the fun I get anymore. You men haven't been getting shot up lately." Doc laughed as he leaned back in his chair and crossed his legs.

Jonathan looked up at his old friend. "So, are you now telling me you want me to send my men out and get them shot up so you can occupy your time?"

Nathan Thomas grinned. "Well, it might help. When Washington gets report on my work here they may decide I'm not needed and relocate me."

Jonathan shook his head. "I don't think you have anything to worry about. I don't think Washington will ever decide that a fort in the middle of the untamed west can do without a doctor."

Jonathan looked into Sonora's smiling face. "Sonora, maybe in a few days, I could take you and Timmy for a ride to see how the cabin's coming along,"

Sonora forced the smile to stay on her face as she told him she would like that, but in her head, she wondered if she would still be there in a few days.

Amanda put a halt to the conversation between Jonathan and Sonora when she asked, "Jonathan, how about coming to supper tonight? I really have some things I need to talk over with you."

Reluctantly, Jonathan agreed but he turned his gaze to Sonora and gave her a warm smile.

Doc looked from Amanda to Sonora. "Well, Sonora, I guess that leaves you and me. May I escort you to the mess hall tonight?"

Sonora smiled at the doctor. "I have an even better idea. Why don't I cook for you and Timmy? I bet I could scrounge up something for a meal from Zeke."

Doc could see a hint of jealousy in Jonathan's face as he and Sonora discussed supper. Doc smiled at Sonora as he said. "That sounds like the best offer I've had lately. I accept. Your place or mine?"

"Since mine doesn't have kitchen facilities, I guess it'll have to be yours." Sonora smiled.

****

Amanda looked across the table at Jonathan as he pushed his food around on his plate. "Jonathan, you've hardly touched your food. Don't you like it?"

Her voice drew him from his thoughts and Jonathan looked up and smiled at Amanda. "I'm sorry. The food's very good. I guess I'm just a little distracted tonight, I'm sorry."

Jonathan's mind was across the compound with Sonora and Nathan. He couldn't help longing to be there with them instead of here with Amanda and he hadn't been able to stop the jealous feeling that had been rising in his heart since this afternoon. The pangs of jealousy had started to rise in him when he had listened to Sonora and Doc make plans for the evening.

Amanda lay her fork on her plate. "I fixed a big peach pie for desert. I know it's your favorite." She gave him a warm smile.

"That's nice." Jonathan offered rather matter of fact as he continued to stir his food around on his plate.

Amanda stood and walked to the counter. She cut Jonathan a large slice of pie and filled his coffee cup before she took her seat back at the table. Any attempt she made at conversation with the distracted young army captain failed miserably.

Wiping his mouth, Jonathan seemed to realize where he was. He looked across the table at Amanda and forced a faint smile. "Amanda, I'm sorry. I've been such poor company tonight, but I'll try and do better. You said you had something you needed to talk over with me. What is it?"

"Could we move into the parlor? We would be much more comfortable." She pushed her chair back from the table. "Bring your coffee and follow me." Amanda was out of her chair and headed into the parlor before Jonathan could respond. He grabbed his coffee cup and followed his young hostess into the other room.

Amanda was seated on the sofa and indicated for Jonathan to take the seat beside her, but in his gallantry, he seated himself in the stuffed chair facing her. He looked into her eyes. "Okay, now, what's on your mind?"

Amanda could feel the heat in her face but she had decided to do this and she wouldn't back down now. She had to make her feelings known before it was too late. She just hoped it wasn't already too late.

Clearing her throat, she began to speak softly. "Jonathan, we've known each other for a few years now and I believe we have become close friends."

Jonathan nodded. "I agree, Amanda; we are friends."

Amanda stood and began to pace the room.

Jonathan noticed her nervousness and tried to offer his assurance. "Amanda, whatever is bothering you can't be too bad. You know you can share anything with me."

Amanda stopped and looked directly at him. "Jonathan, it's not bad at all, at least I don't think it's bad. I just don't know how you'll respond to it."

"Well, neither of us will know how I respond until you tell me what it is." Jonathan smiled.

She couldn't hide the nervousness in her voice as she spoke. "Okay, here goes. Jonathan Parker, I'm in love with you."

Jonathan choked on the swallow of coffee he had just taken and began to cough violently.

"Oh, Jonathan, I'm so sorry." Amanda rushed to his side and knelt down beside his chair. "Here," she said as she handed him a napkin. "I didn't mean for you to get all choked up."

He finally composed himself and took a deep breath before he spoke. "Did I hear you right?"

Amanda smiled as she looked into his dark green eyes. "I hope you did. I just told you I'm in love with you. I know it's not very ladylike for the woman to admit it first, but Jonathan, I just couldn't wait any longer. I love you."

Jonathan was speechless. He could have thought of a million things Amanda might want to talk to him about but this would have never come to his mind. What could he say to her?

Amanda stood to her feet and then seated herself on the sofa across from the man she loved. "Jonathan, I know I've taken you by surprise. You don't have to say anything to me right now. I just wanted you to know how I feel. I'd hoped you'd return my feelings right away but I can wait for you. Jonathan, I can wait forever for you if I have to."

Jonathan could hardly stand the wistful look on her face. He stood to his feet and walked to stand in front of her. He took her arms and assisted her to rise to her feet.

Looking her in the eyes, he finally gave voice to part of his feelings. "Amanda, like I said I consider you a very good friend, but I have never thought of us in any other capacity." Tears began to appear in Amanda's blue eyes and he added, "I'm sorry."

"It's her, isn't it?" Amanda choked out as she pulled away from Jonathan.

A puzzled look covered his face as he asked. "Who?"

When Amanda turned to face him again, Jonathan could see that her blue eyes had fire in them. "Sonora...you're in love with Sonora." The tears began to flow freely down Amanda's cheeks.

Jonathan's voice was weak and maybe not as convincing as it should be. "I don't know what you're talking about. There's no one else, Amanda. I don't even know Sonora well enough to be anything but a friend to her."

Amanda stepped closer to him. She placed her hands on his arms. "If you're not in love with Sonora, then give us a chance. We could be good together."

Jonathan tried to pull away but her grip was strong. "Amanda, I consider you a good friend. That's all."

Amanda flung her arms around the neck of the unsuspecting captain and begged. "It could be more if you'd just give us a chance. I love you, Jonathan Parker. Don't you understand? I love you."

Jonathan firmly took her arms with his hands and removed them from his body. He continued to hold her at arm's length as he spoke with authority. "Amanda, get control of yourself. I know it's lonely out here, and since you lost Russ, you've had a hard time. I think you have just confused friendship with love. You're trying to fill the void left in your life when your husband died."

"I know my own feelings." Tears continued to flow down her cheeks but there was an edge of anger in her voice. "Don't you try and tell me how I feel. Sure I've been lonely but I could have satisfied that loneliness with any number of willing able-bodied men. I know what love feels like; I've been in love before so don't try and define my feelings for me."

Jonathan released his grip on her and walked away. "Amanda, you don't mean what you're saying. You wouldn't settle for just any man and you know that."

Now anger covered her face and filled her voice. "Oh, don't flatter yourself, Captain Parker." She lifted her arm and pointed toward the door. "Now get out."

"But..."

Amanda interrupted before he could get anymore out; "I *said* get out."

Jonathan removed his hat from the peg by the door and took his exit. As he stepped out into the night air, he shook his head. Maybe if he shook it hard enough, he'd be able to figure out what had just happened inside Amanda's parlor.

****

"It's a little cool, isn't it?" Doc commented, when he met Jonathan in front of the captain's quarters.

Still disturbed by the recent events, Jonathan grunted, "Hadn't really noticed."

"How was your supper with Amanda?" Doc wanted to know.

Not wanting to reveal the details of the evening, Jonathan just answered, "It was fine." Then he remembered that Nathan had supper with Sonora so he returned the question.

"We had a wonderful time. I just walked them back to their quarters." Doc smiled. "That Timmy is a great kid. Sonora was a little quiet but I guess with all she's been through lately she needs time to recover."

Jonathan nodded. "Yeah, she's really been through a lot. Well, it's late, think I'll turn in."

"Yeah, me too. See you in the morning," Doc called as he walked on toward his own living quarters.

Jonathan stood for a moment on the porch of his office and gazed up at the star-filled sky. "Lord, please forgive me if I was too harsh or too blunt with Amanda. I was just so shocked when I heard her put her feelings into words. Sure, I knew she was a little attracted to me and I have in the past toyed with the idea of maybe there being something serious between the two of us. Lord, please forgive me if I ever gave Amanda reason to think I thought of her as more than a friend. And Lord, please help Amanda deal with her feelings for me and send her someone who will love her as she deserves."

He went into his sleeping quarters and got ready for bed. As he lay in the darkness of his room, he continued talking with the Good Lord. His turmoil lessened somewhat as he opened his heart in prayer.

"Lord, please help me with my growing feelings for Sonora. I didn't exactly lie to Amanda when she asked me if I was in love with Sonora because I don't know what it is that I feel for her. Lord, help me sort it out and show me your will in this situation. Lord, I pray Sonora will turn her life back to you. At one time, she followed you and your teaching, but somewhere along the way, she has taken a different path. Please help her find the right road again. In Jesus name, I ask all these things"

****

Sonora lay in the darkness listening to the slow, even breathing of her son. Easing out of bed. she crossed the room to the window. Looking out over the fort, she saw the sentries as they made their continual rounds. She looked heavenward and saw a clear sky. The moon was almost full and the stars twinkled like flickering candles in the night.

"God, I know you're still there. You've always been there; it's me who's been lost. It's me; I turned my back on You. I know You didn't turn away from me." Sonora choked back the tears. "God, it was just easier to blame You than to take all the blame on myself. I'm the one that ran away instead of staying and fighting Daniel Forrester. I don't know if it was so much I didn't trust You to help me or I just didn't trust the human beings that would be deciding a little boy's fate." Again she paused as she wiped the tears that had begun to trickle down her cheeks. "Now I'm faced with the same situation. In a few days, the marshal will be here and when they run a check on Daniel they'll find out that he is the boy's father. Although I didn't give birth to Timmy, I'm the only mother he's ever known and I love him as if he's my own son." Sonora fell to her knees. "Oh, Father God, what do I do? I don't know if I have the strength to run away again but I also don't know if I have the strength to stay and fight the likes of Daniel Forrester. Help me make the right decision. Just make sure whatever happens that I get to keep my son."

Sonora finally stood to her feet again and looked out the window. For what seemed like hours, her gaze stayed glued to the sky. It was as if she expected God to write the answer to her prayer across the heaven. Sonora finally returned to her bed. She had been very sincere when she began her prayer to God and she hoped He would help her do the right thing. Sonora just knew her way had to be the right way and she hoped God was in agreement with that. She had hoped for the peace Jesus said passes all understanding after she had prayed, but she still felt very scared and very confused about the days to come.

Chapter Fourteen

It had been ten days since Uncle Tobias had left the confines of the fort. Sonora didn't know how the progress on the cabin was coming but she knew she had to make a decision and soon. If she stayed anywhere in this territory, she knew she'd lose Timmy. *What would happen if I ran? How can I take care of myself much less a little boy?* Sonora had no skills, no money, and she was out of relatives to run to. Uncle Tobias was her only living relative, other than her father, and she certainly couldn't go back home to him. Daniel would find her there in no time. *What should I do?*

Sonora's thoughts were interrupted by the sound of a knock on the door. Opening the door, she found Jonathan standing on the other side.

"It's a beautiful morning," Jonathan said as he removed his hat.

Sonora stepped out onto the porch to join him. "Yes, I guess it is." She quickly glanced around the compound. "Timmy's off enjoying the sunshine with Private Johnson."

Jonathan could hear a touch of anxiety or maybe a little depression in her voice. "You sound a little down. Are you under the weather?"

Afraid that if she opened her mouth at all she would say entirely too much, Sonora just kept silent.

Jonathan had a scowl on his face as he looked down into hers. "Sonora, is something wrong?"

Sonora shook her head. "Just daydreaming, I suppose."

A smile covered Jonathan's face. "I know something that might cheer you up. How about taking a ride out to the cabin site? I thought you and Timmy might enjoy getting a look at your new home."

Sonora managed a faint smile but was lacking in

enthusiasm at Jonathan's offer. She finally agreed and went back into her quarters to fetch her bonnet and a light shawl. Jonathan headed across the compound toward the horse barn to find Timmy and get a buggy hitched for their little adventure.

****

The Dakota Territory

"Boy, Captain Parker, I never saw this stream before." Timmy ran up to the edge of the water, his eyes wide with excitement. "Reckon there's any fish in it?"

Jonathan had pulled the buggy to a stop beside a quiet mountain stream. The breeze was cool and the trees were filled with the contented chirps of what sounded like hundreds of birds, probably on a southbound course before the weather got really cold.

"Timmy, this stream is full of trout. I sneak off out here as often as I can get away and fish." Jonathan had walked up to stand beside the lad. He patted Timmy on the head. "Why don't you sit down here and check it out. The water's clear enough you can see the fish swimming."

"Timmy, you be careful," Sonora called to her son as he eased a little closer to the water.

Jonathan walked back to the buggy where Sonora sat waiting. He offered her his hand to assist her down from the buggy. "I thought we'd rest and enjoy the sounds of nature for just a little while." His smile was captivating.

Sonora caught her breath, as his gaze seemed to look deep inside her. Her heart started to speed up its pace as she timidly lay her small hand into his strong one. This man was getting close and she had to do something about it before it was too late.

As soon as her feet touched the ground, she quickly pulled her hand from his tender grasp. "Do you think it's safe here?" She was desperately trying to draw her mind away from any romantic thoughts of the handsome army captain beside her.

"Do you think I'd risk your safety, not to mention Timmy's?" The tone in Jonathan's voice indicated her question might have slightly offended him.

"No," Sonora quickly returned as she glanced up to look him in the face. "I know you would guard us with your life. You've proven that on more than one occasion." Her voice was betraying her. It was showing more tenderness for this man than she intended. Trying to bring indifference back in her voice, she added, "I guess I'm just a little on edge these days."

A soft smile covered Jonathan's clean shaven face and his voice took on a softness that was hard to resist. "Sonora, you have every right to be on edge after all you've been through."

He took her hand once again. For a brief moment, Sonora thought he might pull her into his arms and kiss her, but the sound of her son calling drew their attention away from one another and to the young boy standing in water up to his knees.

"Timothy Allan Grimes, what do you think you're doing? You were just supposed to look at the fish not go swimming with them."

Jonathan couldn't hold back his laughter as he saw the sparkle that came into Sonora's eyes when her small son gave her an innocent smile.

"But, Mommy, I almost had one. A really big one." Timmy spread his little hands about a foot and a half apart to indicate the size of the fish.

Sonora shook her head as she tried to reprimand Timmy without showing the smile that was threatening. "Timmy, what are we going to do with you? Look at you, you're all wet.

Timmy pointed to the bank. "I pulled off my shoes and socks."

Jonathan could restrain himself no longer and his laughter filled the morning air.

Sonora gave a heavy sigh as she glanced from Jonathan to her son. "It's not funny," Sonora scolded as she tried to choke back her own laughter. "Now, Timmy, you get out of there this minute before you catch a cold."

The boy carefully stepped on the small rocks at the creek's edge and pulled himself from the cold stream. His little body began to shiver as the morning breeze blew across his wet pant's legs.

Laughing, Jonathan pointed out, "Timmy, the next time you decide to go diving for fish, maybe you'd better pull off more than just your shoes and socks."

Sonora walked over to her son and placed her shawl around his shoulders. She looked up at Jonathan who was standing beside her and the boy. "Don't encourage him." She pushed Timmy's hair back from his face. "Timmy, what am I gonna do with you?"

"I was just trying to catch a fish, Mommy." Timmy's teeth chattered as he talked. "I'm all right."

"Sonora, he was just being a boy." Jonathan smiled as he started walking toward the buggy. "He's a might chilly right now. I'll go get the blanket from the buggy."

As soon as Jonathan returned with the blanket, Timmy shed his clothing and Sonora wrapped him in the blanket.

Jonathan looked down at the little boy. "Timmy, go stand over there in the sun for a few minutes and warm up a little."

Timmy made his way to a large rock and seated himself in the sun. As he walked away, his mother was finally able to let the chuckle she had been choking back escape from her lips.

Jonathan placed his hand on her arm and escorted her to a fallen tree beside the water. "Let's sit a spell." As she seated herself on the log he added, "He's a fine boy, Sonora. You have a lot to be thankful for."

Sonora glanced over at her son who was now lying on his stomach on the huge rock raking a long stick through the water. She knew she had a lot to be thankful for but she also knew her past was about to catch up with her and then what would she have? The smile was now replaced with tears that filled her dark eyes and spilled onto her soft cheeks. If something didn't change and soon, she would loose her son.

Jonathan pulled his kerchief from his back pocket and handed it to Sonora. With the tears still spilling down her face, she took it but refused to lift her eyes to meet his. Sonora could feel his gaze on her and once again her heart started to pound in her chest. How she longed to tell him everything but she just couldn't bring herself to do it.

****

As Jonathan drove the buggy down the bumpy path that led to the cabin Tobias was building, his mind was on the beautiful dark-haired lady beside him. How he wished he could stop the hurting she was feeling. He thought back to those moments by the stream when he had longed to pull her into his arms and kiss away her tears but he couldn't do that. He was finding it very difficult to suppress the feelings he had for Sonora but he had to keep them at bay. He had prayed for a strong Christian wife and in his head he knew Sonora was not the one. He was finding it very difficult to convince his heart of that.

****

Tobias walked up to the buggy. He stroked his beard as he looked at his small nephew wrapped in a wool blanket. "Well, boy, that a new kind of outfit for young fellers?"

The lad shared the story of what had happened with his great-uncle. Tobias couldn't hold back the laughter as he pictured the scene in his mind. The older man reached out his arms for Timmy. "Come over here. I'll build a fire and have those clothes dry in no time at all."

Timmy watched as his uncle built a nice, big fire. With the fire going and the young boy's clothes laid out to dry, Tobias picked up Timmy and walked toward the cabin. The men had accomplished a lot in the ten days they had been working.

"Still a long way to go, but should be finished in a couple of weeks, if the weather holds," Tobias offered as he sat Timmy down on the porch.

"It's bigger than the other cabin," Sonora observed as she walked though the three- foot high shell.

Tobias chuckled. "Yeah, the boys decided you and Timmy needed a room to yourself. They are real pushy fellers, Capt'n."

Jonathan nodded in agreement. "You're right about that. Ben Tivy is one of the pushiest men I've ever met." Jonathan glanced around at the work that had been completed. "Looks good though. Should keep you nice and warm this winter."

Tobias noticed something strange in the young captain's face and voice. Somehow his expression didn't match the words he was saying. Could it be the young man would be sorry to see Sonora and Timmy leave the fort? Tobias knew his niece needed a good man to look after her and Timmy and he prayed that just maybe

Jonathan Parker would be that man.

Sonora interrupted her uncle's thoughts when she spoke. "We brought lunch. Zeke packed enough for an army." Everyone laughed at her statement. She blushed when she realized what she had said and she added, "I meant the whole army."

The men made a makeshift table and pulled up stumps for chairs. As they gathered around the table, Jonathan offered grace before they began to eat.

"Sure is good food," Tivy said just after he'd swallowed a big bite of fried chicken. "I thought Zeke was crazy when he said he was gonna raise chickens at an army fort but I'm real glad now he was crazy enough to try it."

Everyone nodded agreement, then talk switched to the soon arrival of the U.S. Marshal. Sonora grew very uncomfortable as talk of an eventual trial continued. She knew the marshal would have to come soon.

"Oh, Tivy, I almost forgot," Jonathan said as he reached into the breast pocket of his coat. "You got a letter the other day. Thought I'd bring it out to you. Might be important."

"Who'd be writin' to me? I haven't got a letter since my mother died." The corporal took the cream colored envelope from the captain's out- stretched hand. He had a puzzled look on his face as he looked at the writing on the front of the letter.

Jonathan took a sip of coffee and then set his cup on the table. "Looks and smells like it could be from a woman." He smiled as he teased the corporal.

The other men picked up on the good-natured ribbing. "Tivy, what you been hidin' from us." Aubrey Calhoun grinned.

Ben Tivy couldn't hide the blush that covered his face as he opened the letter and noticed it was from Willow Ingram.

"Ah look, his face is bright red," Pete Baker pointed out.

"Why don't you men leave him alone and let him read his letter in peace," Sonora scolded as she stood and started to clear the plates from the table.

Tivy tucked the letter back inside the envelope.

"Don't mind them, Miss Sonora. They got no manners and I'm used to that." The corporal tucked the letter in his pocket.

Aubrey glanced over at his friend. "Well, aren't you gonna read it?"

"I think I'll wait 'til later when I don't have such a big audience." Tivy stood up from his place at the makeshift table and pulled his hat on his head. "Now I guess it's time we get back to cuttin' some trees. This cabin won't build itself ya know."

The men went back to the work at hand while Sonora cleaned the dishes they had used for their noon meal. Her thoughts, as usual, were on her plight and what she should do. As she began to work, she found her thoughts turned to prayers but they were too soon interrupted by the sound of her uncle's voice.

"Sonora girl, you're a million miles away. Care to share your thoughts?" Tobias placed his arm around his niece's shoulders.

Sonora choked back tears as she shook her head. Finally finding her voice, she tried to focus her attention in a different direction. "I'll leave this food for you and the other men. There's plenty here for your supper tonight."

Tobias would not be put off. Taking both her shoulders in his hands, he turned her to face him. "Girl, it's time we did some talkin'. Let's sit a spell." He led her back to the table and they seated themselves on the stump chairs. "Sonora, what are your plans?"

Sonora tried to pretend she didn't know what he was talking about. She refused to look him in the face as she played with the fabric of her skirt. "What are you talking about? What plans?"

Tobias reached over and gently lifted her chin with his hand. "Now, girl, you know well as I do what I'm talkin' about. I've kept my mouth shut just hopin' you'd come to me but guess that's not to be so I'm askin'. What do you plan to do about this whole situation with Timmy?"

Sonora turned and propped her elbows on the table and lowered her face into her hands. After a long pause, she finally murmured, "I have no idea." Another pause, she lifted her head and looked her uncle in the eyes. "You know when the marshal gets here and hears all the facts,

I'll lose Timmy."

Hoping to lift his niece's spirits, Tobias reached over and took her small hand in his. "You don't know that for a fact. After all, you're the one that's raised the boy, not that Daniel Forrester. You're Timmy's mother in every way that matters."

Sonora sighed deeply. "I know that and you know that, but how would I ever convince anyone else of that fact. I can't fight Daniel's money and power or the fact he is Timmy's real father." The loss of hope was weighing heavy on her heart and she felt just like she did when she had left her father's house in Mississippi. She looked around at this little homestead. She remembered the peace she had finally come to know after several months here with her uncle but that peace was gone now. She knew her uncle was concerned about her and Timmy but there was nothing he could do to stop the feelings she was having now.

Tobias looked into her dark eyes.

"Sonora, why don't you talk to the Captain? Maybe he could help. I know he cares an awful lot about you and Timmy."

Sonora shook her head. "I can't tell him the truth. What would he think of me then? He'd probably help Daniel take Timmy from me."

"Why would anyone think bad of you? You just took a little boy who lost his mother and raised him as your own." Tobias smiled. "There's nothin' wrong with that and you've got to have some help from someone."

"Not if Timmy and me just up and leave," Sonora mumbled as she turned away from her uncle.

Tobias lowered his voice and leaned in a little closer to Sonora. "Just where do you think you'd go this time?"

Looking desperately into her uncle's eyes, Sonora pleaded. "If you could see your way clear to lend me some money, we could go somewhere and make a new start for ourselves."

He could see the desperation in Sonora's face. He shook his head as he spoke to her. "Girl, how many new starts do you plan on makin'? If Daniel Forrester is dead-set on gettin' that boy, do you think he'll stop here? Look at the lengths he went to this time to get Timmy. If he could find you out here in the middle of nowhere, then do you really think you'll be able to get away from him?"

Sonora jumped to her feet. "Well, what else can I do? Just give Timmy to the man?" With those words said, Sonora stomped off into the woods.

Tobias followed Sonora the short distance into the trees. When he caught her, he forced her to look at him. "You can quit runnin'. Tell the truth. The only way you and Timmy will ever know peace is to come clean. When a court declares Timmy can remain with you, then and only then will you find peace."

"That's a wonderful thought, Uncle, but it's really not very realistic, now is it?" Sonora's words were cut short by the sound of Timmy's voice calling her name. She answered her son and walked away from her frustrated uncle.

Chapter Fifteen

Fort Benton

The ride back to the fort was very quiet. Timmy drifted off to sleep and Sonora kept all her thoughts to herself. Jonathan could sense something was wrong but decided for the time being to just leave well enough alone. He silently prayed for God to intervene and help Sonora with whatever was troubling her.

The big gate swung open and Jonathan drove the buggy into Fort Benton. He pulled it to a stop in front of the visitor's quarters and assisted Sonora to the ground. He picked up Timmy's sleeping body and carried him into the small cabin. As he started to leave, Sonora thanked him for the day and taking the time to drive her and Timmy out to the cabin.

Jonathan started out the door, but stopped and turned to face Sonora. "I know something is troubling you and if you need someone to talk to, I'm always willing to listen."

Sonora gave him a faint smile and tried to assure him she was only tired. "I guess seeing our future home just made me a little anxious to get back out there and try to put our lives back on some kind of normal basis. Thank you for your offer." She hesitated for a moment. As she looked up into Jonathan's eyes, she added. "I really appreciate all you've done for us."

Jonathan stepped out onto the porch and started to pull the door closed when Sonora's voice once again stopped him. "Captain." Sonora waited for Jonathan to turn and look at her before she continued. "No matter what happens, I really do thank you for all you've tried to do for us. You've been a good friend and I will never forget you."

The young captain smiled. "Sonora, if I didn't know

better I'd say you were trying to tell me goodbye, but it's a little early for that." He paused as she stepped out onto the porch and stood in front of him. "What I've done for you and Timmy was my pleasure and I thank God it turned out for the best and you got your son back."

Jonathan's smile grew broader. "You know it was more God's doing than mine. He's the one that kept Timmy safe and led us to him. So, Sonora, give God all the glory for the way things have turned out."

Placing his hat on his head, Jonathan said as almost an afterthought, "Sonora, trust God to take care of whatever lies ahead." He turned, stepped off the porch and then walked across the compound to his office before Sonora had a chance to respond to his comments.

****

Sonora walked back inside her quarters where she pulled a handkerchief out of her skirt pocket. Carefully she untied the small cloth bundle. Even though Tobias had been dead-set against her running away again, just as she and Jonathan were getting ready to leave, he took her hand and pressed the handkerchief into her palm. Sonora stared at the ten large gold coins. This was probably all her uncle had in the world and Sonora felt a pang of guilt for even thinking of taking advantage of her uncle, but what else could she do? If she stayed until the marshal came, then she would surely lose Timmy again and this time for good.

She walked out onto the porch of the little cabin that set safely in the confines of Fort Benton. She walked to the edge of the plank porch and leaned her body against one of the post that supported the roof. Gazing up she saw the sun setting over the far wall of the fort. The sky was alive with various shades of red and orange. Any God who could paint a picture like that surely could handle Sonora's problem. Sonora started to feel a swell of peace in her heart, but just before she gave in to the comfort of the peace, the old questions and doubts started to shove the peace out of her heart and her mind.

A voice was telling her, *if you stay you know you'll lose Timmy because he's not really your son. Daniel Forrester will take him away and you'll never see him again.* The voice seemed to get louder and louder and

Sonora put her hands over her ears to try and stop the unwanted words. Nothing seemed to help and she gave in to the depression that had plagued her for months. She had to form a plan. How would she ever slip away from Fort Benton without the army following fast on her trail? Jonathan Parker had already proven he wasn't a man who gave up easily. If she left with Timmy, she knew it would only be a short time before Jonathan found her and brought her back to stand before the U.S. Marshal. Her plan had to be good.

****

"What do you mean you're going to Rapid City?" Jonathan questioned Sonora the next morning at breakfast.

"I have a friend that lives there. She has wanted Timmy and me to come visit ever since I came to this territory and I just never have gone. I thought now would be a good time. Timmy and I have been a burden on you and the army long enough. We could visit her until the cabin is ready." Sonora turned away so the captain could not see her face. She was ashamed that lying had become all too easy for her these past months.

Jonathan stood close beside her. "Sonora, the marshal will be here any day and you and Timmy will need to be here to talk to him."

Sonora began to walk slowly toward her quarters with Jonathan keeping step beside her. "Well, you could wire us and we could take the next stage back or I could write out my statement for you to give to the marshal."

She paused in mid-stride for just a moment. "I just feel like a change would be good for both Timmy and me right now. You know, get away from the scene of the crime so to speak."

Jonathan shook his head, his confusion and concern evident on his face. "I can understand your wanting to get away but wouldn't it be better for you to go after the marshal has come and gone with Daniel Forrester?"

Once again she began to ambulate slowly toward her cabin. "Captain Parker, is there a legal problem with us going?"

Jonathan sighed deeply. "If you're asking if I can force you to stay here until the marshal comes, no, I don't guess I can. But Sonora..."

Sonora stepped up onto the porch in front of the guest quarters. "Well then, I had better go and get our bags packed right now. The stage will be leaving shortly and I don't want to miss it." She looked deep into Jonathan's eyes before she turned to enter the little cabin. She didn't realize until then how deep her feelings had become for the brown-haired, green-eyed captain. Sonora saw something akin to love shinning in the young captain's eyes.

What she wanted to do was rush into his arms and beg him to make everything all right for her and her son, but Sonora knew that was impossible. Jonathan still thought of her as an unwed mother, and she also knew that was not the kind of woman Jonathan Parker wanted to spend his life with. Her only choice was to run. Even if Jonathan truly cared about her, she knew he didn't have the power to beat a man like Daniel Forrester.

****

Timmy set cross-legged on the bed. "But, Mommy, why do we have to leave the fort?"

Sonora placed their clothing into the carpetbag. "Son, I explained that; we're going to visit a friend of mine who lives in Rapid City." She hated lying to her son but she couldn't tell him there was no friend or he would surely give her away. They were headed to Rapid City but only to catch another stage that would take them farther west.

Timmy sighed deeply and then with a childish whine he spoke. "But I like it here. I don't want to go to Rapid City."

Sonora closed the bag and looked around the room one last time. "Timmy, that's enough. Now put on your jacket and let's go. The stage is ready to leave."

Reluctantly the young man did as his mother instructed. Sonora grabbed their luggage and the two walked to the general store where the stage waited. Everyone was there to see them off.

"Sonora, I will miss you and Timmy. Please hurry back to us and take care of yourself." Nathan Thomas hugged her and kissed her gently on the cheek.

Sonora fought back the tears as each soldier wished her and her son well. Even Amanda gave her a hug, although Sonora sensed Amanda was really glad she would not be in the fort any longer.

Jonathan walked up and scooped Timmy into his arms. He hugged the young lad and then deposited him inside the waiting stagecoach. Turning to Sonora, Jonathan's voice was soft as he spoke. "Be careful and hurry back."

Sonora forced a smile but there was definitely sorrow showing in her eyes. Jonathan extended his hand and assisted Sonora up into the stage. When he secured the stage door, the driver slapped the reins and the coach began to lunge forward. Timmy hung out the window and called good-bye, waving to all his friends. Sonora sat back in her seat and for the first time allowed a few tears to trickle down her cheeks.

****

Doc looked at the long-faced captain. "How about a sarsaparilla?" He slapped Jonathan on the back. "You look like you could use one. As a matter of fact, the look on your face looks like a fellow who just lost his best friend or something."

"Or something," Jonathan mumbled. Once again choking back his feelings, Jonathan replied, "I'll take you up on that drink." The two men walked into the general store just as the big gates closed and the stage disappeared from their view.

"So why did you let her leave?" Doc asked as he opened his soft drink.

Jonathan stared down at the counter. "Just how would I have kept her here?"

Doc took a sip of his sarsaparilla before he answered. "The marshal should be here soon and he will want to question her and Timmy."

"That's true but she can come back for that." Jonathan took a sip of his drink. "That alone isn't a good enough reason to make her stay at the fort."

"You could have told her how you feel about her."

Jonathan turned to look at his friend. "And just how do I feel about her?"

Nathan laughed. "It's evident to everyone but you apparently. You have some very strong feelings for her."

Jonathan was quiet for several minutes. "Doc, I

honestly don't know what my feelings for her are. I won't deny that I'm very attracted to her but I don't know if she's the one God has picked out for me."

Doc was thoughtful for a moment. "Jonathan, I sure don't know much about God. But I do know Sonora's a good woman and any man would be lucky to have her for his wife and Timmy would be just an added bonus."

Jonathan sighed deeply and then looked into Doc's face. "But Doc, I have to be sure she's the one God wants me have for a wife."

****

"Mommy, why are you crying?" Timmy asked as he looked up into his mother's face.

Sonora pulled a handkerchief from her reticule and wiped the tears from her eyes and face. "Oh, girls just sometimes cry for no reason." She forced a faint smile as she looked down into her son's confused little face. "I guess I'll miss our friends." She reached over and smoothed back her son's hair.

The boy's face was alight with glee. "We could make the driver stop and take us back to the fort."

Again Sonora smiled into the face of her innocent son. "No, son, we have to go on; we can't go back. Now you settle back into this seat. We have a long ride ahead of us."

Sonora reached into the small bag in her lap and pulled out a slate and chalk for her son to occupy his time. They both settled back into the leather seats in the bouncing coach. Sonora was thankful that at least for now they were the only passengers on board.

****

Rapid City, Dakota Territory

It was late the next day when the stagecoach arrived in Rapid City. Sonora secured a room, then she and Timmy went to the little café in the hotel for supper. Once back in their room, she decided it was time to tell her son the truth. After they dressed for bed, Sonora tucked Timmy in and then sat down on the edge of the bed beside him.

"Son, I need to talk to you a minute." Timmy's eyes became wide as she started telling him her story. "Timmy,

I don't have a friend here in Rapid City. I just said that so Captain Parker wouldn't follow us when we left the fort."

Timmy quickly set up. "Mommy, you told a lie?" He asked in childlike innocence.

Sonora nodded her head. "Yes Timmy, I did." She took a deep breath and swallowed hard to keep from crying. "I'm sorry I had to lie but I did it to protect you. You see there was another man coming to the fort and I was afraid he might try to take you away from me. I couldn't stand the thought of you being taken from me again, so you see we had to leave before he got there. Do you understand?" She hated the mixture of fear and confusion she saw on her son's face.

"No, ma'am, I don't. You mean there are other bad men coming that want to take me away from you? Who are they?" Timmy wanted to know.

"It was just a man that would take you away." She paused. Oh how she hated what all this was doing to her son but she couldn't take any more chances. "You know how the man that took you first said you were his son?" Timmy nodded and Sonora continued. "Well the marshal that was coming to get him would have believed his story and he would have taken you from me and given you to Mr. Forrester."

Timmy moved closer to his mother. "Well, you could have told him my daddy lives in heaven and you're my mommy. The marshal would have to believe you, Mommy."

Sonora put her arms around Timmy and pulled him close. "Son, I'm afraid they would never believe me. I couldn't take the chance they would believe him so we had to leave."

"When the marshal takes Mr. Forrester away, then we can go back?" Timmy wanted to know.

Sonora sighed and hugged Timmy a little tighter. "No, Timmy, I'm afraid we can never go back there again."

Neither mother nor son could fight back the tears as the two held each other and cried themselves to sleep.

****

Fort Benton

The days wore on for Jonathan. It had been a week

since Sonora and Timmy had left and he had gotten a telegram from the marshal stating he would be delayed for another week or so.

Daniel Forrester was becoming a very unhappy prisoner and threatened to contact everyone from the governor of the Dakota Territory to the President of the United States unless Jonathan freed him immediately. Jonathan had finally allowed the man to wire his father in New Orleans. Seemed the older Forrester was expected to arrive at the fort any day now. Jonathan knew he was in for a very unpleasant time if the father was anything like the son, and from the few things Sonora had told him about this family, he was certain the elder Forrester was even worse than the younger one.

Jonathan saw Doc and Amanda sitting on the bench in front of the general store. Amanda had said very little to the army captain since the night she had declared her love for him. Jonathan had tried to remain cordial but the strain between them was evident to anyone who knew of their previous relationship.

As Jonathan neared the store, Amanda excused herself and disappeared inside the building.

"You sure have a way with women," Nathan teased his friend. "First Sonora leaves, and now every time you get in the vicinity, Mandy runs like a scared rabbit."

Jonathan pulled off his hat and wiped his brow with a handkerchief. "Well, I had nothing to do with Sonora leaving," he moaned softly, "and I'm real sorry about Amanda. I didn't know how else to handle the situation."

Doc watched as Jonathan seated himself on the edge of the porch. "Just what is the situation between Mandy and you, if I may be so bold as to ask?"

Jonathan glanced up at the doctor. "You can ask but I don't know that I'm ready to talk about it." Then an idea occurred to him. "Doc, why haven't you ever tried to court Amanda? I know you're fond of her."

Doc almost blushed at the captain's words. Jonathan could tell many thoughts and emotions were running through his friend's mind before he finally answered Jonathan's question. "Oh, Mandy doesn't have any feelings for me in that way. I think she's kind of sweet on you."

Jonathan shook his head and gave a soft chuckle. "No, she has no feelings like that for me, at least not anymore."

Doc pulled his pipe from his pocket and began to fill it with tobacco. "So did she finally realize you're in love with Sonora?"

Taken aback, Jonathan tried to deny what he knew in his heart was true. Somewhere along the way he had fallen in love with the dark-haired beauty he had rescued a few months back.

"It really has nothing to do with Sonora. My feelings for Amanda are strictly friendship and she deserves a man who will truly love her and take care of her." Jonathan watched as Nathan lit his pipe. "I think that man is you, Doc, but don't wait too long. She might up and do something real stupid." Jonathan cautioned. He waited for Doc to make a comment but the man just sat there and puffed on his pipe, although he did have a strange little gleam in his eyes.

The troop assembled in the middle of the fort. They were ready to ride on a routine scouting trip and Jonathan was going to lead them. He stood as Corporal Tivy rode up with Jonathan's horse in tow. The captain looked at the doctor. "See you in a few days, Doc." The captain mounted his waiting horse. He gave the doctor a quick salute and then gave the order for the troop to move out.

Chapter Sixteen

Wyoming Territory

Sonora and Timmy were on yet another stage taking them even farther away from the Dakota Territory and Daniel Forrester. Sonora gazed out the window at the sagebrush-covered mountains. True this coach was taking her farther away from Daniel Forrester but it also took her farther away from the army captain who had stolen her heart. She looked at her young son. Even though she had come to realize how much she loved Jonathan Parker, she loved her son even more. She could never sacrifice Timmy for Jonathan and that's what she'd have to do if she returned to Fort Benton. California was a big place, surely she could get lost there.

The stagecoach lumbered on across the rugged terrain. They had been headed southwest from Rapid City, but somewhere in the Wyoming Territory, they had started a westerly course. The view out the window never seemed to change. There was dust, sagebrush and mountains. Sagebrush covered mountains. From a distance the mountains were beautiful, rugged peaks reaching up into the azure blue sky but up close they were just dark rocks covered with the ever-abundant sagebrush. Sonora smiled to herself. She knew the view wasn't that bad, God had created all of this wonderful country but she did long to see some trees.

Timmy awoke from his nap and began to watch for the wildlife out the windows of the coach. They spotted antelope, elk, coyotes, and a sage hen now and then. It really was unique scenery, and for a while, Sonora's mind was on her son and not her fear of loosing him or how much her heart missed Jonathan Parker.

Sonora saw a huge wooden fence in the distance; it must be Fort Bridger. She had heard of it and knew it was the fort opened by the famous Jim Bridger. The stage would stop here for a couple of days before they continued their journey west. She was glad to have a break from the jostling of the coach. She knew the older couple who had joined them in Rapid City would also be happy for the rest.

As Sonora stepped from the stage, her heart raced. The sights, the sounds, all the men in uniform seemed so familiar. The atmosphere of being in an army fort once again brought a terrible longing to see Captain Jonathan Parker.

****

Fort Benton

U.S. Marshal Reuben Jeffress rode into Fort Benton. He was an intimidating man to most people who met him. He stood well over six-foot and weighed in excess of two hundred pounds. Jonathan had known him for several years and knew him to be a tough but fair man.

"Good to see you, Reuben," Jonathan spoke as he extended his hand to the marshal.

Reuben pulled off his gloves before he shook hands with the army officer. "Good to see you, Captain. Sorry I couldn't get here no sooner. I knew you could keep the prisoner here under wraps so I took care of some more pressing problems on the way." The marshal took off his wide-brim hat and hung it on the rack by the door before seating himself in a chair in front of Jonathan's desk. "Now tell me what ya got."

Jonathan told Reuben all the details of the story. He told him of finding Sonora along with the search for and the hanging of at least part of the comancheros. He gave the marshal all the details of the search and rescue of little Timmy, and then filled him in on the details Sonora had shared with him about the birth of her son. He told the marshal how Daniel Forrester had sent her packing instead of taking responsibility for the child she was carrying at the time.

Reuben Jeffress looked thoughtful. "So why did a man like that finally decide to claim the boy as his son and try to get him away from his mother?"

Jonathan leaned back in his chair. "Well, seems

Daniel wasn't blessed with a son by his wife and his father wasn't happy about not having a male heir to the Forrester fortune. So that left finding Timmy and bringing him to New Orleans to become the one and only male heir to the wealth of the family."

The marshal nodded his head. He leaned back in his chair and stretched his long legs out in front of him, crossing them at the ankles. "So just to please the old man, this Daniel character has comancheros steal his son and take the boy away from his mother, who has raised him since birth. The only parent the little fellow has known. This Daniel must be some character."

"He is that, but he's a character with power." Jonathan stood and walked to the door of his office. He gazed across at the guest quarters. "His papa, Mr. Samuel Forrester, is here. Arrived last week and has been stirring up a fuss since the minute he rode through the gates." Jonathan turned to face the marshal, who still sat in a very relaxed position. "He's sent telegrams to everyone from the governor of Louisiana, to the governor of this territory, even one to the President himself. I can't count the number of senators and congressmen he's telegraphed." Jonathan shook his head in dismay.

The marshal placed his elbows on the arms of the chair and formed a triangle with his fingers, resting them on his chin. "So what good does he think that's gonna do. His son clearly stole the boy, and even if he is the boy's father, that's against the law. 'Specially since he didn't want nothing to do with the lad until just recently."

Jonathan walked over and sat down on the edge of his desk facing Reuben. "Well, he and his father are claiming Sonora isn't Timmy's mother. Daniel has been saying that since the night we picked him up." The captain took a deep breath. "He claims Sonora's sister was Timmy's mother, and he had just recently found out she died giving birth to the boy. He claims Sonora took the child to raise as her own after her sister died and that since he is the real father he should get the boy."

The marshal nodded. "You think there's any truth to it?" Jonathan shook his head and the marshal continued. "What does Sonora have to say about all this?"

Jonathan slowly moved back around his desk and sat

down in his chair. "Well, Sonora and Timmy aren't here right now. They went to Rapid City to visit a friend. I've already sent a wire to tell her to come back to the fort." Jonathan looked the U.S. Marshal in the eyes. "But, Reuben, I've seen Sonora with Timmy; she is his mother."

Jonathan knew the lawman in Reuben Jeffress wouldn't rest until he got all the answers he needed. "Then why did she run in the first place?"

"Afraid of the power this Forrester family has. She said she knew she couldn't win against them. She's a lot like a frightened rabbit, just trying to protect her little one." Jonathan paused a moment before he continued. "But in some ways, she has probably frightened him more, especially since he was taken by those renegades. It would have been better for both of them if she had just faced Forrester in a courtroom right at the beginning of this whole mess."

Reuben stood to his feet. "Well, guess I'd better question this Forrester." He walked to the door and pulled his hat from the rack.

The dinner bell sounded from the mess hall as Jonathan walked around his desk. "How about something to eat first?"

Reuben Jeffress agreed and the two men set out across the compound.

****

Nathan was seated in one of the chairs in front of Jonathan's desk when Reuben Jeffress entered the captain's office. "Well, what do you think of our distinguished guest?" Reuben had just finished interrogating the prisoner.

The marshal pulled his hat from his head and walked over to the little wood stove. "He's either telling the truth or he's the best liar I've run across in years. He has his story down pat, down to the last detail. Dates, times, and everything. He, of course, denies hiring the comancheros to steal Timmy. Claims they heard about his search, found the boy, kidnapped him and then contacted Forrester for ransom." Reuben poured himself a cup of coffee before he sat down with the other two men in the room.

Jonathan looked directly at the marshal. "Do you

believe that?"

The marshal shrugged. "Don't know what to believe yet. I'll have to talk to Sonora before I can get a good feel of this case. I need to hear her story from her own lips and look into her face when she tells me how she gave birth to this little boy. Then maybe I can tell who's lying and who's telling the truth." The marshal took a long drink of the hot liquid in the cup he held.

Jonathan stood and walked to the window and looked out. "Reuben, what do you think will happen if Forrester's story is true and Sonora's sister was really Timmy's mother?" Jonathan wasn't sure he really wanted an answer to that question.

Before the marshal could answer, Doc jumped to his feet and almost shouted. "I don't believe you could even think such a thing." Nathan pounded his hand on the desk. "Jonathan, you've seen that woman with her son. You saw her before you found him and how she suffered. Sonora is Timmy's mother and there's no question about it. You can't take the word of a scoundrel like Daniel Forrester."

"And how do you know he's a scoundrel?" The marshal asked before taking another sip of coffee.

"Sonora says he is and that's good enough for me," Doc replied as he stomped out of the office.

Reuben and Jonathan watched as the doctor left the office. "A might touchy isn't he?" the marshal observed. "Could he have more than a casual interest in our young mother and her son?"

Jonathan hesitated before he answered. He knew Doc's feelings for Sonora were purely friendship but his own feelings were of a deeper nature. For now, he had to try to remain neutral.

"No. Doc cares about Sonora and Timmy, as we all do. He really saved her life and nursed her back to health. I guess he feels a little like a father to her."

The marshal stood to his feet. He walked over and hung his cup on a nail above the stove. "Well, I'd better send a wire to the federal judge and see what he wants me to do here. I'll talk to you later." Reuben started out the door and then paused. "Have any idea when Sonora and the boy will be here?"

"No, haven't gotten an answer to my telegram yet. Should hear real soon though." Jonathan fought hard not to let the emotion in his heart show. He could hardly wait to see Sonora once again.

****

Fort Bridger, Wyoming

Sonora felt much better. She had been able to take a bath in a real tub and was free of dust for the first time in many days. She walked out of the little cabin into the cool night air. Timmy was in the yard playing with a little boy and a big collie dog.

The mother of the other child approached Sonora. "Hello, I'm Willamena Applegate, Captain Applegate's wife. I just wanted to see if you or your son needed anything."

Sonora smiled at the woman. "That is very kind of you, Mrs. Applegate, but we're fine. I got a good bath so I feel like a human being again."

The woman returned Sonora's smile. "Please call me Mena, everyone does. I'd like for you and your son to join us for supper."

Sonora glanced at her son, then back at the lady standing before her. "That's very kind of you but I don't want you to have to go to a lot of trouble on our account."

Willamena reached out her hand and gently touched Sonora on the arm. "I assure you it's my pleasure. I don't get a chance to entertain very often and especially another woman. You can tell me about life away from Fort Bridger."

Sonora finally accepted her kind invitation and then called Timmy to come inside the small quarters they had been assigned for the next couple of days.

"Now, son, you understand why you must not say anything to the Applegates about us running away from the bad man, don't you?" Sonora said as she wiped the dirt from her son's face.

Timmy grimaced as his mother scrubbed his face. "I guess so, Mommy, but if we told somebody, like Captain Parker, maybe he could help us and get rid of the bad man."

Sonora checked behind Timmy's ears for more grime.

"I don't think so, son. It's best if we just keep it to ourselves and keep going until we reach California." She pulled her son into her arms and hugged him close.

How she wished it was that simple. How she longed to tell Jonathan the truth and have him be able to work everything out for the three of them to be together forever. But Sonora knew that was impossible. If Jonathan knew how many times she had lied to him, he would never forgive her, and even if by some miracle he could forgive her for her lies, Daniel would take Timmy away from her. There was nothing to do but continue on to California and forget she ever met Captain Parker.

****

Sonora liked Willamena Applegate. She was a very kind and caring person. But tonight, at supper, Sonora had felt somewhat uncomfortable. The Applegates were fine Christian people; maybe that was the problem. Sonora had attempted to make everything right with God back at Fort Benton. She had been sincere when she had asked for forgiveness and she knew God had forgiven her. For a very brief time, she was even able to pray again but she could not seem to release Timmy into the hands of the Lord. She wasn't certain God was on her side when it came to Timmy and she just couldn't risk losing him again—this time for good.

All the lies and deception made her feel guilty and pushed her farther away from the safe keeping of the Almighty. She especially felt guilty when she was around people of faith. It had been that way with Jonathan and now with the Applegates. The guilt was a heavy burden to bear but for now Sonora would just suffer. Keeping Timmy was the only thing that mattered.

When they reached California, she would attempt to once again set things right with God. Maybe God was somewhat on her side after all. She had gotten hundreds of miles away from Fort Benton without problems. Even that thought did little to free Sonora of the guilt she felt. She knew the secrets she had buried in her heart and the lie she still lived on a daily basis was keeping her from knowing true peace and forgiveness.

****

Fort Benton

Sonora

Jonathan gazed into the eyes of Sonora's uncle. "What do you mean, Sonora's not in Rapid City?"

Tobias looked down at the floor. "She has no friends anywhere in the Dakota Territory, except here at the fort."

Jonathan fell more than sat down in his chair. "Tobias, maybe you'd better tell me what's going on here."

Tobias began to pace the small office. He didn't know just how much he should say. He wanted the captain to know the whole story but it would be a lot better if the truth came from Sonora. What good would it do at this time if he told Captain Parker Sonora was not Timmy's blood mother? For now he would keep his niece's secret.

"Well, Capt'n, you know Sonora's afraid of loosing her son. That's why she came to me in the first place. Now that Daniel Forrester is here, then naturally Sonora wants to be somewhere else." The old man sighed deeply but still wouldn't look at the army captain. "The day you brought her and Timmy out to the cabin she told me how scared she was and she was thinking of leaving but didn't have any money. I told her to talk to you and let you help her. I got the feeling she wouldn't do that so I gave her some money, just in case." Tobias stopped his pacing and looked the young captain in the eye. Jonathan's displeasure was very evident.

Jonathan shook his head. "You gave her money so she could run away."

Once again, Tobias hung his head. "I guess so. I hoped she wouldn't run but I guess fear won out over good sense."

"I wish I had known she wasn't really going to Rapid City." Jonathan ran his fingers through his hair and then leaned his elbows on his desk. "I wish you had told me the truth sooner."

Tobias sat down. "Capt'n, how was I supposed to do that? I didn't even know she was gone. But, if you'd sent someone out to the cabin, I could have told you her plans."

Jonathan looked at the distraught older man. "I'm sorry, Tobias. I didn't mean to blame you. I know you want her and Timmy to be safe even more than I do."

Tobias did want his niece to be safe but he didn't

know if it was possible for him to want that more than the captain did. Tobias looked into the concerned eyes of the young captain. It was plain to the old man that Jonathan Parker was in love with Sonora, whether he would admit it or not. Yes, Jonathan loved Sonora very much.

"Do you have any idea where she might be headed?" Jonathan asked Tobias.

"Probably as far west as she can go."

"I guess that means California," Jonathan said and Tobias nodded in agreement.

****

Jonathan paced the floor of his office. *What do I do now?* Sonora had to be found and brought back to Fort Benton. Her running away only gave credibility to Daniel Forrester's story. If she were really Timmy's mother, why would she run away; why wouldn't she stay and fight for her son?

The young captain continued to pace. His mind went back to the night they had rescued Timmy. The picture he remembered so vividly in his mind made him smile. Sonora was the little boy's mother, at least in every way that mattered. The love between the two was the kind only a mother and child have for one another.

Sonora had to be found and brought back, but what would happen then?

Would a judge be cold hearted enough to take Timmy away from the arms of a loving mother, even if the mother wasn't the one who gave birth to the child? Jonathan was afraid Sonora had tipped the scales of justice in Forrester's favor when she ran. The captain was tempted to do nothing, to allow her and her son to escape the possible consequences of her actions.

As Jonathan considered that possibility, the longing in his heart grew stronger. He ached to see Sonora and Timmy once again. He had missed Sonora from the moment the huge gate had closed behind the stagecoach the day she had left for Rapid City. He found himself missing Timmy almost as much as he missed Sonora. The army captain had grown very fond of the little lad, and as much as he tried to avoid the thoughts of such things, Jonathan could picture himself as the little boy's adoring father.

Jonathan tried to shake all thoughts of a personal nature away. Right now he had to do what was right for Timmy and Sonora. He just had to decide what that was. Jonathan had been a Christian long enough to know he wasn't capable of making such a decision alone. He had to call on his Heavenly Father for guidance.

A knock on the office door interrupted Jonathan's prayer. After calling out for the person to enter, Jonathan looked up to see Doc Thomas standing before him.

"What are you going to do?" Doc wanted to know as he seated himself in the chair in front of Jonathan's desk.

"Don't know," was Jonathan's simple reply.

"Why do you think she ran off?"

"Don't know that either," Jonathan answered.

Doc smiled. "You're really a wealth of information today."

"Sorry." Jonathan looked across the desk at his friend. "Why do you think she might have run?"

Doc shrugged. "Probably because she was scared."

"Scared of what?" Jonathan pushed.

"Losing the boy I reckon."

"So you think she might lose him?"

The doctor rose to his feet and began to pace in front of Jonathan's desk. "I know you're trying to get me to say that scoundrel might be right about Sonora not being Timmy's birth mother." Doc paused and looked Jonathan directly in the eyes, "You and I both know she is the mother of that child."

"We know she's the mother in every way that really counts, but did she give birth to him? That's the question a judge will want an answer to."

"Only if she's found and brought back to face a judge," Doc reminded the captain. "What are you going to do about that?"

"Don't know. Been praying about it." Jonathan stared into the face of his friend as if seeking an answer to his prayer.

Before the conversation could continue further, there was another knock on Jonathan's office door. "Enter," Jonathan called.

"Just dropped by to let you know I've wired every stop along the stage route that the young woman took,"

Marshal Jeffress said. "Hopefully we'll get a lead on her whereabouts. Least ways we should be able to have her and the boy picked up and held until we can arrange for her return to Fort Benton."

Doc Thomas rose to his feet. Before he left the office, he turned to Jonathan and murmured, "Guess God answered your prayer."

The marshal looked confused by the doctor's words but made no comment of his own. He turned to look at the young captain still seated behind his desk.

Jonathan offered no explanation but knew in his heart that he no longer had to worry about what to do. The decision had been made for him. Now all he could do was pray for Sonora and Timmy.

Chapter Seventeen

Fort Benton

"What's wrong with you this morning?" Amanda asked when Doc Thomas stormed into the general store.

"Nothing," Doc spit out, slamming the door behind him.

"Well, I'm glad you're in a good mood. I'd have to replace that door if you were upset." Amanda couldn't hide her grin.

Nathan ran his fingers through his hair. "Sorry, Mandy. Guess things just aren't going as I'd hoped they would."

"Must have something to do with Sonora." Amanda poured a cup of coffee, then walked to stand beside the doctor as she handed him the hot brew.

"What makes you say that?" Doc asked as he took the coffee from the pretty storeowner. The doctor crossed to a small table and seated himself in the straight-back wooden chair.

Amanda walked back to the stove and poured herself some coffee. "Lately every time you or Jonathan have been out of sorts it's been because of that woman." She took a sip of the hot liquid, then walked over and sat down across from Doc Thomas at the little wooden table. "She's been a plague on this fort since Jonathan and Corporal Tivy brought her here."

Doc shook his head and spoke a little more strongly than he normally did. "Mandy, don't talk like that. Sonora did nothing to you. She's just a woman desperately trying to keep her son with her. She's been through a lot and really there's been no one to help her."

Nathan sighed deeply and then took a sip of the dark liquid. As he slowly drank his coffee, he looked across the table and into Amanda's dark blue eyes. "Mandy, what do you have against Sonora? The look in your eyes is something akin to hatred."

Amanda set her mug down onto the table. "It's not akin to hatred, Doc; it is hatred." Amanda hung her head.

Doc waited for several moments before he spoke. "But why, Mandy? She has done nothing to you. At least as far as I can tell."

"She stole Johnny from me," Amanda whispered. Amanda hadn't meant to let her nickname for Captain Parker slip out, much less let that confession be heard by anyone but herself.

Confusion was obvious on the doctor's face. "Who's Johnny?"

Amanda cleared her throat. She had to talk to someone. She had kept all the secrets and hurt buried inside since the night Jonathan Parker had rejected her love. Now she had to pour out her heart to someone so she told Doctor Nathan Thomas the whole story. She told him how she had pined for the young captain for months and how she had made a fool of herself and been completely rejected.

"Don't you see? If Sonora hadn't shown up here, Johnny would have been mine." Amanda wiped the tears from her eyes with the handkerchief Nathan handed to her.

"Oh, Mandy." Doc stood, and then reached down and pulled Amanda into his arms. He held her close; her tears flowed with ease as he whispered words of comfort.

Finally Amanda's tears subsided and Nathan held her at arm's length. He brushed her hair back from her face and gently stroked her cheek with his thumbs.

"Mandy, do you really think Sonora came between you and Jonathan? Had Jonathan ever given you any sign he felt more than friendship for you?" Doc asked.

Amanda hesitated. She had searched her heart for weeks ever since that horrible night. She knew Jonathan had never given her any reason to think he loved her. He had always treated her like a sister and friend, but oh, how she hated to admit that out loud. It just seemed easier to blame Sonora for her heartache. Maybe if she did admit it, at least to the doctor, then she would feel better.

"No, Jonathan always treated me as a friend. It was just my wishful thinking that there might be more between us." She let out a slight chuckle and then took a deep breath. Amanda realized that, for the first time in months, she did feel better. The torch she had been carrying didn't seem to be burning nearly so bright right now and the weight of misery that had been resting on her shoulders seemed to be lighter as she had shared all her feelings with Doc Thomas.

Amanda finally looked up into the doctor's sympathetic face. "Nathan, you won't tell anyone about this conversation will you?"

"Not a soul," the doctor promised. Smiling broadly, he repeated. "Not a soul. You feel better now?" Nathan reached over and wiped the last stray tear from Amanda's cheek.

Amanda gave him a smile. "I really do. Thanks, Doc." She picked up the coffee cups and started to take them to the back of the store but stopped. "How about sharing dinner with me? I've got a pot of soup on the stove."

"That would be great. Soup sounds good to me," Doc answered as he followed her into her home quarters in the back of the store.

****

Fort Bridger, Wyoming

Sonora stretched as she walked out onto the porch of the tiny cabin she and Timmy shared at Fort Bridger. She needed to locate the stagecoach driver and find out when they would be on their way. They had already been here two days and she was getting anxious to be traveling once again. Staying still made her very nervous. It just gave somebody more time to find her. She felt sure Daniel Forrester had someone on her trail by now.

Sonora scanned her surroundings. Fort Bridger was much larger than Fort Benton. There were stone buildings and a large parade area. A small creek ran through the middle of the fort, and there was even a school on the premises. It would be nice to be somewhere that had a school so Timmy could get a real education. She shook that thought from her mind. Of course, she could teach him if she had to once she got settled in

California, somewhere safe, some place she wouldn't have to run anymore. Everything would be better then.

Of course, that was probably wishful thinking. Sonora knew deep down that Daniel Forrester could find her wherever she went. She just prayed that with a new identity and in a place as big as California she could dodge him for awhile. At least she had been successful so far but that was probably because Daniel was still in jail.

Sonora wondered what was happening back at Fort Benton. Had the United States Marshal arrived yet? Had Jonathan now learned the truth about her? It wouldn't be hard for Daniel to convince all of them of the truth since she had taken Timmy and ran. Jonathan would know all about her lies. Even if by some miracle she could go back, Jonathan would want nothing to do with her.

"Just as well," Sonora whispered to no one but herself. "Now where's that stage driver?" She started across the compound to look for the man.

****

"I'm sorry, miss, but it's taking longer than I figgered." The stage driver wiped his brow with the sleeve of his shirt. "We're lucky we got here without breakin' down. That there axle was almost plum near broke into. The smithy is gonna make us a new one but it takes time."

The older man walked over and picked up a harness. "He had some other stuff he had to finish first. He'll git to us soon as he can. I wired the next stop to let them know about the delay. If you got kin, you can send them a wire, but that's all we can do now." The driver hung the harness he held on a nail on the wall. "I'm gonna go make sure the horses are fed and watered. You best git you some vittles fore the cook throws them away and starts dinner."

Sonora watched the driver head toward the corral. There was nothing she could do now but wait. She would go wake up Timmy and go to the mess hall for breakfast.

On her way back to the cabin, she saw Willamena come out of the fort store carrying a small parcel. If she walked fast maybe the captain's wife wouldn't speak to her. Sonora was not in the mood for a cheerful conversation this morning.

"Sonora, you're out early," Willamena called as she stepped into the early morning sunshine.

Sonora sighed and then turned to look at the woman who greeted her. "Not really. I'm usually up a lot earlier."

Willamena smiled. "But you're on a little vacation now. No need to get up early. You can be a lady of leisure until you reach your home in California."

Sonora couldn't help but smile at the thought of being someone on a vacation. "Can't say I'd even know how to be a lady of leisure. Never had the opportunity to do that before."

"I know what you mean. Seems a woman's work is never done," Willamena walked over to stand beside Sonora. "Have you and Timmy had breakfast?"

Sonora shook her head. "No. I was on my way back to the cabin to wake Timmy and then we'll go to the mess hall and see if the cook has anything left."

"Why don't you go get your son and come over to my cabin? I have biscuits left from our breakfast and I could fry a couple of eggs and cook up some bacon."

"Oh, we couldn't put you to that much trouble. We'll just go to the mess hall." Sonora began to walk back toward her cabin.

Willamena strolled along beside her. "It's no trouble and I'd feel better. You and that little boy don't need to be in the mess hall with all those soldiers."

"I think most of the soldiers have already eaten."

"Well, I'd just feel better if you came to my cabin, besides Timmy can play with Joey. I won't hear anymore about it and I'll go start cooking the bacon now. You go get Timmy. I'll be expecting you in just a little while." Willamena gave her instructions and walked toward her own cabin before Sonora could protest anymore.

Sonora had no choice but to go and wake Timmy to go to the Applegate's. At least this morning, the captain wouldn't be there. She would try to enjoy a visit with the captain's wife. She might as well since it appeared she would be at Fort Bridger for a few more days.

Sonora did enjoy her visit with Willamena in spite of herself. Willamena Applegate was a woman you just couldn't help but like. After breakfast, the two women sat down and Sonora helped do some mending. It was nice to share another woman's company. Timmy and Joey had gone outside to play so the ladies had time alone.

"Sonora, I hope I'm not being too personal but is your husband waiting for you in California? I know, with the big gold strike out there, lots of men got the gold fever and left their families behind." Willamena asked as she sewed a patch on the knee of a pair of Joey's pants.

Sonora swallowed hard. *Here we go again; now, I have to come up with another lie to satisfy this woman's curiosity.* Sonora kept her eyes on the shirt she was mending. "No. Timmy's father is dead," Sonora lied. "We're going to California to start a new life."

"That's a long way to travel for a woman and child alone to start a new life," Willamena looked across at Sonora. "Didn't you have family back where you came from?"

"No. There was no one." The lies just kept coming. Sonora was actually surprised at how easy it had become to make up these stories. The problem, as with all lies, was keeping them straight and remembering whom she had told what.

"You see, I just wanted to escape all the memories. I don't know why I picked California; maybe it just seemed exciting to me." At least part of that was the truth; she did want to escape.

"Well, I wish you luck and I'll pray for you and Timmy." Willamena smiled. She picked up a shirt and began to repair the sleeve where it had pulled away from the shoulder. "I would never be brave enough to do something like that. If anything ever happened to my husband, I'd just be lost. I guess I'd have to go back home to my parents.

Willamena smiled as she placed a stitch in the material. "Maybe it's not so good for a woman to be that dependent on a man."

Sonora tried to sound confident as she spoke. "Oh, I think it's all right for some women, but not for me. I have learned I can function just fine without a man." She glanced up to see if Willamena was looking her way but the woman was intent on her work. "The only male I need in my life is Timmy and I'll not give him up for anyone or anything."

Willamena glanced up at Sonora. "I can see you're a good mother to Timmy and maybe one day the Lord will send a good man your way who can be a husband to you and a father to Timmy." Willamena smiled before she started her mending once again.

"I doubt that," Sonora whispered. Then in a louder voice she added, "Well, I'll not count on that. I'll just continue to take care of the two of us for now."

"Oh you never know. California's full of eligible men, so they say." Willamena turned and looked at the clock on the mantle when she heard it chime. "My, the time has sure flown by this morning. It's been so nice to have someone to help me with my chores and to visit with. I'd better get some dinner started so it will be ready when Milton gets here."

Sonora placed the last stitch in the shirt in her hand, folded it and placed it in the basket beside her chair. "Timmy and I had better go so you can do your work. Thank you so much for breakfast."

"Now, no need for you to go. You two stay for dinner." Willamena placed some logs in the wooden cookstove.

"Mena, Timmy and I can't eat every meal with you while we're here at the fort. We'll be fine eating in the mess hall." Sonora took a couple of steps toward the door.

Willamena turned to look at the young woman. "Now, I told you this morning that you didn't need to be over there with all those men."

Sonora smiled at her new friend. "Actually I would really like to cook for Timmy and myself if I had a few pots and pans in that little cabin."

"Say no more." Willamena walked over to her cupboards and began to pull items from the shelves. She returned to stand in front of Sonora, her arms loaded with pots and dishes, enough to prepare any meal for two people. "You can get most any food stuff you need at the store but if there's something they don't have that you need just let me know. I might have it or I can get it from the cook at the mess hall."

Sonora thanked her hostess. She and Timmy took the kitchen utensils to their cabin before making their way to the general store for supplies.

Chapter Eighteen

Fort Benton

"How long do you think it will be before Sonora and Timmy are found?" Tobias asked Captain Parker.

"I don't know. It shouldn't take long though, not if Sonora stayed on the stage for California," Jonathan told the old man.

The older man began to pace the room. "What if she didn't go to California or what if she signed on with a wagon train?"

That thought had occurred to Jonathan but he hadn't voiced it to anyone. "Guess then it might take a while to find her. My guess would be she wanted to travel fast and the stage would be faster than a wagon train. I still think she headed for California."

The old man nodded in agreement. "Well, I thought I might as well head back to my cabin. Nothing I can do around here."

Jonathan nodded in agreement. "I'll send word out to you when we hear something."

Jonathan walked out of the office with Tobias and he watched as the old miner left the fort. The old man's shoulders seemed to sag as he rode away. Jonathan knew how dismayed and worried Tobias was because he felt that way, too. He felt helpless. That was becoming a normal feeling for him, at least since Sonora had come into his life. The captain went back to his office. There was some paper work that needed his attention and maybe for a few minutes it would take his mind off Sonora and Timmy.

A gentle knock sounded on Jonathan's door. "Enter," he called.

Jonathan looked up to see Amanda standing before him. She looked rather shy and unsure of herself.

"Amanda, can I help you?"

"I wanted to tell you I am sorry," Amanda said softly.

Jonathan stood to his feet and walked around his desk. "Amanda, won't you sit down." He pointed to the chair in front of his desk. As she sat down, he asked. "What are you sorry about?"

"The way I've been treating you." Amanda kept her eyes on her hands. She tried to still their trembling as she straightened the folds of her skirt.

Jonathan seated himself on the edge of his desk. He looked down at the woman seated in front of him. He had never seen Amanda this venerable. "Amanda, you don't have to tell me you're sorry. I know things have been a little strained between us lately."

"Yes, and it's all my fault." Her voice trembled as she spoke.

"Well, I wouldn't say that." Jonathan smiled when Amanda finally lifted her face and looked at him.

"Yes, it is my fault and I wanted to apologize for that, too. I acted like a complete idiot. You were always a gentleman and friend to me and I treated you badly."

"Amanda, you just told me your feelings and I guess I overreacted a bit." Jonathan still kept a smile on his face. "Why don't we just put all that behind us now and move on."

"I'd like that." Amanda smiled and extended her hand to Jonathan.

The captain stood to his feet as he shook hands with Amanda. "Why don't I walk you back to the store? I need some more ink so I can finish this paperwork."

"That would be nice." Amanda smiled as she stood to her feet.

Jonathan opened the door and Amanda walked through it in front of him. Once outside, Jonathan offered the pretty redhead his arm. Placing her hand in the bend of his arm, Amanda was surprised to realize she was truly comfortable just being the handsome captain's friend. Maybe it just took getting her feelings out in the open for her to realize it wasn't love she felt for Jonathan Parker but a deep sense of gratitude and friendship. A big smile covered her face when she noticed Nathan Thomas standing on the porch in front of her store.

****

Fort Bridger, Wyoming

Sonora washed the few dishes she had used to prepare supper for herself and Timmy. It almost felt like they were home, but of course, Fort Bridger in the Wyoming Territory was not home. How she wished they could move on to California, then maybe they could have a real home, at least for a while.

The sun was setting as Sonora walked out onto the little porch attached to the cabin. Timmy and Joey were playing with Joey's dog; it was good to hear Timmy's laughter. Sonora's heart broke at the thought of all her son had been through. Guilt riddled her for her part in the distress Timmy had suffered.

"Miss, sorry to have to tell ya this but looks like we'll be here fer a few more days." The stagecoach driver said as he walked up in front of the cabin. "The stage needs more repair than we first figgered. Must have been the Good Lord that got us this far safely. Can't figger no other reason. Had to be Him looking out for us." The old man scratched his beard and then added, "Well, I'll be goin' now. Hope you and the boy won't be put out too much."

"Thank you. Timmy and I are fine, just anxious to be on our way again. I guess we'll just have to wait." Sonora assured him. "We'll be fine though."

Sonora hoped they would be fine. It all depended on whether or not Daniel Forrester still remained in jail and if the marshal believed his story. There was also the strong possibility Daniel had hired someone to search for them. Oh well, she couldn't think about that right now. She just had to hope, and maybe even pray, she and Timmy would be in California long before Daniel could be on their trail again.

Sonora was still lost in her thoughts when she heard Willamena calling Joey to come home. The little boy told Timmy goodbye, then ran toward home. Before she and Timmy could get into the cabin, Joey ran back over to them.

"Miss Sonora, Mother wanted me to invite you and Timmy to church in the morning. We meet at the school house at ten o'clock," Joey said. "Please come."

"Can we go Mommy? I'd really like to," Timmy asked.

Sonora didn't see any way to get out of going and besides she had nothing else to do. At least going to church would kill a little time. She told Joey to tell his mother she and Timmy would be happy to go to church with them. Now she just had to work on making her attitude match her words.

****

Sonora awoke early. She decided to repay some of Willamena's kindness. Sonora put a big pot of stew on to cook and made fresh bread. She would invite the Applegates to join her and Timmy for dinner after church.

There were more folks at the worship service than Sonora expected. The school- house was almost full. The minister preached a good sermon but Sonora would have preferred a different topic. The preacher talked about deception and how it can ruin a person's life. She tried to block his words from her ears but was not very successful. She knew what she was doing was wrong but she had to do it to keep her son. Again, she reminded herself that she would try to make things right with God when she reached California.

****

"Sonora, this is such a treat for me. Not having to go home after church and worry about feeding these two hungry men of mine," Willamena said as the little group walked toward Sonora's cabin. "Thank you for going to all this trouble for us."

"Oh it was no trouble. I just wanted to repay some of your kindness toward us." Sonora smiled.

Upon arriving at their temporary home, Willamena helped Sonora get the food on the table. Once they were all seated, Sonora asked the captain to say grace over the food.

"Sonora, tell me. What did you think of our minister?" Captain Applegate asked as he placed his napkin in his lap.

Sonora hesitated for just a moment as she dipped stew into a bowl and passed it to the captain. "I enjoyed him very much."

"He was in rare form this morning. I think he gets better every time I hear him. We only get him once a month." The captain took a bite of his stew. "He pastors all through these parts."

Sonora made no comment as she continued to fill bowls and pass them around the table. She listened as Captain Applegate continued. "I really liked the message this morning. I've always said if people would just learn to tell the truth, at all times, then their life would always work out for the best. The Bible says the truth will set you free."

"You're right about that." Willamena nodded in agreement. "I knew a woman one time who had lied to her husband for years. Seems she had been married before and never told anyone. She had moved to a new town where no one knew about her past and she kept it her secret."

Milton Applegate took a sip of his coffee before he asked, "Well, did her husband ever find out about her past?"

"Yes. Her first husband showed up one day. Seems the man had been in prison. The woman had divorced him or at least thought she had. Her lawyer took her money but never filed the papers." Willamena looked across the table at her husband. "When her first husband got out of prison, he came looking for her. Ruined not only her life but also that of her present husband and their two children. If only she had told the truth from the beginning." Willamena shook her head as she picked up her cup of water and took a sip.

Timmy had apparently been listening to Willamena's comments very closely. "Mommy, maybe you should...."

Sonora cut him off before he could say anymore. She was afraid she knew what was about to come out of his mouth. "Timmy, I think if you and Joey are finished eating you should get the two of you some of those molasses cookies and run outside to play for a while."

The two young men didn't hesitate at the mention of cookies and disappeared out the door.

Sonora passed the cookies to Captain Applegate and Willamena. She hoped the two of them hadn't paid any attention to how quickly she had cut off her son when he started to speak.

After enjoying a couple of cookies and a cup of coffee,

Milton Applegate excused himself. He thanked Sonora for the delicious meal and then went outside to join the boys. Sonora could tell by the look in his eyes as he thanked her that the captain was very astute and had some questions on his mind but at least for now he would not pursue them.

For that Sonora was grateful.

****

"Mena, where did Sonora say she and the boy had come from?" The captain asked his wife after they had settled into bed for the evening.

"Georgia, I think. Why?" Willamena blew out the lamp on the table by the bed.

"Oh I don't know. Just had a feeling at dinner that Timmy was about to tell something when Sonora cut him off. Had a funny feeling since the first time I met her that something wasn't just right with her."

"Of course, something isn't right; she lost her husband and is traveling alone with her son to a new land to start a new life. That's enough to make anyone act a little strange." Willamena snuggled up next to her husband.

Milton placed his arm around his wife. "Maybe, but if I was a bettin' man I'd bet she was hiding something."

"I think you have just become too suspicious of folks. Sonora is a nice woman. Don't go borrowing trouble. She won't be here much longer." Willamena lifted her head and kissed her husband goodnight. "Now let's get some sleep. It's getting late."

"Maybe you're right," the captain mumbled. He pulled the cover up over his shoulders but sleep did not come quickly. Milton Applegate still believed Sonora was hiding something but he might never know what it was.

****

The Dakota Territory

"Capt'n Parker, you must have had word from Sonora," Tobias said as the young army captain dismounted in front of the old man's cabin.

"No. No word yet." Jonathan tied the reins to the hitching post. "Just wanted to get out of the fort for awhile. Started riding and found myself here. Guess I wanted to talk to you."

Tobias smiled. "Well, come in and I'll fix us a cup of coffee."

Jonathan followed the older man into the cabin. Tobias poured two cups of coffee and set them on the wooden table. Jonathan seated himself in one of the chairs at the table.

"You did a good job on this furniture," Jonathan observed as he rubbed his hand over the handmade table.

"Thank you. I like working with my hands; always prided myself in my furniture making." Tobias sat down across from the captain. "Now, Capt'n, what's on your mind?"

Jonathan took a sip of the hot coffee. After a few moments, he looked across at Tobias and spoke. "Sonora."

Tobias smiled. "I figured that much." The old miner sipped on his coffee before he spoke again. "But don't know how I can help you with that subject."

Jonathan gazed into his cup for a long time as if expecting to find an answer there. "Tobias, why does she keep running away? If she had stayed here, this whole mess could have been over. The judge would rule against Daniel Forrester and then Sonora and Timmy would be safe from him forever." Jonathan stood and walked to the little window and looked out into the woods.

"You really think Sonora would win against a fellow like Daniel Forrester?"

Jonathan turned and looked at the old man seated at the table. "Don't you think she could win? After all she is the boy's mother."

Tobias looked thoughtful for a moment. "She's his mother all right, but Forrester is a man of wealth and power. The judge might think he and his wife could give Timmy a better life than a woman alone could."

Jonathan looked out the window once again. "Money doesn't mean a child would have a good life. Love is much more important than money." The captain walked back to the table. "Sonora loves Timmy. That's better than all the money in the world." He picked up his coffee mug and took a sip.

Tobias nodded. "True. But the judge might look at the circumstances of Timmy's birth and rule against

Sonora."

"You talk like there's no way Sonora could win in court." Jonathan set his mug back on the table and again walked to the window.

"Just trying to point out why Sonora might think so." Tobias pointed out before taking another sip of his coffee. "That's why she keeps running."

"Well, if she would have just stayed here, maybe I could have helped her." Jonathan sighed as he seated himself back at the table.

"You're in love with her, aren't you Capt'n?"

Jonathan couldn't stop the blush that covered his face. "I think I may be. I've tried to fight these feelings—tried real hard. But they just won't go away; I don't know what to do."

"Hard to fight matters of the heart." Tobias smiled. "What do you want to do about Sonora?"

Once again, Jonathan stood and began to pace around the room. "I don't know. It may not matter what I want to do. I may never see her again. She may disappear for good this time."

"You don't think the marshal will be able to track her down with all those telegrams he sent out?" Tobias walked over to the fireplace, stirred the ashes, and then added another log to the fire.

"Oh, he may, but we don't know for sure she stayed on the stage. If she didn't, it could be a long time before we find her."

"Now, Capt'n, you know she and the boy probably stayed on the stagecoach. It really all depends on if she gets all the way to California before the telegrams catch up with her."

Jonathan faced the old man. "Tobias, do you think Daniel Forrester will continue to try and take Timmy from her?"

Tobias had seated himself in a large rocking chair in front of the fire. "Don't rightly know. Don't know the man. What do you think?"

Jonathan squatted in front of the fireplace and gazed into the flames. "I hope that since this time got him into such trouble that he will give up and go back to New Orleans before Sonora is found."

"I pray you're right but I'm afraid that's wishful thinkin'. I can't see him givin' up so easy. Not after all the trouble he's gone to as he's tried to get the boy."

Jonathan pulled a chair up in front of Tobias. "You know what I'd really like to do. I'd like to head straight for California and find her myself and bring her and Timmy back. Beat that Daniel in court and make everything all right for her."

"You got honorable intentions in mind for my niece?" Tobias smiled.

"I'd like to have." Again Jonathan blushed. "But all this with Timmy has to be settled first."

"Son, you know you can't take off after her, not with your obligations to the army. The only thing either one of us can do is pray."

"I know. God is the only one that can take care of this." Jonathan stood and walked toward the door. Pulling his hat from the peg on the wall, he added, "Guess I'd better be heading back. It's been good visiting with you."

"Capt'n, you come back anytime. I enjoy your company. We'll pray it won't be long before Sonora and Timmy can be with us again. Like you said, maybe Forrester will give up and go back where he came from. Then Sonora and Timmy can live in peace."

"I pray if that happens we can get word to her and she will know she can safely come back," Jonathan said.

Jonathan mounted his horse and rode back to the fort. As the horse trotted along he prayed to his Heavenly Father. Jonathan tried to pray that God's will be done but he knew his own will was very prominent in his prayers for Sonora and this situation.

Chapter Nineteen

Fort Bridger, Wyoming

Sonora listened to the rush of the water in the little creek that ran through the middle of Fort Bridger. She seated herself on the bank and pulled her shawl tightly around her shoulders. If the chill in the air was any indication, winter was approaching fast. She hoped they could be on their way tomorrow as the stage driver had promised. If not it was possible they could find themselves snowed in.

Sonora's thoughts turned to Jonathan Parker. She could picture his handsome face and warm smile. How she longed to see him again. Sonora sighed deeply.

How did my life get to be such a mess? Sonora's thoughts drifted back to her sister, Maryanne. When Maryanne had died giving birth to Timmy, Sonora's life had changed forever. Sonora took on the role of mother. It was a role that fit her well. Even as a child, Sonora had played with her doll and dreamed of marrying the handsome prince and having a large family.

She thought back to Harper Mayfield. She hadn't thought of him in years. She and Harper had never been formally promised to each other but it was understood they would someday marry. When Harper did finally pop the question, it was just a few weeks after Maryanne's death. He ran like a scared jackrabbit when he realized Timmy now came along with Sonora. Harper didn't want to raise another man's child.

Sonora couldn't really say her heart was broken. She liked Harper but had never truly been in love with him. She would have married him though and done her best to make him a good wife while trying to be content in that situation. Back then, Sonora had decided, maybe it was for the best when Harper took off. During that time of her life, she believed God had control of things and probably had someone else in mind for her to marry. Someone she could truly love.

As time passed Sonora contented herself with being Timmy's mother. She decided all the men in the world must be like Harper; none of them seemed to want a ready-made family. That was fine with Sonora because no man had really gotten to her heart. That is...until Jonathan Parker.

When Harper left, she trusted God to bring a man into her life, and when that didn't happen, she thought maybe it was not meant for her to marry. Even though she had remained alone all those years, it didn't weaken her faith in a Heavenly Father who loved her.

Sonora began to ponder in her mind just when she had stopped believing in God. Actually she still believed in God, she had just stopped trusting Him. She had taken control of her life instead of allowing God to be in control. *When did that happen?*

It was when Daniel Forrester had showed up at her door. That day all faith and all common sense left her life. Up until that point, she had trusted God for all her needs and He had never let her down.

Why couldn't she trust God with the biggest problem in her life? Her way of trying to solve the problem wasn't working. So far her way had taken her and Timmy away from all their friends, her father, and their only other relative, Uncle Tobias. They were away from every familiar thing in their life. Her way had gotten Timmy kidnapped and now they were on the run again. No, her way wasn't working well at all.

How long would it be before Daniel Forrester hired another band of renegades to find Timmy? He may already have someone looking for them. Even if Daniel was still in jail, Sonora was sure that Samuel Forrester had come to his son's aide. With that man's power and wealth, they could have dozens of men on her trail.

Sonora's heart began to race as fear gripped her being. "What do I do now?" she asked aloud.

"What do you do about what?" a male voice asked.

Sonora turned quickly and saw Captain Applegate standing behind her.

"I'm sorry if I frightened you," he said. "I saw you sitting alone and just wandered over." Milton Applegate looked directly into Sonora's eyes, and then seated himself on the cold ground beside her. "Sonora is there something I can do to help you?"

Sonora turned her tear-filled eyes back toward the creek. "No, nothing," she choked out.

Captain Applegate picked up a small stone and tossed it into the water. "Sonora, I've had a feeling you need help ever since you arrived. I don't think all is just as you say it is."

Again Sonora choked back the tears. This army captain was very astute and she was afraid he was on to her. She had to think fast.

"I've just had a rough time lately. It's not easy starting a new life."

"That's very true," the captain agreed. "It's even harder if you're trying to start a new life without God's guidance."

There was silence. Sonora barely breathed and tried to ignore the gaze coming her way from the captain. This man beside her was beginning to encroach in her feelings where he certainly didn't belong.

"Sonora, I know you're hurting." He paused, but Sonora did not turn her head to look at him. "I also know that once you were close to God but for some reason you've drifted away from Him." Again Captain Applegate hesitated before he spoke. "Now you're in a place where you can see no way out. You don't want to be where you are but you think you're stuck where you are right now."

Sonora was stunned by his comments. "How do you know that?"

The captain tossed another small rock into the creek. "Sometimes the Holy Spirit just reveals things to me." The captain turned to look at her. "Sonora, won't you please let me try to help you?"

Sonora sighed and choked back tears. "There's nothing you or anyone else can do."

"Maybe no human being can help you, but God can if you'll just let him."

Sonora could hear the compassion in the captain's voice. Tears began running down her cheeks. How she wished someone could take this burden from her. She was bone weary from the weight she had been under for so long. She didn't know how much longer she could stand under the strain of all her troubles.

Without permission from anyone, Captain Applegate began to pray. "Our wonderful Heavenly Father, you alone know what Sonora's going through and you alone know the answers for her. Father, I beseech you on her behalf, help her, Father. I pray she will allow you to lift these burdens from her. She is so weary and you are so strong. Now watch over her and her young son. Keep them safe from any harm. In Jesus name I pray, Amen."

Milton Applegate said nothing more after he finished his prayer. After a few moments, he stood and walked away leaving Sonora all alone.

Sonora's thoughts once again turned to days gone by. She remembered from the Scripture that Jesus taught to cast your burdens upon Him. She remembered a lot of things she had read in the Bible or heard in church. Didn't God protect those three fellows in the fiery furnace? Didn't he save Jonah from that big fish? Didn't Jesus come to give us abundant life? Didn't the Bible say He would be a father to the fatherless and a husband to the widow?

Well, Timmy had a birth father but had never had a real father. Sonora was not a widow, but maybe in her case, God would still be a husband to her. How she longed to be rid of this burden. She ached for someone to tell her what to do next. Sonora was tired of making all the decisions and all the wrong decisions at that. Maybe it was time she truly put her life, and also the life of her son, into the hands of God.

"God, I need you," Sonora began. "Please help me and my son. Forgive me of my sins. Jesus, I need you to come back into my heart. I can't do this anymore. I need you, Father." Sonora began to cry. She didn't know how long she had cried, but all of a sudden, it was as though she could feel loving arms around her. She knew, for the first time in a long time everything would be just fine.

****

Fort Benton

"I got a telegram from Cheyenne, Wyoming. Seems there was a woman with a little boy on the stage when it came through there," Marshal Jeffress told Jonathan.

Jonathan looked across his desk at the U.S. Marshal. "How long ago was that?"

"Three weeks."

Jonathan nodded. "Well, the stage should be well out of Wyoming by now."

"I reckon, but I wired Fort Bridger just to see if she and the boy were still on board when the stage stopped there. I understand they have a layover there for a couple of days so the passengers can rest."

Jonathan leaned his elbows on the desk. "If they were still on board, what then?"

"Thought I'd see if the captain there could send a patrol to pick up Sonora and the boy," Marshal Jeffress told him.

Again Jonathan nodded. "Let me know what the captain says. Milton Applegate is an old friend of mine. I'd like to be the one to ask him to go after Sonora if you have no objections."

The marshal stood and walked to the door. "Soon as I hear from him, I'll let you know."

****

"Captain, are you all right?" Ben Tivy asked as he walked up to the coral.

Captain Parker stood at the fence with one foot propped up on the bottom rung. "I'm fine."

"Sir, I don't mean to be disrespectful but I think you're lying. I don't think you're fine at all." The corporal leaned on the fence beside Jonathan. "I think you lost your heart to a little dark-haired woman, and when she left, she took your heart with her."

Jonathan smiled. "Corporal, I wouldn't admit this to just anyone, but I think you're right."

"What are you gonna do about it?" Tivy asked as he straddled the top rung of the coral and seated himself.

Jonathan looked up at the corporal. "What can I do?"

"I don't know, sir. I guess pray is about all you can do right now."

"Corporal, why do you think I'd fall for a woman like Sonora? She's got way too many problems and she isn't even close to God?"

"Well, sir, there's one thing I've noticed through the years. Most folks make strange picks to be attracted to, besides the fact she has so many problems brought out the protector in you."

"You know, Corporal Tivy, you are smarter than you look." Jonathan laughed. He was ready to take the conversation in a different direction. "Let's talk about you now. Have you gotten any more of those good smelling letters?"

Corporal Tivy looked toward the horses stirring around in the coral. "As a matter of fact, got one today."

Jonathan jumped up on the fence and took a seat. "So tell me about this lady. She seemed nice but all I saw of her was when she brought the message from you."

The corporal told Jonathan all he knew about Willow Ingram and how he had come to meet her. "Captain, it bothers me that she runs a saloon."

"Is she planning on staying in the same line of work now that she's back in the states?"

Tivy jumped down from the fence. "Don't know."

"Have you told her it bothers you for her to run a saloon?"

"Nope. Captain, don't know if I have the right to express my feelings to her about that. After all, we just barely know each other."

The captain jumped down to the ground and the two men started walking toward his office. "Well, are her letters of a serious nature or just letters from a friend?"

The corporal began to blush as he answered, "Sort of serious."

Jonathan gave the corporal a sidelong glance. "Well, are you serious?"

Tivy smiled. "I could be."

"Then you need to tell her your feelings before things go any further." Jonathan stopped just outside his office. "You want your relationship to start off on the right foot."

Tivy smiled. "I think maybe we'd better go back to talking about you and Sonora. I felt much more comfortable with that subject."

Both men laughed at Tivy's statement before they said goodnight.

****

Jonathan awoke to the first light snowfall of the season. He wished this kind of weather had held off for a few more weeks, getting Sonora and Timmy back now would be even more difficult. Jonathan took his heavy coat from the peg in his bedroom and pulled it on. Walking out into the cold air, he noticed Doc Thomas going into the general store. The doctor seemed to be making more trips than usual to the store. Maybe things were beginning to look up for his old friend.

Jonathan made his way across the compound. The bell above the door jingled as he stepped into the general store. Amanda and Nathan looked up from their place at the small wooden table.

"Captain, come in and have a cup of coffee with us," Doc offered.

"Sounds good," Jonathan said as he pulled off the heavy coat. He warmed his hands over the wood stove as Amanda disappeared into the back for another cup.

Jonathan looked over at the doctor and smiled. "Things are looking up for you, I'd say."

"Could be," Doc agreed just as Amanda came back through the door.

"Thank you very much." Jonathan told Amanda as she handed him the hot cup of coffee.

Doc looked up at the captain. "Think this weather will last long?"

Jonathan sat down at the small table. "I hope not. Sure will put a damper on things if it does."

Amanda glanced over at Jonathan. "Such as getting Sonora back?"

Jonathan was a little hesitant but finally answered her question. "Yes. If this is truly the beginning of winter, it may be spring before we can proceed with finding her and Timmy and bringing them back to Fort Benton."

Doc took a sip of his coffee before he spoke. "Have you heard anything from Fort Bridger yet?"

"Not yet." Jonathan stood and walked over to the stove and poured more coffee into his mug. "I know Milton Applegate will get back to us as soon as he gets the telegram though."

"Well, I'd love to stay here and chat all day, but

Private Baker came in this morning. He's having a lot of trouble breathing and has a pretty high fever. I need to go check on him." Doc stood and pulled on his heavy coat. "After that, I'll go over to the barracks. If Baker's come down with this, some of the rest of the men will before long. Hope it doesn't reach epidemic proportions." Doc took his hat from the rack by the door, and then turned back and smiled at Amanda.

"Mandy, I'll see you later," Doc called.

"All right. Nathan, let me know if you need my help," she returned.

As the doctor opened the front door, Jonathan called to him. "Let me know what I can do to help. I'll be over to check on Baker a little later." Jonathan took the last sip of coffee from his cup. "Amanda, thanks for the coffee. Guess I'd better get on over to the mess hall before Zeke throws breakfast out." The captain stood to follow the doctor outside.

Once safely outside Doc wanted to know. "Jonathan, if nothing can be done until spring, what do you think the marshal will do with Daniel Forrester?"

"Don't know. Guess we'll have to ask him that question? I'll see you later, Doc." Jonathan stepped off the porch and began to walk toward the mess hall.

Chapter Twenty

Fort Bridger, Wyoming

Captain Milton Applegate sat at the desk in his sparsely furnished office. A chill ran through him and it wasn't just from the cold of the early morning hour. The telegram he held in his hand made him shiver. Why would a U.S. Marshal be looking for Sonora and her son? The captain had known in his spirit that Sonora was hiding something but he never dreamed she might be on the wrong side of the law. *What could she have done?*

He would think the marshal was looking for another woman and child if the law officer hadn't asked specifically about Sonora. He could sit and speculate all day but that would do him little good. The only way to get answers to his questions was to go to the source—Sonora.

It was still very early so Captain Applegate decided to go back to his cabin and have another cup of coffee before talking with Sonora. It would give him time to pray about the situation.

"Milton, something's wrong. What is it?" Willamena wanted to know as she set a cup of warm coffee down on the table in front of her husband.

Milton looked up into his wife's warm eyes and smiled. "It's nothing for you to worry about."

Willamena seated herself across the table from him. "If it's got you concerned, then it's something for me to worry about."

The captain decided to let his wife in on what was troubling him. Maybe she could shed some light on the problem. "Mena, I got a telegram this morning from a marshal in the Dakota Territory." He pulled the paper from his pocket and pushed it across the table to his wife. Willamena picked it up and began to read.

After reading the telegram, Willamena looked across

the table. "Maybe, there's just some family that's concerned about her and the boy. This doesn't mean she's done anything bad."

"But Sonora says she has no family." The captain picked up his coffee and took a sip.

"We could sit here all day and try to figure out what this means and get no where, so why don't we talk to Sonora." Willamena stood, walked to the door and pulled her cape from the peg.

"Just where do you think you're going?" Milton asked his wife.

"To get Sonora. I'll go get her and bring her over here. I think that would be more proper than you going to her cabin." Willamena said as she opened the cabin door.

Captain Applegate couldn't help but smile. "And that way you can find out right away what's going on."

Willamena flashed her husband a smile just before exiting the cabin. "Well, that too."

****

It seemed like no time at all had passed until Willamena came back through the door with Sonora. Sonora couldn't help the anxious feeling that came over her as she walked into the room.

"Sonora, sit down and let me pour you a hot cup of coffee," Willamena instructed as the two ladies hung their cloaks on pegs by the door.

Sonora did as she was told. She had a feeling of doom lurking over her head. Silently she prayed for God to take care of whatever was about to happen. This would be the first test to see if the peace she had felt since re-dedicating her life to Christ was real and here to stay.

"Sonora, I got a telegram this morning." The captain handed the wrinkled piece of paper to the young woman.

With trembling hands, Sonora took the paper and began to read. When she finished, she breathed a long sigh. For some very strange reason, she felt this was the beginning of the end of her struggle. This was her opening to tell the truth and see just what would happen.

Sonora looked at Willamena, and then shifted her gaze to the captain. "I knew this would come, I just didn't know when."

Milton took a deep breath. "Would you like to tell us

your story?"

Sonora picked up the china cup in front of her and took a sip of the hot coffee. She began to tell her story to the captain and his wife. For the first time in months, she told the truth, the complete truth which felt so good.

The captain walked over to the stove and filled his cup with coffee. "So, this Daniel Forrester is Timmy's birth father?"

"Yes, he is the natural father," Sonora nodded.

"I can't believe a father would stoop so low as to have his son kidnapped, even a father who never had anything to do with his son." Willamena's anger was clearly evident as she spoke. "The man should be hung for putting that little boy through such an ordeal."

"My dear, I think that might be a little drastic, but he deserves some kind of punishment." Milton Applegate reached over and covered his wife's hand with his. "Sonora, this marshal probably wants to talk to you about the kidnapping and you'll have to testify at Forrester's trial."

Sonora glanced from Milton to Willamena. "Do you think that's the only reason he's looking for me?"

"What else could he want?" Willamena asked.

Sonora stood and began to pace the floor. "I told you I'm not Timmy's birth mother. What if the court decides to give Timmy to his natural father?"

The captain leaned forward and propped his elbows on the table. "I will pray that doesn't happen. Sonora, you are the boy's mother whether you gave birth to him or not. That's what should matter to a judge."

Sonora turned to face him. "Captain, I sure hope you're right." She sat back down in the straight back chair at the table. "What are you going to do now?"

"I'll send a wire back and ask what they want you for. I won't tell them you're still here at the fort."

"Won't you be lying?" Sonora frowned. "I want to get all the lies out of my life."

"I'd rather not say it's a lie." Milton smiled. "I'll tell them you were on the stage when it arrived here. I just won't mention the stage hasn't left yet."

"But it's supposed to leave today." Willamena reminded her husband. She looked at Sonora as she asked. "Sonora, do you plan on leaving today?"

Sonora ran the finger of her hand around the rim of her cup. "What good would that do now? I think I'm ready to face the music whatever that may be. I just pray I won't have to give up my son."

****

Tears filled Willamena's eyes as she looked into her new friend's face. She admired Sonora for being willing to go back and face her past but she wondered if she would have the courage to do the same thing if she were in Sonora's shoes. Willamena knew she would do whatever she had to in order to keep Joey with her.

Captain Applegate left to send the telegram to Fort Benton and Sonora went back to her little cabin to prepare breakfast for Timmy. Willamena Applegate began a prayer vigil. She knew Sonora and Timmy could use all the prayers they could get.

****

Fort Benton

"Now we know she and Timmy made it as far as Fort Bridger, but the captain doesn't say how long ago the stagecoach left there," Marshal Jeffress observed. "Our prisoner is getting restless and I can't keep hanging around here forever. We need to get this matter settled."

Jonathan nodded agreement, and then shrugged. "Just how do you plan on getting it settled?"

The marshal seated himself in front of Jonathan's desk. "I don't know. The territorial judge got here this morning, as you know. I'll talk to him. Maybe he would agree to let Sonora give Captain Applegate her statement if he can catch up to her. If he agrees, we can proceed from there."

Jonathan leaned back in his chair. "Then she and Timmy wouldn't have to come back here?"

"Not unless she wanted to." The marshal stood to his feet. "I'll go talk to the judge. Do you still want to be the one to send the wire to Fort Bridger?"

"If you don't mind." Jonathan stood and walked around his desk to stand in front of the marshal. "If you need to wire the captain yourself, I can send Milton a personal note."

"I'll let you know after I talk to the judge." With that the marshal pulled his hat on his head. "Get back to you as soon as I can."

It could all be over soon and Sonora might not even have to come back to Fort Benton. For Sonora that would be wonderful, but for Jonathan, it might not be so good. If everything got cleared up without her having to come back to the Dakota Territory, he might never see her again and never be able to tell her how he felt about her. He would just have to wait and pray.

****

Fort Bridger, Wyoming

"Enter," Captain Applegate called when he heard the soft knock on his office door. Looking up he stood to his feet and started around his desk. "Sonora, take this chair close to the fire. Get the chill out of your bones."

"Thank you, Captain. You must have heard from Fort Benton."

The captain pulled a chair up beside the young woman and smiled. "I did and I think it's better news than we expected."

"What do you mean?" Sonora rubbed her hands together in front of the fire.

"The marshal says that if I can catch up to you, I can take your statement and send it back to them. The judge will take it as admissible evidence against Forrester if you and I both sign it."

Sonora stood and walked closer to the fire. "Just what does he want me to testify too?"

The captain could tell by the tone of her voice and her actions that Sonora was nervous. "Just about the night Timmy was taken from you."

Sonora turned to face Captain Applegate. "You mean I don't have to say anything about not being Timmy's birth mother?"

The captain smiled. "No, you don't. You just have to testify to the facts about that night. See God is working everything out for the best."

Sonora gave a big sigh of relief as she sat back down in the chair. "That's hard to believe. It's wonderful, just hard to believe."

"Oh, by the way, I got two telegrams. One from the marshal and one from the captain of the fort." Again a big smile covered the captain's face as he stood and walked to his desk.

"Jonathan sent you a telegram?"

"Well, he sent it to me because he assumed you were long gone from here, but really it's to you." Captain Applegate handed her the telegram.

Sonora's hand shook and she could feel her heart start to beat faster as she took the paper from the captain's hand. She took a deep breath before she began to read.

To Captain Applegate, United States Army, Fort Bridger, Wyoming Territory. Stop

The young woman Sonora and her son, Timmy, are very special to me. Stop

They have been through a lot. Stop

When you find her, please treat her as friend. Stop

She will need a lot of support and help. Stop

Tell her my thoughts and prayers are with her.

Jonathan Parker, Captain United States Army, Fort Benton, Dakota Territory

"I'd say my friend Jonathan Parker has a special interest in you and Timmy," Captain Applegate observed as he seated himself once again in the chair across from Sonora.

A blush covered Sonora's face. "You know Captain Parker?"

The captain smiled. "Yes, I've known him for several years. He's a fine man."

"Yes, he is very nice. He was very kind to both Timmy and me."

"I'd say he took a special interest in the two of you." The captain leaned back in his chair as he looked at Sonora. "If I could read between the lines, knowing Jonathan, I'd say he's in love with you."

Again Sonora blushed. She stood and walked up to the fireplace turning her back to the captain. "I doubt that. I'm not the kind of woman Captain Parker could be interested in."

"What makes you say that, Sonora?"

Sonora turned to face him. "You see. I have lied to

Jonathan at every turn. I told him I had Timmy without the benefit of marriage. I have told him so many lies he could never forgive me."

Captain Applegate stood and walked to Sonora's side. "Sonora, I know Jonathan Parker and he's one of the finest Christian men I have ever met. It's not in him not to forgive."

Sonora kept her eyes on the fire. "Maybe he could forgive me, but he would never want anything to do with me. I'm not the type of woman he would want to marry. After I give you my testimony, I'll just continue on my way to California."

"Sonora, that would be a big mistake. I think you should go back to Fort Benton next spring when the weather permits and tell Jonathan the story as you told Willamena and me. You might be pleasantly surprised."

"I'll have to think about that." She looked up into the captain's kind face. "Now when do I give you my statement?"

Captain Applegate walked around his desk and pulled some paper from the drawer. Laying it on the top of the desk, he looked at Sonora. "Why don't you sit down right here and write out everything you can recall about that night. I'll go send another wire and let them know you're still here and that your statement will be in tomorrow's post. Lucky thing the mail rider is scheduled to be through here tomorrow."

The captain waited until he saw Sonora do as he requested. It appeared to take several moments for her to gather her courage to pick up the quill and start writing. Knowing she would complete the task, the captain opened the front door as the cold air rushed in to greet him.

****

Fort Benton

It had been a month since the telegram had arrived at Fort Benton informing them Sonora was still in Wyoming at Fort Bridger and that her statement would be leaving the next day. Marshal Jeffress had left the confines of the fort to take care of other duties. The judge had continued on his circuit and Daniel Forrester remained in the guardhouse much to the dismay of himself and his father. Samuel Forrester was still making life miserable for anyone and everyone he could. Jonathan had wanted to ask him to leave but thought better of making the request.

Finally the mail arrived from the west. The long awaited letter was in Jonathan's hands. He sent telegram's to the marshal and the judge. The ordeal should be over anytime now.

****

The day of Daniel Forrester's trial finally arrived and it went much like Jonathan and the marshal had suspected. Daniel could not be tied to the actual kidnapping. Sonora's testimony, of course, could not put Forrester at the scene. Willow Ingram had made her way back to the fort to testify Daniel was the man who had given her the money to give to the comancheros but even that was not as damaging as Jonathan would have liked. His claim that it was ransom was almost impossible to contradict.

Both Forrester men testified Daniel was the natural father of the little boy. Daniel again said Sonora's sister, Maryanne, was the boy's birth mother. This was very hard for Jonathan to swallow but something in his spirit told him that it was probably the truth. The story Sonora had told about going to New Orleans and returning in a motherly way must have been her sister's story. At this point, it didn't really matter since Sonora was more than likely gone for good.

The judge declared the parentage of Timmy was not relevant to the case except if Daniel were the birth father. If so, he wouldn't charge him with kidnapping. The charges were dropped with a stern warning from the judge that taking a little boy from the only mother he had ever known whether she gave birth to him or not was a very low deed for sure. He didn't seem to think a man who had denied his son for so long should suddenly develop a fatherly interest in him. The judge advised the Forresters go back to New Orleans, tend to their business there and leave the young boy and his mother alone to get on with their lives.

The trial ended and the Forresters did leave even though the snow covered the land. Jonathan was thankful for that but Daniel had promised his quest to get his son was not over. He would find a judge somewhere who would be sympathetic to his cause. Of course, he would have to find Sonora and Timmy first or it wouldn't matter what kind of judge Forrester found.

Willow had come for the trial. The weather had gotten worse since she arrived and she decided it was best to spend the winter in Fort Benton. Jonathan knew Corporal Tivy, more than the weather, was the deciding factor in Willow's staying at the fort. Willow was provided a small cabin for her stay and she and Corporal Tivy began a very special courtship.

It seemed love was blossoming all across the fort. Nathan and Amanda had let the fort in on their secret romance. Seemed a wedding was in their plans for spring. Love was everywhere but life for Jonathan proceeded as normal. He led the men out on patrol, and then came back to the emptiness he felt every time he entered through the big wooden gates. His heart was with Sonora, wherever she was.

Chapter Twenty One

Fort Benton

The winter was extremely cold. Jonathan was thankful it had been a peaceful season for the fort. Christmas was next week and the fort was a bustle of activities. Amanda had a new outlook on life since she and Nathan had become engaged and she had planned a big Christmas day celebration for the entire fort. Willow and Amanda had become fast friends and were decorating every building on the fort with greenery. Jonathan had a feeling if he stood still very long they would put some kind of greenery on him.

"Come in, Captain, and pull up a chair," Doc called as Jonathan entered the general store.

Jonathan brushed the snow from his hat and then hung it on a peg by the door. "I thought I smelled popcorn."

"Hang your coat up and get over here and help us." Willow called. "We can use all the hands we can get."

"Yeah, I've found out I'm not very good at sewing, even if it is just stringing popcorn." Corporal Tivy smiled as he looked at Willow.

Jonathan laughed as he watched the corporal's large awkward hands try to thread the popcorn on the string. "Well, Corporal, sewing may not be your strong suit, but I do know a few things you do well." Jonathan turned his gaze to Nathan. "Doc, looks like you have the process down pretty good."

"The advantages of being a doctor. We have to learn to sew. I just pretend like each kernel of corn is a stitch I have to make so it's going just fine."

"Don't be shy Jonathan. If you don't want to string popcorn, you can start stringing that pan of berries." Amanda indicated the pan of red berries sitting on the floor by the table.

"Guess I'm drafted." Jonathan laughed as he seated himself in a chair at the table.

Corporal Tivy stood and walked to the fireplace where Willow held the long handle of the pan she was popping corn in. "Willow, I'll trade jobs with you for a while."

Willow smiled broadly. "Do you think you can do it without burning it?"

The corporal returned her smile. "I'll do my best."

The conversation was light-hearted. Willow informed the assembled work crew that she planned on having a party on the twenty-second—just a pre-Christmas celebration.

Jonathan opened the discussion as to the true meaning of Christmas and hoped that at sometime before the season was over they could celebrate the birth of Jesus. Corporal Tivy agreed with that idea and the two of them were put in charge of coming up with an idea for the celebration of the birth of Christ.

"Guess you'll learn not to open your mouth," Doc Thomas teased.

"Guess so, but I think I can come up with something. Pastor Howard will be here this Sunday, and with his help, we'll figure out some way to honor Jesus." Jonathan smiled as he threaded another red berry onto his string.

"That's cheating." Amanda continued teasing the captain. "Getting the preacher to do your job."

"Didn't say I'd get him to do it, just said I'd enlist his help." Jonathan smiled. It was good to be with friends.

****

Fort Bridger, Wyoming

Fort Bridger, Wyoming was alive with Christmas preparations also. The children were doing a play reliving the birth of Jesus. Willamena and Sonora were busy baking, sewing, and making plans for Christmas day. Sonora had made Timmy and Joey both new shirts for Christmas and had helped sew the costumes for the play. She had also made a new shawl for Willamena and had sewn several new bandanas for Captain Applegate.

Milton had carved a couple of small wooden horses

and several small wooden soldiers for both boys. Sonora felt very blessed that Milton and Willamena had taken her and Timmy in as though they were family. It would be a good Christmas but something was missing. Sonora longed to spend Christmas with Jonathan but that was not possible. At least, it wasn't possible this year, and she feared this longing might be a dream that would never become a reality.

Willamena looked up as she started to roll the dough out on the table. "Sonora, why don't you write to Jonathan and tell him your story. Then you would know how he felt and if there might be a future for the two of you."

The two women were busy baking gingerbread men for all the children in school.

"I've thought about that and even started a couple of letters but threw them in the fireplace." Sonora cut another figure from the dough on the table.

"This one looks a little handicapped." Willamena laughed as she picked up the gingerbread man she had just cut out.

Sonora also laughed at the lopsided cookie. "Well, none of them are perfect but that one is a little funny."

Willamena picked up the rolling pin. "I'll roll it back out and try again."

"Don't bother. We can bake it and its imperfection will give us a good reason to taste one." Sonora giggled.

Willamena laughed. "I like the way you think." She placed the deformed cookie man on the baking tin.

****

Timmy was snuggled warmly into bed when Sonora sank her tired body into one of the straight-back wooden chairs at the small dining table in her cabin. She stared at the blank pages of paper lying in front of her. She picked up the quill pen and dipped it into the ink. Slowly she began to write. She poured out her heart to Jonathan on that dull white paper. Sonora told him the entire story of her life before and since Timmy.

It was a long letter and took Sonora some time to write. When finished, she picked it up and read it through again. It sounded fine but should she mail it? She carefully folded the paper and slipped it into an envelope and then addressed the envelope to Jonathan. She slid the envelope into her Bible, deciding she would pray about it until the mail rider came through. Sonora would let God direct her in whether or not she should go ahead and post her letter.

****

Fort Benton

Nathan pulled his heavy coat from the rack by the door. He stepped out of his office into the cold crisp morning air and looked around the fort. Christmas day was finally here, and for the first time in many days, there was no snow falling in the Dakota Territory. Nathan smiled. *It might be cold but I can still admire the beauty around me, especially today. For the first time in a long time, I love Christmas.*

Christmas morning started with a small service honoring the birth of Jesus. Pastor Howard led the service with Jonathan's assistance. The Christmas story was read and then the service was opened to anyone who wanted to comment on what Christmas meant to them.

Jonathan began. "Christmas was always a special time for me. My parents are Christians and we always honored Jesus on the day of His birth. As I grew older and accepted Jesus as my Savior, Christmas took on a very special meaning. Without the birth of Jesus, there could have been no death, no resurrection and no salvation. I'm thankful Jesus loved me enough to come to earth and suffer all he did so I could have eternal life." To close he added, "I hope to someday have a family and pass the love of Jesus on to my children as my parents passed it to me."

Corporal Tivy shared his faith in Jesus with the group and had some of the same sentiments Jonathan had shared. When he was finished, Willow Ingram made an unexpected request.

"I've listened to Captain Parker and to Ben as they shared their love for Jesus. I've heard about Jesus but never thought much about Him. I wasn't raised in a home that went to church, and in my adult life, I have lived about as far away from the church as a person can get."

Willow looked at Ben sitting beside her and smiled. "In getting to know Ben better and watching him live his life, I have come to realize he has something very special.

I've seen that same thing in the life of Captain Parker. I want what they have. How do I get Jesus to come into my life?"

Pastor Howard looked at the young woman and smiled. "You just have to ask."

Willow jumped to her feet. "Well, let's do it."

The preacher and Willow knelt together and he led her in a sinner's prayer as tears filled the corporal's eyes.

Doc glanced over at Amanda and noticed that it looked like she was deep in prayer. As Willow repeated the words asking Jesus to forgive her of her sins and come into her life as Lord and Savior, Amanda's lips were forming the same words.

When the prayer was finished, Corporal Tivy was the first to pull Willow into his arms for a hug. Willow looked into his eyes and smiled broadly. "Guess this means I will have to find a new line of work."

"I think I might have a job in mind for you." Ben Tivy smiled.

Before the corporal could say more, Willow was being pulled toward Jonathan as the captain hugged her and welcomed her into the family of God.

The Doc and Amanda were seated quietly toward the back of the meeting room. "Amanda, what has happened to you?" Doc asked the red head beside him.

Amanda turned to face her future husband. Tears rolled down her face as she whispered. "I asked Jesus to forgive me of my sins, too, and to come into my life and He did."

Amanda lay her head on Doc's shoulder. "It is such a relief. I feel like the weight of the world has been lifted off me, Nathan. It's wonderful."

"I'm happy for you, Mandy." Doc whispered. He was hoping inside that this change in Amanda didn't change things between the two of them. The doctor found himself in a rapidly growing minority here at Fort Benton. Seems the place was becoming overrun with Christians.

The service ended with most of the assembled troop coming by and wishing Willow their best. Dinner followed in the mess hall with the entire fort in attendance. Zeke and the ladies of the fort had out done themselves. The men had not been able to kill any turkeys but there was elk and moose for everyone, along with apple pie and spice cake. No one went away hungry.

****

Fort Bridger, Wyoming

"Mommy, look the soldiers can ride on the horses." Timmy shouted as he and Joey played with their Christmas presents. "This one is Captain Parker."

"That's nice," Sonora told her son as she checked the roast baking in the oven. Her heart felt like it had skipped a couple of beats at the mention of Jonathan's name.

"Sonora, did you send that letter out with the rider?" Willamena whispered.

"Yes," Sonora answered, dropping the empty frying pan on the floor. "I guess that's why I'm so clumsy today. I haven't been able to calm my nerves since the rider left the fort."

"You might as well calm down because it will take at least a month for Captain Parker to get the mail. This weather slows down the mail considerably." Willamena picked up the pan from the floor. "At least, you dropped an empty pan. Why don't you sit down and slice up those potatoes, unless you think using a knife might be dangerous." Willamena laughed.

"I know you meant that as a joke but it could be dangerous the way I feel." Sonora laughed with her friend. "But you're right. There's no way Jonathan could have gotten the letter by now. It will be at least a couple of months before I hear anything from him—if he cares enough to write to me in return."

The two ladies finished Christmas dinner and everything was on the table. Before they sat down to eat, Milton read the Christmas story from his Bible and then offered grace. It was a wonderful meal with friends.

Chapter Twenty Two

Fort Bridger, Wyoming

The days after Christmas drug by slowly. The snow kept falling and the drifts got higher. Sonora was getting cabin fever. She felt more isolated than she ever had in her life and she didn't know why. Of course, the snow could be a major part of the problem. Growing up in the south and living there until last April, she had never seen much snow. Until this winter, she had never seen enough to build a snowman.

Sonora watched out the window of her cabin as Timmy and Joey played in the snow. They both laughed as they threw soft balls of snow at one another. It was good for her son to have a friend. She turned and walked over to the fireplace to check on the pot of stew she was preparing for dinner. Her thoughts turned to Fort Benton and Jonathan. In her mind she could see him standing tall with his green eyes sparkling as he smiled. She loved the way his wavy, brown hair fell slightly over his forehead when he took off his hat. She wondered what he might be doing right now. She prayed that whatever it was he was safe and sound. Sonora shook her head as she tried to get the picture from her mind but she was afraid Captain Jonathan was in her mind and heart to stay for a very long time.

The door burst open and two snow covered little boys came through the door. "Mommy, can we have some cookies and milk. Playing in the snow sure makes a kid hungry." Timmy grinned as he pulled his stocking cap from his head.

Sonora looked at her son. She couldn't believe how much he had grown. "You two get over here by the fire and warm up. I'll get you some milk and you can have one cookie each. It's almost time for lunch."

****

Fort Benton

Jonathan looked out his office window. The ground was covered with snow but life at the fort went on as normal. He looked at the pages of paper he held in his hand. He had read her letter at least a hundred times, but he read it again. Sonora told him the complete truth and she even indicated she had feelings for him. She also shared how she had rededicated her life to Jesus and was letting God take control of things from now on.

"Now what do I do? Oh, how I wish she was right here at the fort but she's clear across Wyoming."

Maybe a walk in the cold brisk air would clear his head. He put on his coat and pulled his hat on his head as he opened the door of his office. The air was frigid and took his breath away for a second. He started to walk briskly toward the stable and the soldier's barracks. Everything at the fort was neat and tidy, nothing like his personal life. He knew he loved Sonora but there were a lot of obstacles in their way; the main one being Timmy's future. Would Daniel Forrester stay out of the picture? Jonathan knew if Sonora lost Timmy it would destroy her or at least make a hole so big in her heart he didn't know if he could fill it. Oh, he knew God could but sometimes that even took a long time.

He finished walking the inside perimeter of the fort and then headed back to his office. He loved Sonora and he loved Timmy. What would become of their future was in God's hands.

The only thing he could do was write to her and tell her the feelings he had hidden in his heart. Everything else was up to God.

****

Fort Bridger, Wyoming

There was a knock at the cabin door and Sonora hurried to answer. Captain Applegate stood shivering in the cold. "Mena sent me over to get you and Timmy. She's made a treat and wanted the two of you to come over and share it. I'm here to escort you."

"Oh, that sounds wonderful. I was beginning to feel

like I was going crazy. Timmy get your coat and let's go visit Joey," Sonora called as she pulled her cape from the peg.

"Mrs. Applegate this is terrific," Timmy said after a big bite of the snow ice cream.

Sonora took a bite of the cold confection. "Yes, it is. How did you make it?"

"It's just milk, sugar, flavoring and snow." Willamena smiled as she watched her family and friends enjoy the fruit of her labor.

"This is such a special treat and it's great to get out of the cabin for a while." Sonora watched her son as he scraped the bottom of his bowl.

A knock sounded at the Applegate's front door. The captain opened the door. "Private Black, come in."

"No thanks, sir, just wanted you to know the mail rider just came in." the private told his commanding officer.

"Thank you Private Black. I'll be in my office shortly."

Willamena watched as the young man left her home. "Is that the rider from the east?"

Milton turned and smiled at his wife. "Don't know but probably."

Sonora's stomach began to do flips. She pushed her ice cream away since she couldn't eat anymore right now.

The captain left the ladies to visit while he went to his office. Sonora sat almost motionless staring down at the table.

"Sonora, you have to breathe." Willamena laughed. "We don't even know yet if it's the mail from the east."

"I know, but there is a very large lump in my throat right now," Sonora choked out. "My stomach feels like a million butterflies are in there. I don't remember ever being this nervous."

Joey interrupted the ladies' conversation. "Mommy, can we have some more ice cream?"

"*May* we have more ice cream?" Willamena corrected. "Yes, you may." She dipped more of the cold confection into the boys' bowls.

Timmy walked over to stand by his mother's chair. Concern was very evident on his little face. "Mommy, are you all right?"

Sonora managed a smile for her son. "Yes, Timmy, I'm fine. You go eat your ice cream and then you and Joey can play for a while."

A broad smile covered Timmy's face as he took his treat and sat on the floor in front of the fireplace.

Sonora's voice was quiet as she spoke to her friend. "Mena, what if Jonathan never writes me?"

"Jonathan Parker is not the kind of man who would just ignore a letter." Willamena poured two cups of coffee and then seated herself at the table across from Sonora.

"How about helping me with some mending? Maybe that will keep your mind occupied for awhile."

Sonora readily agreed. "I'll try anything to take my mind off of a certain army captain." Sonora smiled. "I would be more than happy to help you."

Willamena disappeared into the bedroom and returned with a basket full of clothes.

"You must be repairing everything you own."

Willamena laughed. "No. Most of this belongs to the enlisted men. Very few of them have wives, so I offer to sew on buttons and repairs rips; you know how it is."

The two ladies began the repair work. Sonora found herself having to rip out more stitches than she put in but she worked diligently.

Over an hour had passed when Milton finally appeared through the door. Both women held their breath afraid to ask the origin of the mail. The captain shook the snow from his hat and coat and hung them on the pegs by the front door before walking to the fireplace to warm himself.

He looked down at the two lads playing on the floor at his feet. "You boys get enough of that ice cream?"

"No. We could eat a big barrel full," Joey told his father.

He reached down and scooped his son into his arms and tickled him on the stomach. The little boy bent with laughter. "If you ate a barrel full of ice cream you would get too big for me to pick up."

The captain lowered his son back to the floor and then reached over and ruffled Timmy's hair. Looking over at his wife and Sonora, he said, "Hello, ladies. Looks like the two of you are busy."

"Just catching up on some of this mending I promised to do for the men." Willamena looked up at her husband. She watched him carefully for a few moments. "Anything interesting in the mail?"

The captain turned quickly and walked back to where his coat hung. "There were a couple of letters." He pulled two envelopes from his coat pocket. "One from your mother." He handed one of the envelopes to his wife.

He then faced Sonora and smiled broadly. "And one for Sonora."

With trembling hands, Sonora took the letter from the captain's outstretched hand.

Willamena appeared to be as anxious as her counterpart. "Is it from him?"

"Yes." Sonora smiled. "I hope you don't mind but I'd like to be alone when I read it."

"I understand." Willamena looked from Sonora to Timmy. "Why don't you go on home? Timmy can stay here and play with Joey and Milton can bring him home later.

Sonora smiled as she stood and walked to the door. "That would be wonderful; if you're sure you don't mind."

Sonora pulled on her cape, hat, and gloves. She hurried as fast as the weather permitted to her little cabin. It was cold inside the little home she shared with Timmy. The fire had gone out in the fireplace. Sonora quickly built a fire and then pulled a chair over close so she could feel the heat. With trembling hands she opened the letter from Jonathan.

Dear Sonora,

I was so happy to hear from you. You will never know how much I have missed you and Timmy. I am glad you told me the truth about you and your son. Whether you gave birth to him or not makes no difference, you're still Timmy's mother.

I am most excited about your recent decision to rededicate your life to Jesus. It warms my heart to know all is well between you and the Almighty.

Willow Ingram, the lady who brought the message from Canada when we were searching for Timmy, is here at the fort. She came to testify at Daniel Forrester's trial. She gave her life to Jesus on Christmas day. She and

Corporal Tivy have become very serious about one another. I expect a wedding date to be announced any day.

Amanda and Doc finally realized how much they care for each other and have set a wedding date. They will be married April twenty-third. And more important, Amanda also gave her life to Jesus on Christmas day. Doc is still holding out, but one of these days, even our hardheaded doctor friend will give his heart to our Lord and Savior. We must keep praying for him.

Your Uncle Tobias joined us here at the fort for Christmas. He is doing just fine but he sure misses you and Timmy. You should see his cabin. He has turned it into a real home. That is, as much as a man alone can turn a cabin into a home.

Sonora, we all miss you and Timmy. You do need to see Tobias' cabin, so when spring gets here, why don't you come to see it and us.

Give my regards to Milton and Mena. They are very special people.

Give Timmy a big hug for me and have him give you a hug from me also. I would love to hug you both myself but for now that is impossible.

I have rambled on enough for now. Will wait anxiously to hear from you again.

I pray God's protection over you both.

All my love,

Jonathan

Sonora's eyes filled with tears. She couldn't believe what she had read so she read the entire letter again. It was true. It did appear Jonathan had feelings for her.

"Thank you, God. I never dreamed this would be possible. Now just let us have an early spring thaw so I can get back to Fort Benton," Sonora prayed.

****

It was a long, cold winter. Sonora didn't think she would ever see the first signs of spring. She had written Jonathan several letters but had not been able to post any of them. Neither the postal riders nor the stage had been able to get through since early January.

Sonora occupied her time sewing clothes for herself and for Timmy. She earned a little money by helping out at the fort store when Mr. Nevins was sick and she also filled in for the teacher at the fort school when she had been taken ill. Sonora was thankful for not only the money but also the diversion both opportunities presented. When she wasn't busy, she always found her mind wandered back to Fort Benton and Jonathan.

Captain Applegate led the worship services every Sunday since the preacher hadn't been able to get to the fort through all the snow. Sonora enjoyed the captain's teaching and she had been joining Milton and Willamena for Bible studies a couple of times a week. It was amazing, Sonora had gone to church and been reading the Bible for as long as she could remember but she seemed to find something new in God's Word each time she picked it up. She tried to think of this time as a time of preparation and felt she was growing stronger in her faith.

****

Fort Benton

Jonathan longed for spring. He hadn't heard from Sonora since he wrote his letter to her but he wasn't surprised. There was no way the mail could get through in this kind of weather. He just prayed his letter had gotten to her.

At least with the weather so bad, things had been quiet in the territory. He hadn't even sent a patrol out for several weeks. Of course that made for very long days with little to do.

Amanda and Willow were busy planning Doc and Amanda's wedding. Jonathan had been sure Corporal Tivy would have popped the question to Willow by now but for some reason he hadn't. Maybe he was waiting until Doc and Amanda said their "I Do's" and for the excitement to die down.

Jonathan was busy in his office finishing the monthly reports when he heard the strangest sound. It sounded like water dripping. He got up from his chair and crossed the office to the front door. Opening the door and looking outside, he saw steady drips of water falling from the roof to the frozen ground below. The drops he had heard falling were hitting a bucket at the end of the porch.

"Praise the Lord!" Jonathan shouted.

Immediately, doors opened. Doc walked out of his

office. "What are you yelling about?"

"The snow and ice have started to melt. Spring will finally get here." Jonathan called back as he walked out onto his porch.

Nathan laughed. "It does every year just about this time. What's so special about this year?"

"I think our captain is hoping spring will bring more than greenery to the Dakotas this year," Corporal Tivy added as he rounded the corner of the store.

"Yes. I think he is wanting it to bring a certain young woman and little boy back to Fort Benton," Amanda chimed in from the front porch of her store.

"Can't a fellow just be happy about thawing out from the cold without having to take all this ribbing from his so-called friends?" Jonathan smiled.

Sure, but it don't feel like it's thawing much. Still cold out here," Corporal Tivy pointed out as he stepped up onto the porch of the general store.

"Why doesn't everyone come on over to the store? We can finish this conversation over a hot cup of coffee by the fire," Amanda invited.

"Sounds good to me," Doc called as he stepped off the porch in front of his office and headed across the compound to the store.

"Be there shortly." Jonathan turned and walked back into his office. Once alone with the door closed, he prayed. "Father, let the spring get here quickly and please Father, let it bring Sonora and Timmy with it."

****

Fort Bridger, Wyoming

"How long do you think it will be before the stage starts running again?" Sonora asked as she rolled the piecrust into an almost perfect circle.

Willamena smiled broadly. "You in a hurry to leave Fort Bridger?"

"Well, yes." Sonora blushed and looked up at her friend. "Not that I'm anxious to leave you and your little family though."

"I know," Willamena assured her friend as she stirred the stew she had cooking on the back of the stove. "You're just anxious to get to Fort Benton and start a little family of your own."

Sonora blushed again. "Now I don't know if that will happen or not, but I am anxious to get back and find out if Jonathan and I could have a future." Sonora placed the piecrust in the metal pan and crimped the edges of the dough around the pan.

"Oh, the two of you have a future all right and it will be together. I just wish there was some way I could be there for the wedding," Willamena sighed as she removed the pan holding the apples from the stove.

"I'm afraid you're rushing things just a little." Sonora smiled at the thought of marrying Jonathan. "If there is a wedding, I would want you there. You're the first real friend I've had in a long time. I would like it, if I got married, for you to stand up with me."

Willamena placed her arm around Sonora's shoulders and gave her a little hug. "Oh, Sonora, what a sweet thing to say. When you and Jonathan set the date, you send me a telegram and I'll do my best to get there."

The piecrust was ready and Willamena poured the apples mixed with sugar and cinnamon into it. "Milton will be so surprised. He wasn't expecting anything special for his birthday. I had these dried apples safely hidden away in the back of the cellar just to make him a pie for today."

The ladies continued on with their preparations for a special meal for Milton. They talked and laughed and made what Sonora called "just in case plans" if she and Jonathan were to get married.

****

White peaks could still be seen on the mountains surrounding the fort but the snow was gone from Fort Bridger. The captain had received a telegram a couple of days ago saying the stage heading east would arrive at the fort next week. Sonora had everything packed and ready to go. She could scarcely contain her happiness.

"Mommy, do we really have to leave here?" Timmy asked at breakfast on Monday morning.

"I thought you would be excited about seeing Uncle Tobias and our friends back at Fort Benton," Sonora said as she stirred her oatmeal.

"I am, but I will sure miss Joey. There's no kids at

Fort Benton," Timmy pointed out. "I'll miss all the kids at school, too."

"I know you will miss everyone, son. We'll ask God to send a friend for you to Fort Benton."

Timmy looked at his mother. "Would God do that for me?"

"God loves you, Timmy. He's your Heavenly Father. Sure He would send a friend to Fort Benton." Sonora stood and began to clear the dishes from the table.

"Mommy, could we pray for that friend now? If we ask God today to send me a friend there, then He could get busy on it right away. That way maybe my new friend could be at Fort Benton by the time we get back there."

Sonora smiled at her son's practical thinking and his faith. "Sure, Timmy, why don't you pray?"

She knelt beside her son's chair and listened as Timmy prayed a simple prayer of faith for a friend to be waiting when they returned to Fort Benton. Prayer finished, Timmy headed off to school.

Late that same afternoon, the stagecoach arrived at Fort Bridger. Early the next morning, Sonora and Timmy began their journey home. Sonora was surprised but she felt comfortable thinking of Fort Benton in the Dakota Territory as home.

Chapter Twenty Three

It was the middle of April. Jonathan and the men had started routine patrols again but thankfully all was still quiet. He had mailed another letter to Sonora when the stagecoach had come through, but in his heart, he hoped she never got it. He hoped and prayed that while his letter was headed west, Sonora and Timmy would be traveling east.

"Enter," Jonathan called when he heard the knock on his office door.

"Sir," Private Baker said as he saluted his commanding officer. "Mr. Miller was just brought into the fort. He's been hurt. Shot in the shoulder."

"At ease, Baker; tell me what happened?"

Private Baker relaxed. "Been some rustling out at his place. He and his men set a trap for the rustlers. They got three of the cattle thieves before one of the rustlers got Miller. The rest of the bandits got away."

Jonathan stood to his feet. "Let's get over to Doc's and see how Mr. Miller's doing. Then I'll take a patrol out to track down those cow thieves."

"How is he, Doc?" Jonathan asked as he stepped into the doctor's office.

"It's a bad hole but he'll make it." Doc placed a bandage on Miller's shoulder. "That is if he will take it easy for a while."

"Now, Doc, I got a ranch to run. I wouldn't have come in here to see you if Enid hadn't made such a fuss." Eli Miller couldn't hide the grimace that covered his face as he tried to sit up.

"Eli, if you insist on moving around, you'll start the bleeding again and then you will have problems," Doc warned.

Enid Miller walked to her husband's side. "Eli, please do what the doctor says."

Eli looked into the eyes of his concerned wife. "But, Enid honey, I have to get back to the ranch. Those characters aren't gonna drive off any more of my herd."

"Eli," Jonathan interrupted. "Can you tell me anything about the men you saw stealing your cattle?"

The rancher began to describe, as best he could, the men and what had been happening at his ranch.

"You rest up here at the fort. I'm taking a patrol out and we will do our best to round up those fellows," Jonathan told the anxious man.

Miller finally agreed to rest at the fort for a few days. Jonathan, along with Corporal Tivy, led a patrol out of the fort in search of cattle thieves. Miller's description made Jonathan wonder if the band of comancheros who escaped last summer had returned to do more damage in the Dakota Territory.

****

Sonora couldn't stop the elevation of her heart rate or the excitement that rose in her as Fort Benton came into view. In just minutes, she would be face to face with Jonathan again. She began to wonder if she could stop herself from running into his arms the moment she saw him. Sonora could feel the heat rise in her face just thinking about Jonathan's arms around her.

The big gates swung open and the stagecoach entered the fort. The driver pulled it to a stop in front of the store. Moments later, the door of the stage was opened by Nathan Thomas.

"Well, look who's come back." A broad smile covered the doctor's face as he extended his hand to help Sonora from the stage. As soon as Sonora's feet hit the ground, the doctor pulled her into a big bear hug. "I have never been so glad to see anyone in my life."

"It's good to see you, too," Sonora said as her gaze scanned the fort.

"Hey, what about me?" Timmy called as he jumped down from the stagecoach.

Doc scooped the boy up into his arms. "It's extra good to see you, Timmy."

Amanda walked out onto the porch of the store. "Sonora, it's good to see you and Timmy again."

Sonora could see a change in Amanda. She could tell

by the look in Amanda's eyes that the red headed storekeeper was truly glad to see her. "Thank you," Sonora acknowledged as she once again carefully scanned the fort.

Doc smiled and leaned down to whisper in Sonora's ear. "He's not here right now. Took the men out in search of cattle rustlers. Been gone a couple of days." Sonora felt as though someone had just kicked her in the stomach as Doc delivered the unwelcome news. "He'll be back soon and he will be glad to see you. He's been praying for your return since the first sign of spring."

Doc picked up Sonora's bag. "I'll take you over to the guest quarters where you and Timmy can get rested from your long trip."

Sonora and Timmy followed Doc to the familiar little cabin. "Doc, do you think someone could get word to my uncle that we're here?" Sonora asked.

"Sure, no problem. I'll ask Lt. Blake to take care of that for you. Soon as you two feel like it, you and Timmy come over to the store. There's someone over there I would like Timmy to meet." Doc smiled as he patted Timmy's shoulder.

Timmy looked up at Doc. "Who?"

"It's a surprise."

Timmy began to jump up and down. "Can I go with Doc now? I'm not tired. Really I'm not."

Sonora couldn't resist those big brown eyes or the excitement radiating from her son's face. She watched as the doctor and Timmy strolled across the compound to the store.

Once inside the cabin, Sonora fought back the tears and the disappointment she now felt. She had longed to see Jonathan and now she still had to wait. Sonora didn't know how long the wait would be and she wasn't sure she could stand being this close and still so far from the man she had come to love.

She remembered Doc's words. He said Jonathan had prayed for her and Timmy to return. Now she prayed for Jonathan's safe and speedy return. Sonora composed herself. Jonathan would be back any day now and she would be waiting for him.

****

"Mommy, God answered my prayer," Timmy called as his mother entered the fort store.

"Timmy, that's wonderful." Sonora smiled at the sight of her son and another little boy playing with wooden horses in the corner of the store.

"Come and meet my friend Gabe," Timmy said.

Sonora smiled at the freckled-faced little boy who looked up at her. "It's nice to meet you, Gabe."

A faint smile covered the boy's face but he didn't say a word. He just turned his face back to the small black horse in his hand.

"He's shy around new people," Timmy informed his mother. "But he's not shy around me now. We are already friends because God sent him here to be my friend, just like I prayed."

"God is good, Timmy. I'm so thankful He sent you a friend," Sonora patted her son on the head. "Timmy, did you remember to thank God for answering your prayer?"

Timmy hung his little head. "No, Mommy."

"It's fine, son. You gave God the credit for sending Gabe to you when you told me God answered your prayer, but just remember to tell God thank you just like you would me for doing something nice for you."

"I'll do that right now." Timmy looked up toward the ceiling and said, "Thank you God for sending Gabe to Fort Benton so we could be friends."

Sonora smiled broadly and wiped the tear from her cheek. She was so thankful for Timmy. She thanked God everyday for allowing her and Timmy to still remain together.

Amanda had finished with the customer and walked to where Sonora stood watching the boys.

"It seems Nathan and I get to start our marriage with a family," Amanda told Sonora. Turning her gaze from the two little boys to Sonora, Amanda asked, "How about a cup of tea?"

"Tea?" Sonora's face showed evidence of unbelief.

"Yes, tea. Willow Ingram introduced us to the custom of afternoon tea and I really like it. So how about joining me?"

"I'd love to," Sonora smiled.

Amanda disappeared into the living quarters of the

store and returned with a china teapot and cups. As she set them on the table, she said, "It's nice to have a little charm and grace at Fort Benton."

Sonora smiled. "I don't know if I can get used to such luxury."

Amanda began to pour the tea. "You will have to. You will be expected to because you will be the captain's wife."

Sonora could feel her face turning bright red. "I don't know about that."

Amanda set a cup of tea down on the table in front of Sonora. "Well, we folks who have had to put up with Jonathan all winter do. He's been like a caged animal waiting for spring to get here and for you and Timmy to return."

Sonora turned bright red again. "But how did he know Timmy and I would come back?"

"I don't know. Guess the Holy Spirit told him." Amanda laughed. "Would you like sugar in your tea?"

Sonora shook her head and glanced over to where Timmy and Gabe played. "Amanda, I don't mean to pry but just who is Gabe?"

Amanda smiled broadly after taking a sip of her tea and setting the cup back in the saucer. "I see, you want to change the subject."

"Maybe." Again Sonora could feel herself blush. "But I am curious about Gabe."

"He's Nathan's nephew. Gabe's father was killed several years ago. He was the sheriff in a little town in Texas and was killed trying to stop a bank robbery. Gabe's mother, Nathan's sister, died a few months ago from consumption." Amanda looked lovingly toward the little boy and then took another sip of her tea.

"How awful," Sonora responded. "No, wonder he's shy around people."

"Yes, he has been through a lot. Nathan's folks took him in for a while but they felt they were too old to raise another child. When Nathan's mother wrote to him about Gabe, we decided to offer to take him. Now here we are, not even married and already parents."

Sonora sipped her tea. She could not believe this was the same Amanda Stone she had known from before.

"Amanda, being a parent seems to agree with you."

Sonora smiled.

"It does. I love Gabe as if he were my own. I think I am able to love him so much because of Jesus and His love for me. Did you know I asked Jesus into my life at Christmas?"

"Yes, Jonathan told me in his letter." Sonora smiled before taking another sip of her tea. "I am so happy for you."

The little bell over the door of the store jingled and Amanda stood to go assist the rancher and his wife.

Sonora continued to sip her tea and watch the two little boys playing in the corner of the store. She smiled as she thought about Doc, Amanda and Gabe becoming a family. *God is a good God.* Maybe God not only sent Timmy a friend but maybe he sent her one, too, in Amanda.

Now she prayed Doc and Amanda were right. She prayed Jonathan did love her and that soon she and Jonathan would make a home for Timmy.

Chapter Twenty Four

Dakota Territory

"They're back in the Badlands," Corporal Tivy reported as he entered the soldier's camp. "They've got the cows in a little draw to the south. I counted ten men on guard there."

Jonathan poured the corporal a cup of coffee. "That's all?"

"Yeah, the others must be out getting' more cows for their herd." The corporal speculated as he took the hot coffee from his commanding officer.

Jonathan paced the ground. He stared off into the distance searching for answers.

"We could probably take care of the ten men guarding the cows now but what would that accomplish us?" Jonathan went deep in thought, again.

Tivy looked at Jonathan. "Do you want an answer to that question, sir?" Jonathan nodded, so Tivy continued. "Nothin' unless we took their places guardin' the cows and surprised the rest of the bunch when they returned."

Jonathan was thoughtful for a moment. "Do you think we could take them without stirring up too much fuss?"

"I think so, sir. We could take them out one at the time starting with the lookout on the west rim." Tivy took a sip of coffee and stood. "Pick one of our men for each one of theirs. Take out the comanchero and put our man in his place."

Jonathan nodded thoughtfully. "Good plan, Corporal. Now carry it out," Jonathan ordered.

Several minutes passed as Jonathan watched the happenings below from his post high on a hill.

"All taken care of, sir," Tivy spoke softly when he returned to where Jonathan lay in the stillness. "They didn't know what hit 'em."

"Good job, Corporal. Now I guess we wait for the others to return."

Tivy looked to the east. "I don't think we'll have to wait long, sir."

Jonathan gazed in the direction Tivy indicated. A cloud of dust was rising on the horizon.

"Looks like they're comin' our way," Tivy pointed out.

"Let's start moving down the hill, men. When you get into position, let them ride by. Don't fire until they're in the canyon. We want to get them boxed in," Jonathan ordered.

The men did as the captain ordered and lay silently in the shelter of the trees and rocks as the comancheros rode by. Jonathan prayed for God's guidance and protection.

****

Fort Benton

"Sonora girl," Uncle Tobias called as he jumped from his horse and ran toward his niece. He pulled Sonora into his arms. "I could hardly believe it when that private came out to my place and told me you and Timmy were here at the fort."

"Uncle Tobias, it's so good to see you. Timmy and I have missed you so much." Sonora hugged her uncle again. "Come, sit down." Sonora offered indicating the chairs on the porch of the little cabin she and Timmy shared.

"Where's my nephew?"

"He's over at Doc's office playing with Gabe." Sonora seated herself in the rocking chair.

"Oh, I heard about Gabe. Haven't met the little fellow yet, but heard Doc and Amanda were takin' him in." Tobias smiled. "It's wonderful Timmy will have a playmate."

Sonora told her uncle about Timmy's prayer for a friend. Tobias laughed. "That's God. He just can't help but meet the needs of His children. A little boy asks for a friend and God has one waitin' on him when he arrives."

Sonora smiled as she began to rock her chair back and forth. "I'm glad it happened that way. It helps Timmy form a strong faith and trust in God. He will need that as he gets older."

Tobias agreed. "When do you expect Jonathan back?"

Sonora shrugged. "Don't know. Guess that depends on how long it takes to catch the cattle thieves."

"Well, how about you and Timmy comin' out to my place until they get back?"

Sonora hesitated. *All the way out to Uncle Tobias' cabin?* That would mean she had to wait even longer to see Jonathan but how could she refuse her uncle. He had been so good to Timmy and to her. "That would be nice," Sonora finally managed to say.

"Great, we'll leave first thing in the mornin'," Tobias smiled.

****

Dakota Territory

"Corporal, you take your men and start working your way around behind them. I'll give you a few minutes to get into position and then we'll converge and hopefully take them by surprise," Jonathan quietly instructed.

Corporal Tivy took his men and quietly made his way around the bandits. As soon as he was in position, the bugler sounded charge. The comancheros were almost as startled as the cattle. The cows began to stampede in the canyon below. The comancheros tried to escape but found themselves surrounded by soldiers so the bandits opened fire. Rifle fire echoed off the canyon walls as the soldiers and the comancheros engaged in battle.

When the smoke cleared, the soldiers took the few bandits still alive into custody and began to survey their own troops. Private Baker had taken a bullet in the leg. Two soldiers were killed and Jonathan had been hit in the right shoulder.

"Capt'n, let me look at your shoulder," Tivy insisted. "Looks like you're bleedin' mighty bad." Tivy pulled his bandana from around his neck.

"I'll be fine." Jonathan placed his hand over the wound on his shoulder. "Did we have any casualties?"

The corporal knelt in front of the captain. "Two, sir, Hamilton and Spivey."

"Form a burial detail," Jonathan sighed.

"Already taken care of, sir. Now let me look at that shoulder." Tivy opened Jonathan's shirt and placed his bandana over the wound. "I'll be right back, Captain. I've got to get some water."

The corporal cleaned the wound on Jonathan's shoulder as best he could and then bandaged it, holding pressure on it for several minutes. "Looks like the bleedin' has stopped for now but we need to get you and Baker back to the fort so Doc can get those bullets out," Tivy said as he stood to his feet.

"Let's say a few words over the graves we're leaving in this canyon first." Jonathan got to his feet and walked over to where the men had just buried their friends and fellow soldiers.

Jonathan held a short service for his two fallen men and also for the comancheros who had lost their lives that day. As he prayed beside the graves of the bandits, the renegades who had been taken into custody watched in disbelief. The comancheros stood watching the whole thing. It was evident by the look on their faces that they were confused by the service.

Jonathan glanced their way and saw a young Mexican boy wipe a tear from his eye. Jonathan prayed that he had been able to show these bandits the love of Jesus as he read scriptures and prayed over the graves of his enemies.

****

"Company B approaching," the sentry called.

Sonora couldn't stop the increased beat of her heart as she waited for the soldiers to enter the fort. The huge wooden gates finally opened and the soldiers rode in but Jonathan was not in the lead as Sonora had expected. Corporal Tivy was leading the patrol.

The troop halted and Tivy shouted orders. Part of the soldiers took their prisoners to the stockade, part of them were dismissed to go about their own business. Corporal Tivy, Private Calhoun and a couple of other soldiers carried handmade litters into the doctor's office. Sonora's heart picked up even more speed as she ran across the compound. Jonathan was one of the wounded men on the makeshift beds.

Sonora sat up in bed, perspiration streaming down

her face. She knew she had just had a terrible nightmare. She finally got awake enough to start to pray. She prayed fervently for at least an hour for Jonathan's safety but could not shake the feeling something was terribly wrong. She had to get back to the fort. Sonora hated to wake Uncle Tobias and Timmy so early but she knew something was wrong with Jonathan and she had to get to Fort Benton as soon as possible.

"Sonora girl, I pray your dream was just that, a dream, but at first light we will head out to Fort Benton," Tobias told his niece.

Sonora packed a bag for Timmy and one for herself before preparing breakfast. As she worked, she prayed. Jonathan just had to be all right.

****

Corporal Tivy looked down at the captain who was passed out on the litter they had made for him. The captain jostled as the horse pulled the crude bed over the uneven terrain. It was probably a good thing the captain had fallen unconscious right after they had started for the fort. If he were awake, the pain would probably be excruciating.

The soldiers halted for a short rest beside a mountain stream. Corporal Tivy walked down to the stream and took a drink of the cold, clear water. He pulled a kerchief from his pocket, wet it and walked over to the litter where his captain lay. Tivy knelt down and wiped Jonathan's face. The captain groaned and moved a little but never woke up.

"Lord, take care of this man and let us get him back to the fort alive."

****

Fort Benton

"Will he be all right?" Tivy asked Doc Thomas after the doctor had examined Jonathan.

"I'll know more after I get that slug out of his shoulder, but if I know our captain, he'll be fine." Doc smiled as he walked over to the stove and poured hot water into a wash pan and began to wash his hands.

"What about Baker," Tivy wanted to know.

"I'm just fine," Baker called from the bunk in the

corner of the room. "Just take care of the captain. You know Blake will be in charge until the captain gets better and I don't know how long I can handle Lieutenant Blake as the commanding officer around here."

"I know what you mean. It's dangerous to give some people power," Tivy agreed. "Come on, Doc. Let's get that bullet out of the captain."

"I'll take care of the bullet, but there is something you can do." Doc poured more scalding water into a large metal pan. "Tobias has some medicine out at his cabin that will be better for the captain than anything I can do for him."

"You want me to go get it?" Tivy asked. "What is it? An old Indian remedy?"

"It's not a what; it's a who." Doc smiled as he dropped his instruments into the hot water.

A smile covered the corporal's face. "Sonora?"

"Yep. She and Timmy got in here a couple of weeks ago. Tobias took her and the boy out to his place a few days back." Doc walked over to the bed where Jonathan lay.

"You get the captain better. I'm on my way to Tobias'," Tivy said as he pulled his hat on his head.

Just as the corporal started out the door, he met Lt. Blake on his way into the doctor's office. "Corporal, I'm glad I found you. I need a full report from you on this patrol."

"Yes, sir, just as soon as I get back." Tivy stepped down off the porch.

Blake looked at Tivy. "Just a minute, Corporal. Back from where?"

Tivy explained his mission to the lieutenant.

"Well, that's all well and good, but, Corporal, you're in the army and I expect a full report from you within the hour. Now, I will meet you in the captain's office in, shall we say, thirty minutes," Blake ordered.

Tivy saluted, "Yes, sir." After the lieutenant returned his salute, Tivy walked toward the mess hall. He might as well eat since he couldn't ride out to Tobias' right now. "Lord, please get the captain well, and fast, before we all desert under the leadership of Lt. Blake."

****

"That's all, sir. Our mission was a success but we lost two good men," Tivy reported. He watched Lt. Blake carefully. The look on the lieutenant's face spoke volumes. It was plain to see the lieutenant was enjoying sitting behind the captain's desk.

"So we have six of the comancheros in custody?" Blake tapped his fingers on the desk.

"Yes, sir," Tivy answered. He was still standing at attention. Ben Tivy didn't mind military law and protocol, but standing at attention for the last thirty minutes in front of the lieutenant was just a little ridiculous.

Maybe he just doesn't realize he's supposed to say at ease, but Tivy knew the smug look on the lieutenant's face said differently.

"Corporal, you're dismissed," Blake said. Then looking up from the paper he had been taking notes on, he added, "Do not leave the fort. I may need to talk with you later."

"But, sir, what about getting word to Sonora about the captain?" Tivy asked.

"I'll take care of that in due time, Corporal. You're dismissed," Blake stated.

When Tivy left the captain's office, he was none too happy. He walked across the compound to the infirmary.

"How are they doing?" Tivy asked as he entered the doctor's office.

"The captain's lost a lot of blood, but with some rest, he will be fine." Doc answered as he poured himself and Baker a cup of coffee. "The private can be moved to the barracks in the morning. I just want to keep an eye on that leg tonight. How about joining Baker and me for some coffee?"

"Sounds good." Tivy straddled the straight-back wooden chair beside Baker's bunk. He took the cup of coffee Doc offered and then took a sip of the hot liquid. He began to relate his meeting with the lieutenant to the Doc and Baker.

"You mean he won't let you go get Sonora?" A touch of anger could be heard in Doc's voice.

"Sonora? Sonora's here." A weak voice spoke from the other cot in the room.

Doc walked over and sat down in the chair next to

Jonathan. "Just relax, Captain," Doc ordered. "Sonora's out at Tobias' place. We'll get word to her somehow to let her know you're back."

Jonathan tried to sit up but Doc pushed him back down. "Now, it won't do any good for you to move around and open up that wound again. I'll take care of everything."

Jonathan grimaced and then took a couple of deep breaths. "Get Blake over here. I'm still in charge; I'm not dead, yet."

At that Tivy jumped to his feet, almost knocking the chair he was sitting in to the floor. After placing the chair firmly on the floor, he bounded out the door to fetch the lieutenant.

****

"But, sir, I was just following regulations and taking command since the commanding officer had fallen." Blake tried to justify his actions as he stood at attention before the captain's bed.

"You can stand at ease, Lieutenant, but I must point out to you I haven't fallen, just stumbled. Now, you may assume command only to the degree that you clear everything with me—before you act. Is that understood?" Jonathan asked.

"Yes, sir," Blake replied.

"Now your first order is to send Corporal Tivy to get Sonora," Jonathan ordered. "Then the day should progress as usual. Oh yes, wire the judge that we have the prisoners."

"Yes, sir," Blake again answered.

"Oh, and Lieutenant, let me know as soon as the rest of the troop gets in. I want to know if they managed to get the cattle back to Miller."

"Yes, sir," Blake once again responded.

"Fine, that'll be all, Lieutenant."

Lt. Blake saluted and turned on his heels to leave the doctor's office. Jonathan could hear some muffled sounds from Baker and Doc and knew they were trying hard not to laugh out loud.

"You had better get some rest," Doc told Jonathan as he walked toward the captain's cot. "You need to save your strength for when Sonora gets here.

"Doc, do you think she came back to see me?" Jonathan questioned.

Doc couldn't hold back the laugher. He laughed so hard his whole body shook. When he finally was able to compose himself, he said, "I think she probably came back to see me, but when she found out, I was engaged to Amanda she stayed around and decided to settle for second best. That, of course, would be you," Doc teased.

Jonathan laughed at Doc's humor but suffered the pains in his shoulder when he did.

"Now rest," Doc ordered. "Amanda will be here soon with some dinner for both of you."

Chapter Twenty Five

Tivy had just finished saddling his horse when he heard the sentry call, "Wagon approaching."

The corporal led his mount out into the compound just in time to see Sonora and her son, along with Tobias, enter the fort. He quickly tied his horse to the post near him and rushed over to greet them.

"I was just about to ride out to your place," Tivy called as Tobias pulled the wagon to a halt.

"And why would you be comin' to see us?" Tobias questioned as he jumped down from the wagon.

"The captain's back. I was comin' to get Sonora." Tivy smiled.

Sonora paled. "Is Jonathan all right?"

The corporal reached up to help Sonora from the wagon. "He will be now." Tivy smiled as he lifted the dark-haired young woman to the ground. "He took a bullet to the shoulder but he's doing fine. He's well enough to still give orders."

Sonora could wait no longer. She ran toward Doc's office and burst through the door without knocking. She knew that wasn't good manners but she didn't care right now.

Doc was changing the dressing on Jonathan's shoulder when Sonora burst into the room. "Well, hello," Doc turned to look at her. "How did you get here so soon? Tivy couldn't have been gone more than a few minutes."

"He hadn't left at all. We met him outside." Sonora slowly walked toward the cot. Concern and love was showing in those dark brown eyes of hers.

Doc finished his task and moved away from the captain's bed. A big smile covered Jonathan's face.

"Hello." Jonathan stretched out his hand toward the young woman.

Sonora hurried to his side. She took his hand as she

seated herself in the chair beside his cot. "Hello."

Doc looked at the two star-crossed lovers. "Baker," he said. "You look like you could use some fresh air and you need to try out these crutches."

Baker nodded in agreement. With the crutches Doc handed him, Baker stood and the two men made their way out onto the porch.

"It's good to see you," Jonathan said still holding tightly to Sonora's hand. "I was afraid I might never see you again."

"I was afraid of that same thing, but God is good and here we are." Sonora said. She then told Jonathan about her dream.

"Thank God. He told you I needed you." Jonathan paused before speaking again. "When I didn't hear from you, I was afraid you didn't get my letter but then I knew the weather was probably the reason. Did you get my letter, Sonora?"

Sonora slipped her hand into her purse and pulled out the small bundle of letters she had written to Jonathan. "Yes, I got your letter and here are the ones I couldn't mail to you."

Jonathan took the letters from Sonora and then she filled him in on the happenings at Fort Bridger. "Milton and Mena send you their regards."

"They are wonderful people. I'm glad you were stranded with them. I knew as long as you stayed there you would be safe." Jonathan smiled. "We have a lot more to talk about." Jonathan released Sonora's hand and pushed himself up into a sitting position.

"Jonathan, be careful," Sonora cautioned as she reached over to assist him. "You should lie back down."

"I have something to do first." Jonathan managed to stabilize himself on the side of the cot and then looked into Sonora's eyes. He reached across to her, took her hand and pulled her to him. He put his good arm around her shoulder and drew her close enough to cover her lips with his. It was a warm and tender kiss.

Jonathan pulled away and gazed deeply into Sonora's eyes. "That's something I have wanted to do for a long time. I love you, Sonora."

"Oh, Jonathan, I love you, too," Sonora returned.

Once again, Jonathan captured her lips with his.

****

"Nathan, you may kiss your bride," Pastor Howard said.

Nathan and Amanda's wedding was just perfect. The bride was radiant in her light blue lace gown and the groom was very handsome in his dress uniform. The happy couple exited the chapel under the crossed sabers of the troop lined up on either side, just outside the front door of the chapel.

For the entire service, Sonora's eyes had been focused on the best man. Jonathan stood tall and handsome at Doc's side. Sonora's heart swelled with pride as she thought about standing at that same altar and pledging her love to Jonathan. Of course, he had not officially proposed, yet.

Jonathan had just been back in full command of the fort for a couple of days and Sonora didn't want to rush anything. Just knowing Jonathan loved her was enough for now. They had all the time they needed to plan their future.

"All you single girls, line up," Doc called. "Mandy is ready to throw the bouquet."

"There are only thee of us," Willow pointed out. Looking at Sonora, she added, "And we all know who will be next to get married."

Sonora blushed. Jonathan just smiled.

"Oh I don't know about that. What do you think, Corporal?" Doc asked.

Now it was Willow's turn to blush and Corporal Tivy's turn to smile.

****

"Do you have to go back out to Tobias' place?" Jonathan asked as he and Sonora strolled around the compound in the moonlight.

"I think it would be best. After all, he is family," Sonora replied.

They walked in silence for a short time. The moon cast a romantic glow over the evening. Jonathan squeezed Sonora's hand. The couple stopped in front of the cabin Sonora and Timmy were staying in while at the fort. Tonight they had a visitor though; Gabe was staying with them so Doc and Amanda could have their wedding night alone.

"Sounds like the boys must be asleep," Jonathan commented.

"I'm sure Uncle Tobias saw to that before he went to the barracks to rest."

Jonathan shuffled his feet around in the dirt like a little boy. "Sonora, I'll miss you. I just get back on my feet and you leave the fort."

"Well, since you are back on your feet, you can come visit us." Sonora smiled. She stepped up onto the porch and sat down in one of the wooden chairs there.

Jonathan followed her. He leaned against the rail and looked down at Sonora. She seemed to get more beautiful each time he looked at her. He couldn't believe all his dreams for a Christian woman to love had finally come true.

Shaking the dreams from the forefront of his mind, he said, "I may visit so much that Tobias runs me off with a shotgun."

"I don't think there's a chance of that. Uncle Toby likes you very much." Sonora began to rock the chair slowly.

Jonathan closed the distance between them and sat down beside Sonora. "I'm proud your uncle likes me but I'm more thankful you like me." Jonathan reached over and took Sonora's hand in his.

Sonora closed her fingers around Jonathan's strong hand. She smiled up at him in the moonlight. Words failed her right now.

"I'll be out one day next week. I want to take Timmy fishing if that's all right with you."

Sonora smiled again. It appeared her son would finally have a father. "That would be just fine with me and I know Timmy would love it."

"I think Timmy and I need to spend some time alone together," Jonathan replied. "You know man-to-man kind of time." Jonathan ran his thumb across the top of her hand as he held on gently.

"I'm glad you want to spend time with my son."

Jonathan stood to his feet. He looked down into her lovely face. "Of course I want to spend time alone with

Timmy's mother, also. You know, man and woman type stuff." He reached down and pulled Sonora to her feet. "But, for tonight, I guess it's time to say good-night."

Jonathan kissed her softly and whispered, "I love you."

Sonora returned the sentiment and Jonathan crossed the compound to his office. Pausing once along the way, he gazed back at the woman he adored standing on the porch.

****

"You must be heading out to see Sonora," Doc observed as he watched Jonathan get ready to mount his horse.

"Yeah, thought I'd take Timmy fishing."

"That sounds like fun. Maybe one of these days soon I can take Gabe." Doc walked over and stroked the long neck of Jonathan's horse.

"See you later." Jonathan mounted his horse and rode out of the fort.

It had been almost a week since he had seen Sonora but it seemed a lot longer. He had to change things between them. There was no reason for this to be a long courtship. Jonathan knew what he wanted and he thought he knew what Sonora wanted also.

****

The Dakota Territory

"Timmy, how about eating some of the lunch your mother packed for us?" Jonathan asked as he laid his fishing pole aside.

"That's a good idea. I'm really hungry." Timmy placed his pole beside the captain's. "Fishing is hard work."

"That it is. Especially when you catch as many fish as you have." Jonathan smiled at the boy. He opened the basket and pulled out a sandwich for Timmy and one for himself. The two settled down on the grassy bank and ate their lunch.

Jonathan took a sip of water before he spoke. "Timmy, could I talk to you about something important?"

Timmy's little face showed some confusion but he nodded his head to the captain.

"Timmy, I know it's just been you and your mother

for most of your life so that sort of makes you the man of the house." Jonathan fought back a chuckle as he looked at the little boy's face. Timmy still had no idea what Jonathan was talking about.

"You see, Timmy. I have come to love you and your mother very much and I would like to ask your mother to marry me." Jonathan paused. The expression on Timmy's face had changed from confusion to pleasure.

"Does that mean you would be my daddy?" Timmy asked.

Jonathan smiled broadly. "It sure does. Would you like that?"

Timmy jumped to his feet and threw himself into Jonathan's arms. "You bet. I love you, Captain Parker."

Tears filled Jonathan's eyes as he held the little boy close. "I love you, Timmy."

Timmy pulled away. "Let's go tell Mommy that you're going to be my daddy."

"Whoa, son. That's not the way it's usually done. You see I have to ask your mother to be my wife and she has to say yes before I can become your daddy," Jonathan tried to explain.

"That's not a problem. Mommy loves you and she wants us to be a family."

Jonathan chuckled. "And just how do you know that?"

"I heard her praying about it the other night." Timmy smiled. "She thought I was asleep but I wasn't."

Jonathan's heart began to beat faster as he packed up the picnic basket. *Sonora had prayed about their becoming a family.* He had prayed that same prayer and now it looked as though he was about to get his answer.

****

Sonora had just finished the laundry when Jonathan and Timmy returned home. Jonathan dismounted and helped Timmy down from his horse. Before Jonathan could retrieve the basket, Timmy was off like a flash to see his mother.

"Mommy, Captain Parker wants you to marry him," Timmy called as he ran into his mother's waiting arms. "Isn't that terrific? Now he will be my daddy."

Sonora could feel herself blush from her head down

to her toes as she looked from her son's excited face to Jonathan's.

"Well, it's not exactly the way I had planned to ask you." Jonathan closed the distance between them. "I had thought I'd wait until tonight after supper and take you for a romantic walk in the moonlight but since Timmy brought the matter up…" Jonathan knelt in the dirt in front of Sonora and took her hand. "Sonora, will you marry me?"

"What are you doing kneeling in the dirt?" Timmy wanted to know.

"It's just something men do when they ask a lady to marry them," Jonathan explained. Then he looked up into Sonora's eyes. "Well?"

"Yes, Jonathan, I will marry you," Sonora finally managed to say.

Jonathan stood, took her into his arms and kissed her. Then he picked Timmy up and the three embraced.

"Now we'll be a family." Timmy had one arm around his mother's neck and one around Jonathan's.

Jonathan and Sonora shared their news with Tobias over supper. Of course, Tobias gave his hearty approval. After supper, the newly engaged couple finally got to take that romantic walk.

Alone under the stars, once again, he asked Sonora to be his wife and she, once again, accepted. They shared a warm tender kiss. "Now, that's the way I had it planned," Jonathan told her.

"Well, I will always have two special proposals to remember, and either way, I love you very much and can hardly wait to become your wife."

"So let's not wait. Let's get married real soon." Jonathan placed Sonora's hand in the bend of his arm and the two began to slowly walk back toward the cabin.

"We have to wait for Pastor Howard to come back to the fort."

"That will be next month." Jonathan stopped to look down into Sonora's dark eyes.

"Well then, I will become Mrs. Jonathan Parker next month. That will give me time to make a dress and get ready." Sonora smiled as she looked up into Jonathan's handsome face.

Chapter Twenty Six

Dakota Territory

Sonora couldn't believe how happy she was when just a few months ago she thought her life was over. Her love for Jonathan grew stronger each day, as did his love for her. Her heart leapt with joy as she thought about how close Timmy and Jonathan had become. Timmy had already asked if he could call Jonathan Daddy. *Life just couldn't get any better than this,* Sonora stitched lace to the bodice of her wedding dress.

"She's a million miles away." Amanda laughed as she looked from Sonora to Willow.

"Probably not a million, but I'd say she's about five miles away, just as far as the fort," Willow added to the laughter.

Sonora drifted to reality. "What's so funny?" she asked looking up from her sewing.

"You," Amanda grinned. She laid the length of fabric she was working on in the basket on the floor.

"Me? Why am I so funny?" Sonora asked.

"We have been trying to get your attention for the last ten minutes," Willow informed. "But you've been so lost in your thoughts, you never heard a word we said."

Sonora blushed. "I'm sorry."

"No need to apologize. Guess that's what love does to us females," Amanda told her friend. "I know before Nathan and I got married I'd get to thinkin' about how much I loved him and I'd just seem to get lost in a world of my own."

"What do you mean before you got married?" Willow asked. "You still do that."

"Well, I am just a newlywed, after all. It's all right if I still love to day dream about my man," Amanda smiled. "You're no better, Willow Ingram. Ben Tivy has you captivated as well."

"How about some tea and cookies?" Sonora stood to her feet. "We need a break from sewing."

"What about your friend from Fort Bridger? Is she coming to the weddin'?" Amanda asked.

"No. I got a letter from her last week. She found out she is going to have another baby and her husband doesn't want her traveling right now."

"That's too bad. Not about her having a baby, but that she can't come," Willow added.

"I know. I wish she could be here but I'm happy for her and the captain. She promised they would visit sometime next summer. Now, how about that tea?" Sonora asked as she set the teapot on the table.

Sonora served the tea and brought out fresh baked teacakes. The ladies continued their discussion of the loves of their lives as they sat around the dining table in Tobias' cabin.

****

"I think fishing has lost its appeal to our boys," Doc observed. Timmy and Gabe had wandered away from the creek and were playing in the shade of a big oak tree.

"Our boys." Jonathan smiled. "That sounds strange, doesn't it?" Jonathan pulled his line from the water and placed another worm on the hook.

"It sure does." Doc agreed as he set his hook in the fish at the end of his line and pulled the wiggling trout from the cool water.

Doc took the fish from the hook and placed it in the basket at the edge of the water. "Just think this time last year, we were just two carefree bachelors and now I'm a married man with a boy to raise and you're almost married with a family, too." Doc baited his hook and cast his line back into the water. "You know, I had almost given up on ever having a family of my own."

"You and Amanda are really happy, aren't you?" Jonathan asked as he pulled a fish from the creek.

Doc's rugged face was instantly covered with a broad smile. "Yes, we are. Jonathan, I've loved that woman for a long time, but never dreamed, she would return my feelings. Finally, she did making my life wonderful."

Jonathan laid his pole on the ground. He stretched

his arms over his head, stood and tried to stretch the kinks out of his back. "Life is wonderful. With God in control, a wonderful woman to love, and a boy who calls me Daddy, what more could a man want?"

Doc felt an uneasiness come over him. His life was wonderful. He had everything Jonathan had, except one thing. He knew God was not in control of his life. Maybe it was time after all these years to do something about that.

****

Fort Benton

"Riders approaching," the sentry called.

Corporal Ben Tivy dismissed the new recruits he had been drilling as the big gates swung open. A coach and four men on horseback entered the fort.

Must be a visitor from Washington, Tivy watched the coach come to a halt in front of the captain's office. Since the captain was out of the fort at the present time and Lt. Blake was out on patrol, the corporal decided he had best extend greetings to the visiting dignitaries.

Tivy was walking across the compound to greet the visitors when the coach door opened. The corporal stopped in his tracks when he saw Daniel Forrester exit the coach. The corporal's heart dropped to his stomach. Of all the times for this man to show up again, just one week before Jonathan and Sonora were to be married could have been one of the worst. Two other men exited the coach. One was Daniel's father, Samuel Forrester, but the other man, Tivy didn't recognize.

The corporal made his legs move again. He walked to where the men stood, and addressing Daniel, he said, "Hello Mr. Forrester. What brings you out our way again?"

"We need to see the captain," Daniel shot back, none to friendly.

"I'm afraid he's out of the fort for the day. Can I be of service?" Tivy asked.

"We got wind my son was back here at the fort," Daniel stated.

Tivy prayed before answering. He didn't want to lie but he didn't want to offer too much information either.

"Well, Timmy's not at the fort," Tivy told the anxious man standing in front of him.

"Where is he?" Daniel demanded.

"Don't rightly know," Tivy returned. The corporal knew he was walking a thin line but so far he had not lied, just evaded the truth a little.

"Have you seen him?" Daniel Forrester was not about to let the matter rest.

"Yeah, I've seen Timmy. Remember I helped rescue him from you late last summer." Tivy knew that was not what the man wanted to know but he was still trying to walk the tightrope.

"You're being very insubordinate, Corporal," Samuel Forrester chimed in. "Now who is next in command with the captain away. We'd like to speak to him, if you don't mind."

"Oh, I don't mind but you have been speakin' to him since you arrived. I'm in command," Tivy explained.

Sighing loudly, Daniel asked. "When do you expect the captain back?"

"It will probably be late this evenin'," Tivy informed them.

"Well, we will wait for him," Daniel stated. "Corporal, will you kindly have someone bring our bags to the guest quarters?"

"I'm sorry, sir. The men are all busy at the moment and I don't have the authority to assign you the guest quarters," Tivy explained.

Now the third man spoke up. "Corporal, I'm Senator William B. Potter. I have the authority to take the guest quarters and I instruct you to bring the bags to that cabin."

"Yes, sir," Tivy choked out. He did as he was instructed but he knew he was not impressed with Senator Potter and he also knew these three men were at Fort Benton to cause as much trouble as they possibly could. Somehow he had to get word to the captain so he could be prepared for what waited him when he arrived back home.

****

Dakota Territory

"Calhoun, what are you doing out here?" Jonathan asked as the private rode up to the creek where he and Doc were fishing.

Calhoun dismounted and then saluted his superior officer. "Sir, Corporal Tivy sent me out to warn you."

"Warn me about what?" Jonathan wanted to know. He laid his fishing pole aside and walked to where the private stood.

"Where are the boys?" Calhoun wanted to know as he scanned the surrounding area.

"They're just over there." Jonathan pointed off to his right. The boys had fallen asleep in the grass under the tree where they had been playing. "Private, what's wrong?"

"It's Daniel Forrester, sir. He just rode into the fort along his father and a Senator from Washington. They've made themselves at home. They got wind Sonora and the boy were back."

"What did Tivy tell them?" Jonathan wanted to know.

"As little as possible but they're waiting for you."

Doc had walked to stand at Jonathan's side. "You go on back to the fort. I'll take Timmy home and tell Sonora that a problem came up and you had to get back. After you find out just what's going on, you can ride back out and talk to her."

"You know what's going on, Doc. He's come back to try and get Timmy away from Sonora. This time, he's brought the big guns from Washington to help him."

Jonathan looked from Doc to Timmy's sleeping form lying under the tree.

"Well, I guess you had better do some major praying while you ride back to the fort." Doc slapped Jonathan on the back. "You've always said your God is bigger than any problem man can throw at you."

Jonathan forced a smile. "Thanks for reminding me, Doc." Jonathan saddled his horse and then rode away with the private at his side.

****

"What kind of problem," Sonora wanted to know. "Is it anything serious?"

"I don't exactly know. Something with some new

Sonora

fellows at the fort," Doc told the troubled young woman. "Jonathan will be out to see you as soon as he can. You know there is no problem that's gonna keep him away from you and Timmy for long."

Doc gave Sonora a brief hug and then turned to Amanda and Willow. "You ladies ready to ride back to the fort?"

Amanda smiled at her husband. She knew more was going on than Nathan had let on to Sonora. She had learned to read her husband well in the past few months. "We're ready. You call Gabe and we'll get started."

Willow hugged Sonora. "Don't worry. You know there's always a problem with new recruits. Probably some guy got homesick and decided the army was not for him."

"You're probably right. Guess I had better get used to my husband having to solve problems for more people than just Timmy and me." Sonora smiled. "Thank you both for helping me finish my dress. Now, all that's left to do is the cooking for the wedding supper."

"Don't you worry about that. Willow and I are going to take care of all that and Sergeant Wilkes' wife, Gloria, said she would help. We have the cookin' all under control. All you have left to do is relax and dream about becomin' Mrs. Jonathan Parker," Amanda informed her friend.

Sonora hugged her friends. "You two have become so special to me. Thank you so much."

****

Sonora wiped the tears from her eyes as she watched the wagon pull away from the cabin.

"Momma, what's for supper?" Timmy wanted to know as he ran to his mother's side.

Sonora wiped the last stray tear away. "Fish, I guess, if you and Uncle Toby will clean them for me."

Just at that time, Tobias rounded the corner of the cabin. "We'll clean them, won't we, boy?" Then looking around, he asked, "But where's everyone else? I expected to have a big fish fry with everyone."

Sonora explained what happened to her uncle. She hoped and prayed the only problem was with some new recruits but something inside of her was very uneasy. She felt a strong need to pray. And pray she did as Timmy and Tobias cleaned the fish for supper.

****

Fort Benton

"Forrester, what do you think you can gain by coming back to Fort Benton?" Jonathan watched at the man paced his office.

"My son," Daniel shot back. "I want my son and I plan on getting him."

"You've tried to make sure of that by bringing Senator Potter with you." Jonathan tried to remain cool. It wouldn't help anything if he let his anger show. "If you think, I would let Sonora walk into a court with a Senator you bought and paid for presiding you're crazy."

At Jonathan's words, the senator jumped to his feet. Slamming his hands on Jonathan's desk, he snarled into Jonathan's face. "I resent that accusation, Captain. I can have your bars for such insubordination."

"I beg your pardon, Senator, but you are here to give your complete support to this man, are you not?" Jonathan asked showing no fear at the senator's threat.

"Yes I am," the senator returned, giving no ground.

Jonathan sat back in his chair. "And you're doing so without hearing both sides of the story, right?"

The senator's face began to turn a little red. He took his hands from the desk and sank back into his chair, but he didn't answer Jonathan's question.

Jonathan took a deep breath. Maybe he was making a little headway with this man from Washington. "You have made up your mind without hearing both sides. So, you are certainly not an impartial judge, right?" Jonathan was defending his lady so he had no fear in making a senator a little uncomfortable.

"I know the story, Captain. I know Daniel Forrester is the boy's father and this Sonora woman is only the boy's aunt." The senator tried to regain some lost ground with the captain.

Now Jonathan rose to his feet, almost knocking his chair over as he did. He could control his anger no longer. "Only the boy's aunt? Only his aunt? Sonora is the woman that has raised Timmy as her own son. She is the one who cared for him as a baby. She's the one who stayed up with him when he was sick. She's the one that has comforted him when he's been afraid and kissed his hurts away. She's the one who has taught him everything he knows. Just his aunt you say. I don't think so. She is Timmy's mother in every way that counts."

The three men in Jonathan's office were quiet for a few moments as they watched Jonathan pace around his office. Jonathan prayed for God to calm his anger before he spoke again. Jonathan finally stopped his pacing and looked from one man to the other. "Gentlemen, I think this meeting has come to an end."

Samuel Forrester stood and faced Jonathan. "This meeting may have come to an end, Captain, but this problem has not. If you insist, we will get the territorial judge here for the hearing. Senator Potter will act as our lawyer, and in the end, justice will prevail and we will get the boy."

Jonathan showed no fear at the senior Forrester's threat. He had to be the defender for Sonora and Timmy. "Yes, sir, justice will prevail. You contact the judge. Until then, you will stay away from Sonora. By the way, the boy has a name. It's Timmy and you will stay away from him, too."

After his three visitors left the office, Jonathan slumped in his chair. "Father, help us. We can't lose Timmy. God intervene in this matter and let Your will be done," Jonathan prayed. "Father, give me the words and the strength to tell Sonora. Please don't let her try to run away again. Let her know she can lean on You and me. In Jesus name I pray, Amen."

****

Dakota Territory

Jonathan held Sonora as she cried. His heart ached at the pain she was feeling. He wanted to whisper words of comfort to her but he didn't know what they would be. Instead he just whispered how much he loved her and placed gentle kisses on the top of her head.

Finally the tears subsided and Sonora looked up into Jonathan's face. She could see the hurt in his eyes. She knew now, without a doubt, this man loved Timmy as much as she did.

"Jonathan, what do we do?" she finally choked out.

"We fight for our son," Jonathan told her as he wiped the tears from her cheeks.

"How do we do that? They have that senator to plead their case. Who do we have?"

"You, Sonora. We have you." Jonathan returned.

"Me?" Sonora pulled away from him and walked over to look out the window. "What can I do?"

"Tell the court how much you love Timmy and how you have taken care of him all of his life." Jonathan walked to stand behind her and placed his arms around her waist.

Sonora laid her head back on his strong chest. "Do you think that will be enough?"

Jonathan turned Sonora to face him. He placed his hands on her shoulders. "We also have our friends who will testify what a good mother you are and I will tell the judge how much I love Timmy and his mother and how I want to make a home for both of you." Jonathan smiled. "I believe we have God on our side."

Sonora looked into Jonathan's reassuring eyes. This time she would stay and fight. This time, she had Jonathan and the Lord to give her strength. She would lean on the two of them and pray everything would turn out for the best. She gave Jonathan a faint smile as she reached up and placed her hand on his cheek.

"Have I told you just how much I love you?" she asked.

"I think you may have mentioned it before but it's always good to hear it again." Jonathan smiled.

"Well, Captain Jonathan Parker, I love you very much. Thank you for being here for me and Timmy."

"Sonora, I love you, I love Timmy and I want to take care of you both." He leaned down and captured her lips with his. Pulling away he added, "I don't want you or Timmy to come to the fort until time for the hearing."

Sonora nodded in agreement. It was good having someone else make the decisions for her.

Chapter Twenty Seven

Sonora and Jonathan postponed their wedding until after the hearing. They didn't want to start their life together with the uncertainty of Timmy's future hanging over them. Two weeks from the day Daniel Forrester arrived at Fort Benton, the territorial judge arrived by stagecoach.

The judge refused to meet with anyone before the hearing and Jonathan was thankful for that. Maybe they would get a fair trial after all.

The day of the hearing finally arrived. Everyone in the fort wanted to attend so the mess hall was used as the courtroom. Tobias had brought Sonora and Timmy into the fort the night before and they had spent the night with Amanda and Doc. Doc had made sure no one but Jonathan had been allowed to see the two of them. Sonora had done her best to explain to Timmy what was going on but the boy seemed oblivious to the whole situation.

Sonora and Jonathan decided it would be best if Timmy did not attend the hearing so he and Gabe were left in the care of Willow. After everyone left for the mess hall, Timmy walked to the window to watch his mother and the man he considered to be his daddy walk away.

Very quietly Timmy prayed, "God, I don't want to go live with that Mr. Forrester who says he's my daddy. I want to be with my real mother and the captain who is now my real daddy. You take care of it, God. I love you, God, and I love Jesus, too. Thank you, God, Amen."

Willow heard Timmy's sincere prayer and she was amazed at the faith this little boy appeared to have. His prayer was short and to the point. He trusted God to take care of everything for him. Tears rolled down Willow's cheeks as she watched Timmy bounce across the room to play with Gabe. The two boys were laughing and playing as if nothing were going on.

"Lord, please answer Timmy's prayer as he prayed it," Willow prayed. She continued to pray without ceasing as the hearing progressed in the mess hall at the edge of the compound.

****

"So you see, Your Honor, this man has been deprived of his child for the last seven years. It's time the boy was placed with his birth father where he belongs." The senator's opening speech had been eloquent and very persuasive.

"Thank you, Senator Potter," the judge said. "Do you wish to call anyone to the stand?"

"Yes, sir, I call Daniel Forrester to the stand."

Daniel took the stand and the judge swore him in. "Mr. Forrester, will you tell us in your own words your feelings for your son," the senator instructed.

Daniel began. He told of his affair with Sonora's sister. He said he had loved Maryanne with all his heart and had pleaded for her to marry him. She had refused and returned to her family shortly after she found out she was with child. Sonora's anger raged. The man was lying. Jonathan grasped her hand; she looked into Jonathan's face and her fury calmed a little.

"Judge, I tried to contact her but her father would not allow it. I finally gave up. I thought it would be best for the boy if I just left things as they were. It was several years before I learned of Maryanne's death. As soon as I did, I tried to get my son but that woman ran away with him." Daniel continued to tell how he had been falsely accused of kidnapping Timmy and how Sonora had run away again. "So you see, Judge, I just want a chance to love my son and raise him. I can give him all the advantages in life."

Daniel finished his tale. Most of which had been fabricated. Now it was Sonora's turn. First, Doc testified to the love he had witnessed between Sonora and Timmy. Then, Tobias testified. Next was Sonora.

After being sworn in, she began, "First, Judge, I'd like to make a correction. The senator said Daniel had been kept away from Timmy for seven years. That is a lie. Timmy is only five. He will be six next month. If Daniel cared so much, you'd think he would know how old his son is."

"I just want your testimony. No elaboration as to the feelings of Mr. Forrester or anyone else," the judge instructed.

Sonora took a deep breath before speaking. "I am sorry, Your Honor. May I tell you what Maryanne told my father and me when she returned home?" The judge nodded approval and Sonora began to tell her sister's side of the story. As Sonora talked the door of the mess hall opened and she watched as her father entered and took a seat in the back of the room. Tears filled her eyes. She wanted to run to the man but continued her testimony.

"Daniel never tried to get in touch with any of us. Since Maryanne died giving birth to Timmy, I've raised him and loved him just as if I had given birth to him. Now, maybe I've made some bad decisions such as running away but I couldn't stand the thought of losing my son." With that, Sonora broke down.

"That was a very touching story, but with the death of the boy's mother, there is no one to collaborate what this woman is saying," the senator pointed out.

Sonora had composed herself enough to say, "Yes, there is. My father just came into the room. He can tell you what happened."

Sonora stepped down and the judge asked her father to take the stand. Ezra Grimes seated himself in the witness chair and told the story of how his daughter had rebelled against everything he had taught her. With tears in his eyes, he told of how she had returned home when she had discovered she was with child. He also explained that he had made up the story of Maryanne's husband being killed. The man could barely speak when he tried to tell about Maryanne dying.

"Judge, Sonora loves Timmy. She raised him. She fed him when he was a baby. She sat up with him when he had the colic. Sonora is Timmy's mother in every way that counts. She's the only mother the boy has ever known. You can't take that little boy away from her for his sake," Ezra Grimes finished his statement.

The judge looked over at the man seated in the witness chair. "Mr. Grimes, at any time, did Daniel Forrester or his family try to get in touch with you or your daughter?"

"No, Your Honor, they did not."

Jonathan finally took the stand. He told the judge of his love for Sonora and Timmy and that he planned to make a home for all of them. It was noon when all the testimony had been heard and the hearing was adjourned. As soon as the mess hall cleared, Zeke and his crew got it set up for dinner and opened again so everyone could eat.

****

"Oh, Daddy, it's so good to see you. I've missed you so much," Sonora said as she hugged her father.

"I've missed you, too, girl. As soon as I got Jonathan's wire, I took the next boat up river and then the stage the rest of the way," Ezra told his daughter.

"You wired him to come?" Sonora asked as she turned and looked at Jonathan.

"Thought you could use some reinforcements." Jonathan smiled. "Let's get over and check on Timmy."

The threesome walked across the compound to the general store. As soon as they entered the living quarters, Timmy jumped from his chair at the dining table and flew into his grandfather's waiting arms.

"Grandpa, when did you get here?"

"Just a little while ago." Ezra gave his grandson a big bear hug. "Timmy, I have missed you so much."

"Me, too, Grandpa," Timmy said. "Have you met my new daddy?"

"Yes, I have and I like him very much." Ezra smiled and then kissed his grandson on the cheek.

"I don't mean to interrupt, but dinner is ready and hot if any of you would like to eat a bite," Willow told the folks assembled in the living quarters of the general store.

They all sat down to eat but Sonora didn't have much of an appetite. She knew she would find it hard to eat or concentrate on anything until the judge rendered his decision. At least she had the four most important men in her life with her now, Timmy, Jonathan, Tobias, and her father. She also knew she had the Lord on her side and she knew she could face the outcome of this hearing no matter what it might be.

****

"I have reviewed all the testimony and this is one of

the most difficult decisions I have ever had to make," the judge told the crowd assembled back in the mess hall that same afternoon. "I have heard and seen the love this young woman has for the little boy she has raised as her own. I know the child is fortunate to have had her for these first years of his young life. I have also heard Mr. Forrester's testimony and he is lacking on many details of his son's life."

The judge paused in his declaration. Sonora began to have hope. She took Jonathan's hand as he smiled down at her.

The judge began again. "I can understand Mr. Forrester's lack of details since he has not been involved in the child's life. Even though I know Miss Grimes has cared for and loved the boy, it is my belief that if a child has a blood parent the child needs to be with that parent. Therefore, I am awarding custody of the boy, Timothy Grimes, to Daniel Forrester. Miss Grimes, you will release custody of the child at eight o'clock in the morning." The judge banged the gavel on the block on the table he sat behind.

"Nooooooo," Sonora screamed. "Please, Judge, don't do this."

The judge continued to bang his gavel. "This hearing is adjourned."

Jonathan pulled the tortured Sonora into his arms. "Sonora, don't. Calm down, baby. We'll fight this." Jonathan tried but none of his words seemed to be getting through. Sonora's crying was out of control. Jonathan continued to hold her as friends and family gathered around.

"Sonora, you've got to get control of yourself. We have to go talk to Timmy," Jonathan pleaded.

Finally Sonora's tears subsided. "Jonathan, why did God let this happen? We prayed."

"I know, baby, but the judge wasn't necessarily listening to God's instructions. We'll fight this. For now, though, we have to go explain to Timmy what happened and get him ready to go with Daniel." Jonathan took his handkerchief from his pocket and wiped the tears from Sonora's eyes and cheeks.

Slowly, Jonathan, Sonora, Tobias, and Ezra walked

into the living quarters of the general store. Their hearts were heavy at the task that stood before them. Timmy and Gabe were playing in Gabe's room.

"Do you want any of us with you when you talk to him?" Ezra asked his daughter.

"Just Jonathan, if that's all right?" Sonora told her father.

Ezra smiled and gave his daughter a kiss on her forehead. "Whatever you want. We'll be out in the store if you need us."

Everyone left the living quarters and walked into the store area and left Jonathan and Sonora alone. In moments, Nathan entered the living room with Gabe and Timmy in tow. "Gabe, you come with me. Miss Sonora and the captain need to talk to Timmy for a few minutes."

Timmy looked at his mother. "What's wrong?"

"Son, let's sit down." Jonathan led Timmy to the sofa. Jonathan sat down and Timmy sat between the captain and his mother.

"Timmy, you know we had the hearing today about whether you get to live with me and Jonathan or if you would have to go live with your real father." Sonora swallowed hard as she fought back the tears.

"I know, Mommy. You told me. So what did the judge say?" The little boy looked with anticipation at his mother.

"Timmy," the tears started and Sonora couldn't speak. She pulled her son into her arms and cried as she held him. She cast a pleading glance Jonathan's way.

Jonathan moved closer and put his arms around Sonora and Timmy. Trying hard to swallow the lump in his throat he said, "Son, the judge said you have to go live with Daniel Forrester for a while."

"I don't want to live with him," Timmy said softly. Sonora continued to cry and hold tight to her son.

"We know you don't want to. Your mother and I don't want you to go either, but for now, Timmy it looks like you will have to. We have to follow the judge's orders," Jonathan told the little boy nestled between himself and Sonora.

Timmy looked up at his mother. "Don't cry, Mommy, it's gonna be all right. I prayed and I won't have to go with that man. I asked God to let me stay here."

Jonathan began to pray. This could be a very touchy situation. This little boy's faith could be destroyed if he didn't say the right thing. "Timmy, sometimes we pray for things and they don't turn out exactly like we want them, too. It doesn't mean God doesn't love us; it's just that at that moment we can't have things our way."

"Oh, I know that, but God answers my prayers. I trusted Him to send me a friend here to Fort Benton and He did. So now, I trust Him to keep me here with you and Mommy. God will do it. You two don't have to worry." Timmy gave his mother and Jonathan a big smile.

Sonora's tears had stopped and she looked over at Jonathan and then back down at Timmy. There was really no use talking any further at this time. She kissed her son and he ran out into the store to find Gabe.

"What happened?" Ezra wanted to know as he and Tobias entered the living room. "Timmy doesn't look upset at all."

"He's not," Jonathan answered as he pulled Sonora closer to him. "He says he prayed and God won't make him go with Daniel. I tried to explain to him that sometimes we don't always get exactly what we pray for but he wouldn't listen. Just told us not to worry and everything would be all right."

Doc, Amanda, Willow, and Tivy had entered the room as Jonathan was explaining what had happened.

"Maybe Timmy has a special connection to God you old folks don't have," Doc said as he sat down in the rocker across from the sofa. "Jonathan, you've always said there's no end to what God can do."

"That's true, Doc, but the judge wasn't listening to God, and for now at least, Timmy has to go with Daniel."

Doc slowly began to move the rocking chair back and forth. "So the judge is more powerful than your God?"

"Nathan, don't make matters worse. You know what the judge ruled," Amanda pointed out as she sat down by Sonora and offered a comforting hand.

"I'm just trying to point out that you Christians should practice what you preach. God says to come to him as a little child and I think there's even something in that Bible of yours about having faith as small as a mustard seed and you can say to the mountain to move and it will move." Doc continued to slowly rock the chair.

Tobias looked over at Nathan Thomas. "For someone who claims not to believe, you sure know a lot about what's in the Good Book."

"Well, been reading up on it a little bit lately." Doc smiled as he looked around the room at the surprised looks on the faces of his friends. "I've watched the captain here all these years and he never wavered in his faith and that got me to thinking. However, now it seems, Timmy is the one with the faith. Maybe Timmy's got the faith to move the mountain the judge put in front of him today."

"Maybe so," Jonathan said as he squeezed Sonora's hand. "But I've never seen a judge come back after he's made a decision and reverse it, so I think we had better all be prepared for Timmy to leave us tomorrow."

Sonora knew there was no use to even try and sleep so everyone stayed awake with her. Amanda and Willow kept the coffee pot filled and they had made bread and cookies so the waiting turned into a time of sharing and visitation although the thought of Timmy having to leave in a few hours was never far from anyone's thoughts.

Periodically through the night Sonora would slip into the room where Timmy slept soundly and sit by his bed. She wanted to memorize every detail about him although she knew that was already the case. She knew her son like the back of her hand. How her heart burst with love for this little boy. She prayed Timmy would never forget her.

****

The sun was just coming up when Jonathan walked out onto the porch. "You all right, Captain?" Tivy asked from the shadows.

"No," Jonathan admitted to the corporal. "No, I'm not sure I'll ever be all right after Timmy leaves with that man. That is not until we get him back."

Corporal Tivy stepped upon the porch and sat down in the rocking chair behind where Jonathan stood. "Do you think you'll be able to get him back?"

Jonathan sighed heavily and then turned to face Tivy. "I don't know. I don't really know where to begin. I've got a little money saved so I guess we'll try to find a good lawyer down south that the Forrester's don't own. Maybe if we find a good one he'll be able to help us."

"Captain, you've got a good lawyer. You've got the Lord on your side," Tivy reminded Jonathan.

"Now you sound like Timmy." Jonathan leaned against the porch rail. Looking down at the corporal, he asked, "Ben, how do we know for sure God wants us to have Timmy? After all, at least some of us were praying for God's will to be done. Maybe it's His will for Timmy to be with his birth father."

"Now, Captain, do you really believe God would want a child to be taken from folks who love him with all their heart and be given to a man who doesn't even know him?"

Jonathan turned again and looked out over the fort that was just beginning to come to life. "I don't know. Right now, I just don't know. All I do know is that in a couple of hours I have to see the little boy I have come to love as my son leave this place. I also know the woman I love more than anything will be heart broken and I don't know if I will be enough for her. I can't stop any of it and I promised to take care of both of them." Jonathan slumped; he could hold back the fear and terror he felt no longer.

"Captain, you can't take care of them, but God can. Give it to Him. Let God comfort Timmy, Sonora and you," Tivy said as he walked to stand by he captain. The corporal put his hand on his captain's shoulder. "God will make it all work out. I don't know how and I don't know when, but the same power that raised Christ from the dead is still alive and working in our lives today."

Jonathan turned to look at the corporal standing beside him. "Ben, thank you. I needed someone to talk to. Someone I could be honest with and not have to be the Rock of Gibraltar for."

"God knew that. That's why he sent me outside ahead of you." Tivy smiled.

****

Sonora walked outside clutching Timmy's hand in hers. Jonathan walked beside them. Stopping a few feet from the coach where Daniel Forrester waited, Sonora knelt before her son. "Timmy, I want you to be good for your father. Remember everything I taught you." Sonora choked back the tears as she added, "And Timmy, don't ever forget I love you."

Timmy threw his arms around his mother's neck. "Everything's gonna be all right, Mommy."

Jonathan picked up the small boy and hugged him, kissed his cheek and then handed him to Ezra. Everyone there took turns saying goodbye to Timmy. Timmy assured everyone that everything would be all right.

At last, Sonora walked Timmy to Daniel and Daniel took the boy's hand to assist him up into the coach. Sonora had walked to where Jonathan stood and was in his arms crying. Timmy jumped from the coach and ran to his mother.

"Mommy, I don't want to go. I love you, Mommy. I want to stay with you." Timmy turned his gaze up toward heaven. "God, where are you; fix this for me," Timmy cried.

Mother and son embraced. Jonathan finally picked Timmy up and carried him to Daniel. Handing the lad to Daniel, Jonathan said, "Now, hurry up and get out of here."

****

Daniel took the boy and looked at Sonora, still slumped to the ground. Timmy continued to cry out for God to fix things. Daniel hesitated. For an instant, he pictured his wife's face and the faces of his two girls. What would he do if someone showed up and tried to take his girls away?

Daniel looked at his father and said, "I'm sorry. I can't do this." He hugged Timmy and walked to stand in front of Jonathan and Sonora. "Sonora, I'm sorry for what I have put you and Timmy through. I just realized I do love Timmy. He's a part of me and I can't do this to him. I can't tear his world apart just because my father wants a male heir. Sonora, take your son."

Sonora was stunned. She looked up into Daniel Forrester's eyes. She reached out for her son and Daniel placed Timmy in her loving arms. "Thank you, Daniel," she finally managed to whisper.

Jonathan extended his hand to Daniel, "Thank you, Daniel. You've made the three of us very happy."

Daniel said nothing but turned and walked toward

the waiting coach. He stopped and turned around. "Sonora, would you write to me from time to time to let me know how Timmy's doing? I know I don't have a right to ask, but I would like it if you would."

Sonora managed a faint smile. "Yes. Daniel, I will."

Daniel mounted the coach and closed the door. The big gates swung open and the coach and outriders left Fort Benton for the last time. Daniel managed one more look back at his son before the gates swung closed.

****

Sonora held Timmy for several moments before she stood and stepped into Jonathan's warm embrace.

"This calls for a celebration," Willow called.

"It sure does. Let's go back to our place and we'll fix that breakfast no one felt like eating earlier." Amanda offered as she smiled up at her husband and took his hand in hers.

"Breakfast is ready and waiting, if you're interested," a voice from the rear of the crowd spoke.

Everyone turned and saw Zeke standing at the back of the crowd wiping his eyes with the apron tied around his waist.

"Zeke, you crying?" Doc asked.

The old cook puffed up his chest. "No, of course not. Just got something in my eyes. Now do you want that breakfast or not?"

The happy crowd followed Zeke to the mess hall for a celebration.

"Told you God would work everything out," Timmy told his mother and Jonathan.

"You sure did, son." Jonathan reached down and swept Timmy up into his arms. "Boy, am I thankful you never give up on God's promises. You just keep praying and believing for whatever you need in life."

"Well, there is something I've been praying for and I sure wish God would hurry up and answer it," Timmy said as Jonathan set him down at the table in the mess hall.

Ezra sat down beside his grandson. "What's that, Timmy my boy?"

"Well, I want Mommy and Daddy to hurry up and get married so we can be a real family." Timmy smiled as he looked up into the happy faces of his mother and the captain.

"That's a good idea," Ezra agreed. Looking at his daughter and future son-in-law, he asked, "Now what do you two plan on doing about it?"

Jonathan smiled at Sonora. "We'll take care of that matter just as soon as we can get Pastor Howard back here to perform the ceremony."

"Someone call my name?" The crowd assembled there turned and saw Pastor Howard standing in the doorway.

Doc looked at Timmy and smiled. "Timmy, if I ever have a need, can I get you to pray for me?"

"Sure, Doc Thomas, any time." Timmy smiled and then took a big bite of his flapjacks. Laughter filled the mess hall that morning.

"You better be careful, Doc. We might get Timmy to start praying for the salvation of your soul," Corporal Tivy chimed in.

"Might not be a bad idea," Doc mumbled.

"A wedding and a baptism. That would be a good day's work for the Lord," the pastor said as Zeke offered him a cup of coffee and plate of flapjacks.

Sonora felt a warm peace fill her entire being. She had her son, the man she loved, her family and her friends. What more could a person ever want. But most of all she knew she was just where God wanted her to be.

Epilogue

The wedding was simple but beautiful. Sonora was radiant in her ivory-colored lace dress coming down the aisle on her father's arm. Jonathan stood tall, handsome, and proud in his dress blue uniform as he waited for his bride. Timmy beamed with joy as he stood beside Jonathan, serving as Jonathan's best man

The couple gazed lovingly into one another's eyes as they repeated their vows. Sonora knew she would love, honor, and cherish this man for the rest of her life.

"Jonathan, you may kiss your bride," Pastor Howard said.

Jonathan tenderly kissed Sonora.

Timmy inched his way in between his mother and Jonathan. "Now, does this mean we're a family?"

Jonathan bent down and picked up his son. "That's exactly what it means, son." Smiling at Sonora, he added, "Thanks to a lot of prayers, *now* we're a real family."

The crowd said, "Amen."

A word about the author...

I am the daughter of a Methodist minister and would not trade that upbringing for anything. I am the mother of two beautiful daughters. My oldest lives in Heaven. She had cystic fibrosis and was a double lung transplant patient and a wonderful Christian young lady. My youngest daughter, a beautiful Christian mother and wife, is the mother of the three most terrific children in the world. Being a grandmother is one of the greatest blessings ever. I am a registered nurse, active in my church and I love to travel.

Printed in the United States
124615LV00001B/4-12/P